CRIMSON ROSE

CRIMSON ROSE

M.J. Trow

CRÈME de la CRIME

This first world edition published 2013
in Great Britain and in the USA by
Crème de la Crime, an imprint of
SEVERN HOUSE PUBLISHERS LTD of
19 Cedar Road, Sutton, Surrey, England, SM2 5DA.

British Library Cataloguing in Publication Data

Trow, M.J.
  Crimson rose. – (A Kit Marlowe mystery; 5)
  1. Marlowe, Christopher, 1564-1593–Fiction.
  2. Shakespeare, William, 1564-1616–Fiction.
  3. Walsingham, Francis, Sir, 1530?-1590–Fiction.
  4. Serial murder investigation–Fiction.
  5. Great Britain–History–Elizabeth, 1558-1603–Fiction.
  6. Detective and mystery stories.
  I. Title II. Series
  823.9'2-dc23

ISBN-13: 978-1-78029-053-9 (cased)

All Severn House titles are printed on acid-free paper.

Severn House Publishers support The Forest Stewardship Council [FSC],
the leading international forest certification organisation. All our titles that
are printed on Greenpeace-approved FSC-certified paper carry the FSC logo.

MIX
Paper from
responsible sources
FSC
www.fsc.org   FSC® C013056

Typeset by Palimpsest Book Production Ltd.,
Falkirk, Stirlingshire, Scotland.
Printed and bound in Great Britain by
TJ International, Padstow, Cornwall.

ONE

The funeral procession blocked the Fleet Ditch and ran all the way up Ludgate Hill. Along Holborn the people lined the route, bareheaded and silent, the brave few crossing themselves as the coffin passed, watching the dead man's cousins and his friends struggling under the weight. A pale sun gilded his arms, the cloth of gold dazzling on the canopy and the tabards of the heralds. Portcullis carried his gilded spurs aloft, Rouge Dragon his great helm with its porcupine crest; Richmond held his shield and Clarenceux, the King of Arms, brought up the rear with his gauntlets.

No one carried his field armour, ripped and peppered with shot, and no one spoke of the thigh defences which, had he worn them that bleak October day at Zutphen, would have saved his life.

At the Ditch, which gave off its putrid smell even in a winter as cold as this, a small knot of horsemen joined the procession, all in black, their beards rimed with frost because they had been there all morning. The oldest of them turned his bay into the winding line alongside a melancholy-looking man on a grey.

'Morning, Francis,' the older man muttered through frozen lips and teeth clenched against chattering. 'Cat got your tongue?'

Francis Walsingham turned to his companion with the kind of contempt he usually reserved for Papists. 'I *am* burying my son-in-law, my Lord,' he hissed.

Perhaps the hiss was a little too loud because Clarenceux turned and frowned at him under his hood.

'Of course you are.' Lord Burghley was the Queen's Chief Secretary, a man of sensitivity, subtlety and understanding. He was usually kinder, but he *had* been sitting on the most uncomfortable saddle in the world for the last hour and he'd lost all feeling in his feet. 'We will all miss Philip.'

Walsingham nodded. They would. Philip Sidney was that rarest of men; a courtier, poet, wit and gentleman. His word was his bond, his hand firm, his eye bright. With Philip, what you saw was what you got. He was perhaps the one man in England who Francis Walsingham would dare turn his back on and that included the Chief Secretary who ambled beside him now, carrying out his civic duty.

With difficulty, Burghley twisted in the saddle. Behind him rode the Privy Council: Hatton, Essex, Leicester, the Lord Admiral – the men who called the tune in Elizabeth's England; the men who knew where the bodies were buried. Beyond them were the hangers-on, the hopefuls who hadn't yet read Philip Sidney's will, the genuinely bereaved who missed already the man's kind words, the lilt of his verse, the thud and crash of his lance in the lists. And beyond that the captains of the Trained Bands, their arquebusiers' butts dragging and bumping in the ruts of the frozen mud, their pikes trailing behind them in respect for the newly dead.

'London's behaving itself today,' the Chief Secretary murmured, eyeing the crowd. He reined in his horse as the procession jolted to another halt. The outriders had reached the Cross now and the great bulk of St Paul's blotted out the sun beyond it. The Queen's Yeomen were here in their scarlet with their halberds lowered. White-surpliced priests fluttered in all directions like so many moths, drawn to Sidney's flame, still burning wherever good men gathered.

'I wanted to talk to you about Marlowe,' Burghley said, resting both hands on the pommel of his saddle. If this delay went on much longer he'd have to whip out the copy of Aristotle he always carried in his saddlebag and to Hell with how it looked.

'Marlowe?' Walsingham blinked.

Burghley turned to him, a little surprised by the apparent absence of mind. This man, after all, was the Queen's Spymaster. He knew everybody. He forgot nothing. That was the way with spymasters.

'Christopher Marlowe,' Burghley reminded him. 'One of your people, isn't he?'

Walsingham turned back to watch the pall-bearers negotiating the steps. Men in the Queen's livery, her rose on their sleeves, gathered at the roadside to take their horses. 'He is,' he nodded. 'What of him?'

'I had a letter,' Burghley told him, 'from a Professor Johns, formerly of the University of Cambridge. Know him?'

The Spymaster was on form again. 'Marlowe's tutor at Corpus Christi. Or he was. I gather there was some sort of falling out.'

Burghley nodded. That was the way of domini. They squabbled like children over anything – Plato, Ramus, Erasmus, Colet, More – anything that was absolutely irrelevant to the real world. Except Aristotle, of course. Burghley fully believed that, of the Ancients, that man alone had got things right.

'What of Johns?' Walsingham asked. He didn't know the man by sight, but he knew Kit Marlowe and, friend or no, *anything* to do with him was likely to be the Spymaster's business too.

'He's heard that the powers that be in Corpus Christi are refusing to grant Marlowe his Masters degree.'

'On what grounds?' Walsingham asked.

'On the grounds that he hasn't been there overmuch of late.'

Walsingham's horse tossed its black-ribboned head and snorted as though it was following the conversation intently. 'We both know why, my lord,' its rider said eventually, studiously looking away to the sky peeping through the rooftops to Burghley's left.

'Oh, quite, quite,' the Chief Secretary agreed, picking a non-existent speck from the back of his glove. 'I've written to Chancellor Copcott.'

'Hmm . . . saying?' Walsingham was now minutely interested in a ribbon in his horse's mane.

'Usual. Dominus Marlowe . . . across the sea to Rheims . . . behaved impeccably and deserves to be rewarded for his faithful service . . . etc, etc. Yes,' Burghley paused, as though rerunning his words back through his head. 'Yes, just the usual. I just wanted to make sure you were happy with that.'

Walsingham tried not to show his surprise. Perhaps Burghley was feeling particularly avuncular today. The Chief Secretary had never bothered about such things before. 'That he was abroad on the Queen's business? Certainly. But I understood Copcott to be sound – one of us?'

'Oh, he is, he is,' Burghley assured him, urging his horse forward as the space became available. 'It's the usual thing, Francis. The University Convocation. God forbid,' he jerked his head towards his Privy Council waiting behind, 'we should ever be governed by committees, eh?'

Walsingham looked out over the heads of the people, standing like an unwashed wave, stunned into silence by the spectacle, by the rich and powerful who were trickling into St Paul's. 'Perhaps we'd be better off with democracy?' He raised an eyebrow at the Chief Secretary, who shuddered at the prospect. Either Walsingham was joking or it was time to look at some sort of rest home for him, perhaps Bedlam.

'I did remind Copcott and his Convocation that they should keep their noses out of affairs about which they knew bugger all, of course.'

'Of course.' Walsingham steadied his grey as the groom took its bridle. 'Now, my lord, if you'll forgive me, I have a son-in-law to bury.'

'Absolutely.' Burghley let himself be helped down from the saddle and slipped the copy of Aristotle from his saddle bag to his sleeve. It was going to be a long day.

TWO

They watched him for a while in Paul's Walk. Ingram Frizer took note of the scarlet doublet, slashed with satin, but he also saw and noted the sword hilt, gleaming at his hip like a coiled snake. The man was . . . what? Twenty-two? Twenty-three? Maybe more; his dark eyes weren't missing much as he took in the sights, looking ever upwards to where the tall pillars disappeared into shadow, pierced with mote-filled shafts of light which ended their journey from the high windows as a twinkle on the trinkets of the market stalls. Nicholas Skeres saw the Collyweston cloak, the elaborate pattens and the brocaded Venetians. A sheep for the fleecing. A lamb to the slaughter.

'Stranger in red,' he muttered out of the corner of his mouth, the trick he had learned in the Compter and Newgate. 'Mediterranean Aisle.'

'I see him,' Frizer mumbled back in the same way. 'I'm not so sure.'

The bigger man looked down at him. 'If that's not a gull, I'll eat my hat. And, talking of eating, we haven't, since yesterday.'

'It *is* Lent,' Frizer pointed out.

'Bollocks. Where's he from?'

'Not from here, that's for sure. He's English, though.'

'How do you know?'

'He's reading the inscriptions on the tombs.'

'Ah.' Skeres smiled the smile of one who has spotted the weakness in an argument. 'But is he reading the English or the Latin?'

Frizer fell back on surer ground. 'He's a gent and no mistake. Doesn't like parting with his money, though.'

They watched the stranger as he drifted past the stalls. He sniffed the cheese, dabbed a damp finger into the tobacco and tasted it. He held a carafe of Burgundy up to the light and shook his head. They started to crowd around him, the lavender sellers and the bakers, the perfume men and the silversmiths. Frizer and Skeres couldn't read his lips in the Babel of St Paul's but he was

smiling at everyone, when he wasn't standing, awe-inspired by
the biggest church in the world.

'Three groats says he's a University wit,' Skeres said, eyes
narrowing.

'Where from?'

Skeres' face contorted with the effort of guesswork. 'Oxford.'

'No.' Frizer folded his arms and leaned against a pillar. 'I
mean, where are you going to get three groats?'

Skeres chuckled. 'Him. Or my name isn't Galamiel Ratsey.'

'Oh, it's the Ratsey Lay, is it?'

'I think it's time. A little bit of Find the Lady first, though,
just to break the ice.'

'Which college?' Frizer asked.

'Oh, come on, Ingram. How the Hell . . .? All right.' Skeres
drew himself up to his full height, knowing a challenge when he
heard one. 'Brasenose. But that's a long shot, mind. You ready?'

'As far as I'll ever be.' Frizer sighed and followed his friend
out into the Aisle, jostling with every trader in London and
keeping their hands tight to their purses. They wove their way
between the clutter of stalls, edging nearer until they parted
company, one to the right, one to the left. It was Skeres who
reached the stranger first and he collided with him, begging his
pardon, pulling off his hat and dusting the man down.

'A thousand pardons, sir,' he beamed. 'I wasn't looking where
I was going.'

'No, no.' The stranger smiled back. 'My fault, I assure you.'

'Couldn't help noticing,' Frizer was at his elbow, penning the
man in between a table and a pillar, 'you were admiring the
architecture. Finest Gothic.'

'Most impressive,' the stranger said.

'Is this your first time to St Paul's, Master . . . er . . .?'

'Marlowe,' the stranger said. 'Christopher Marlowe. And, yes,
indeed. This is my first visit.' He smiled again and stepped to
one side, to move on.

Frizer stepped neatly to stay in front of him. 'Ingram Frizer,' he
said, extending a hand. 'And this is my associate, Nicholas Skeres.'

'Gentlemen.' Marlowe shook hands with them both. 'It has
been delightful, but . . .' He made general motions with his head
and hands, indicating that time was pressing, that he really should

be going, that Skeres' breath could stop the planets in their courses.

Skeres still held his hand. 'It's a little hobby of mine,' he said, 'to try to guess where a stranger has come from. I take you to be a University man? A scholar?'

'Astonishing!' Marlowe was open-mouthed with amazement, but managed at last to prise his hand free. 'I really must . . .'

'Do I detect an Oxford accent, Master Marlowe?'

'Cambridge,' Marlowe corrected him. 'Corpus Christi.'

'Oh.' Skeres' face fell.

'Is there a problem with Corpus Christi, Master Skeres?' Marlowe could think of a long list of them, but how they could concern these two ne'er-do-wells was trickier to guess.

'Corpus Christi, sir, no. But Cambridge. If you're a Cambridge man, you'll know of . . .' He paused for the full effect. 'Galamiel Ratsey.'

Marlowe caught his breath. 'Ratsey the highway robber?'

Skeres turned a shade paler. 'The same. I – and it pains me still – I met Master Ratsey on the road only last week. I'd rather meet the Devil himself.'

'They say he wears a Demon's mask,' Marlowe said.

Skeres clutched his doublet. 'He does, Master Marlowe, he does. Like a basilisk it is, grotesque. But you can't look away.'

Marlowe shook his head in sympathy. 'At least you aren't turned to stone, Master Skeres.'

'No.' Skeres shuddered. 'Just lighter by my entire purse and a ring my father gave me on his deathbed.' He paused to dash away a tear. 'I haven't eaten for nearly three days.'

Marlowe looked back at him. There was care in his face, concern, even. What there wasn't was any coin coming from his purse into Skeres' discreetly extended palm. Frizer knew a dead horse that would take no more flogging and changed tack. 'We do still have a dribble of wine, Master Marlowe. Won't you join us in a goblet? And perhaps a little game?'

Marlowe frowned. 'What, here? In the church?'

'Of course.' Frizer laughed. 'This is Paul's Walk, the antic of tails to tails and back to backs. Look about you, Master Marlowe, the place is busier than parliament. There's nothing you can't buy here.'

'I thought Jesus cleared the temple,' Marlowe said, straight-faced and wide-eyed.

The others looked at each other.

'If it's the Temple you want,' Frizer said, 'that's along the river a way.'

A silence. 'No, no.' Skeres laughed. 'If it's divine service you're after, that's that way,' he waved his hand to his right, 'in the choir stalls.' He closed to his man, laying a firm hand on his shoulder and sitting him down on a stool. It and the table in front of him had a price tag on it. 'I didn't have you down for a Puritan,' he said.

Skeres clicked his fingers and Frizer reached below the table and came up with three grubby goblets and a stone bottle, from which he poured three gurgling draughts of sack. 'Do you know Find the Lady, Master Marlowe?'

Marlowe looked confused. 'Is that a play?' he asked. 'I *do* like a play.'

'A sort of play,' Skeres chuckled. 'Show him, Ingram.'

Frizer sat down at the table, turfing out a begging cripple who was half-sitting on the stool. From nowhere he produced three cards – an Ace, a King and a Queen – which he laid out in front of them.

'Now, Master Marlowe, I will turn these cards over, face down, and you must select the one you think is the Queen.'

'Ah,' Marlowe said as realization dawned. 'Find the *lady*. Yes, I see.'

The cards flipped over in hands that flew and dazzled. Frizer slid them over the polished wood surface. 'So, care to try your luck, Master Marlowe?'

Marlowe hesitated. He sucked in his breath, his fingers hovering over first one, then another card. He gritted his teeth, staring at the cards as Frizer and Skeres grinned at him, like indulgent parents watching their child take his first step. 'That one!' Marlowe tapped a card and Frizer flipped it over. The Queen smiled up at them.

'Well done!' Skeres slapped Marlowe on the shoulder. 'He's a natural, Ing.'

'He is indeed, Nick. Would you care to try again, Master Marlowe? Lady Luck seems to be smiling on you. Shall we have a small wager, just to make it interesting?' A small silver coin had appeared in Frizer's fingers and it hovered invitingly over the cards.

Marlowe scratched his chin and looked doubtfully at Frizer

and then turned his head to look up into Skeres' face. 'Well, I don't know . . .' he said. 'I feel a little uncomfortable . . .'

Skeres gave him a friendly slap on the back. 'Don't worry yourself,' he said. 'Everyone here is fl . . . playing in some way or another. You'd only be joining in.'

Marlowe looked dubious still. 'I thought all of your money had been stolen.'

Frizer flicked Skeres a look, which Marlowe missed as he was looking down at the cards. 'I kept some for emergencies,' he said, quickly. 'I just have three coins, that's all.'

'I don't think you should wager them, then,' said Marlowe. 'What if I win again?'

Frizer smiled a mirthless grin. This was harder work than he had done in weeks. 'Well.' He chuckled. 'I'll have to take that risk. Now . . .?' He raised an eyebrow and held the coin out over the cards.

'Oh.' Marlowe looked again from face to face and seemed to come to a decision. 'Why not? As you say, everyone seems to be doing the same. A thunderbolt can only hit one man at a time, after all.'

Frizer grinned using only his teeth and set down the coin, flipping over the cards and spinning them through their moves. Then he lifted his hands and said, 'Master Marlowe. Find the lady.'

Marlowe looked along the three cards and dithered with his silver coin, which had appeared in his fingers as miraculously as Frizer's had. 'Hmm. You move them very quickly, Master Frizer. I am not at all sure . . .'

Behind his back, Skeres hugged himself with joy. The cards had moved at a snail's pace. His old gammer, dead these last ten years, could spot the lady from her grave in St Olaf's ground.

Still the coin hovered, then with a little shrug Marlowe plonked it down, right on the Queen. Frizer flicked over the cards and pushed the two coins across to Marlowe.

'Well done, Master Marlowe. Shall we try again?'

'I hesitate to take your money, Master Frizer, but why not? Shall we use both coins this time? Is that kind of . . . wager, is it? Is wager the word I am looking for? Yes, is that kind of wager allowed?'

Frizer laughed merrily. 'Indeed it is, Master Marlowe,' he said.

'Well, two coins it is, then,' Marlowe said. 'Move the cards,

Master Frizer. See if I can find the lady again.' He turned to Skeres with a smile. 'I like this game, Master Skeres. Much better than the games at Corpus Christi, such as chess, that kind of thing. Too hard for me. This is much more my style.'

Frizer's fingers flew. His two coins went down, followed without hesitation by Marlowe's. He flipped over the card and almost swallowed his own tongue. Despite his best efforts, the university idiot had found the By Our Lady. Skeres was frozen, as though the basilisk had got him after all.

'Look at that!' Marlowe said, gathering up the coins. 'Lady Luck is certainly on my side.'

'Ready for another go, Master Marlowe?' Frizer's indulgent smile had turned to a rictus grin.

Marlowe leaned back from the table, slipping the coins into his purse, which the two men noticed only now was secreted carefully under his doublet, to keep it safe from people like them. 'I don't think so, gentlemen.' He smiled. 'Now I come to think of it, it is rather *too* simple a game for me. And, listen . . .'

Above the babble in the aisles a clanging tried to make itself heard. 'There's the sacring bell. I must to my devotions.'

'Your devotions?' Skeres scowled, staring the man in the face.

'Why, yes. It *is* Thursday, isn't it? I always pray in St Paul's on Thursdays.'

'But . . .' Frizer couldn't find the words.

'But thank you.' Marlowe clapped the man's arm. 'It's been an education.' And he was gone, waiting until he was lost in the crowd before slipping out of a side door, away from the little trickle of devout souls on their way to the services.

'Gull, indeed!' Skeres rounded on his associate.

'It was your idea,' Frizer snapped. 'I had my doubts.'

'I was going for the Ratsey Lay. You had to find the lady.'

And despite the ringing of the sacring bell, the trading went on and Ingram Frizer and Nicholas Skeres spent the next few minutes wrestling each other ineffectually in the Mediterranean Aisle of the church where they'd buried Philip Sidney a few short weeks before.

Philip Henslowe was shouting. He spent a lot of his time shouting and some of it got heard but usually only as background noise.

Thomas Sledd the stage manager and Ned Alleyn, actor, ladies' man and thoroughgoing Narcissus were talking in normal voices to each other and taking not a whit of notice. Henslowe was yelling at them, gesticulating wildly and eventually Sledd took pity on him.

'Master Henslowe,' he said, marking his place on the page he and the actor had been discussing. 'In what way can I be of assistance?'

'You could try listening to me, for a start,' Henslowe said, truculently but at a more normal level.

'How could we not listen to you?' Alleyn yawned, turning from the manuscript and going in search of a reflective surface. 'You make my bones jump in my body, with your incessant shouting. My emotions are in tatters. Tatters, I tell you.'

Henslowe looked at Sledd. 'What?' he said. 'Tom, explain to me what he just said. It sounded like English, but I am not totally sure.'

'Master Alleyn is in a state of excitement, Master Henslowe,' Sledd said. 'His nerves are, apparently, standing out like the strings of a dulcimer, and your voice is as the hammer with which a maiden plays those strings.'

Henslowe raised a disbelieving eyebrow.

Sledd turned his back on Alleyn very ostentatiously and mouthed, 'Woman trouble' without making a sound.

Henslowe still looked perplexed. Not bothering to lower his voice at all, let alone mouth silently, he said, 'If woman trouble caused him this kind of grief the man would never be upright. What's the matter with the buffoon?'

Alleyn turned tortured eyes on the theatre owner. 'Master Henslowe, Philip, I am in agonies. I met a maiden . . .'

'Temporarily,' Sledd interjected and Henslowe grinned.

Alleyn ignored them. 'A maiden, so fair as to surpass all the suns in the firmament.'

'And?' Henslowe asked. He knew they would get nowhere until Alleyn had given them a blow-by-blow account of his conquest.

'And she—'

A door slammed below at the bottom of the stairs and a voice called, 'Hello above. Is anyone in?'

'Kit!' Sledd ran to the head of the stairs. 'Up here, Kit,' he called, then muttered to himself, 'at last some sanity.'

Kit Marlowe usually kept away from theatres when a play of his was toward. It had nothing to do with superstition; it had to do with the division of labour. He was a poet and a playwright; his tools the quill, ink, parchment and a mind that compassed worlds away from this one. Ned Alleyn was an actor. With a snap of his fingers he had the pampered jades of Asia kneeling gibbering before him because he was Tamburlaine, the scourge of God. He could make an audience forget that the pampered jades bending the knee on stage were all bit players, sweepings of the taverns and spotty boys in sundry stages of puberty; in Ned Alleyn's hands, all things were possible, all tall tales real. Thomas Sledd was a stage manager. A blasted heath? A lovers' bower? A battlefield of the maimed and dying? How many would you like? Sledd was your man. Bearing in mind that he had cut his teeth – almost literally – on the wagons and painted canvas of a travelling player-king's outfit, living off their wits and relying on the flickering and smoky light of torches to hide a multitude of sins, Sledd had grown up fast and now his marvellous mechanical inventions could hold their own with the best in London.

And Philip Henslowe . . . Well, what did Henslowe do, exactly? To the outside world, he was bluff and bluster, a manager of men, maestro of music, maker of the Muse. But behind that he was a prey to nervous disorders, a man who had to make the sums add up, a man who had to tease the fickle multitude to turn up to see a show. He had to pass bribes upward to the Master of the Revels to allow a play to be performed at all; sideways to the other theatre owners all too anxious to pinch his people and his plays; downwards to the grooms and sweet-meat sellers and those hopeless misfits who played fife and tabor while the crowds took their places. He lived his days in the magic of the theatre, with music, noise, wonderful words spinning in the air above his head. He spent his nights staring with hot and sleepless eyes into the dark, where columns of numbers danced and spun and never came to the same sum twice.

'How goes it, Master Henslowe?' Marlowe asked, smiling as he sauntered into the room. He knew Alleyn and Thomas were about their business; it was Henslowe he worried about.

'Oh, very well, Kit, very well.' Henslowe's grin could be seen on any plague victim from here to the Wash. 'Assuming that

Thomas here can do the execution bit with just a threat of realism.' He dropped his voice. 'And that Alleyn can get his lines right in the next twenty-four hours.'

'I heard that!' Alleyn bellowed. He was wearing a huge plumed helmet with the beavor removed so that his vowels and consonants could soar to the heavens. 'Have I not played Tamburlaine to gilded reviews and brought tears to the eyes of grown men? Do women not swoon from my Part One? Do small children not run from me? Have a little faith.' He looked round at them, an eyebrow raised, his arm extended. Then, suddenly, his mood changed. 'Claret, Kit?' Alleyn dropped his declamatory stance and sat back down in an elegant pose on the wide windowsill. He reached across to the trestle covered with plans, pieces of fabric and crumbled sticks of charcoal and poured two goblets of ruby liquid. Marlowe sat alongside him, looking out into the street from their eyrie in the roof of the theatre, on edge, always ready to spring. Ned Alleyn wasn't the sort of man you could always drink with. He had stolen a play of Marlowe's once, had enjoyed more men's wives than Tamburlaine had conquered countries, and knew the inside of the Compter and Newgate like the back of his own hand. But the crowds loved him and tomorrow afternoon, by the grace of Kit Marlowe, Sir Edmund Tilney, Philip Henslowe, Thomas Sledd, Dick and Harry, he would *be* Tamburlaine, the Scythian shepherd, once again in Part Two, adding to his undying fame and making Kit Marlowe's even more secure.

'I'm in love, Kit,' the actor said, face straight, eyebrows knotted, tears in his eyes.

'What, again?' Henslowe said as he went to the head of the stairs, on his way down to supervise the arrival of some timber.

Thomas Sledd was with him. Timber was his concern, flats, for the making of. He wasn't quite sure what the gates of Babylon looked like, but he wasn't telling Henslowe that. *Signing* for the timber was Henslowe's concern, however, and he was there, fussing around the builders' merchants, scratching away with quill on parchment as the costs ran ever higher.

'She's a vision, Kit,' Alleyn said, gazing into the middle distance before gulping his wine.

'Could her face have launched a thousand ships, Ned?' Marlowe asked.

'Hmm?' The actor got up and wandered across the room, striking a romantic pose, head back and leg bent, against the door jamb.

'Nothing.' The playwright smiled. 'How's Tamburlaine coming along?'

'Who? Oh, well, Kit, well.' He cleared his throat. 'Villain, I say!' he growled in a rumbling snarl which carried throughout the theatre and a builders' merchant down below nearly died of fright. '"Should I but touch the rusty gates of Hell, the triple-headed Cerberus would howl and make black Jove to crouch and kneel to me" . . . Pretty good, eh?' Alleyn was himself again.

'Masterly!' Marlowe laughed and took a swig of his claret.

'No, this girl, Kit . . .'

'Now, Ned,' the playwright wagged a playful finger at him, 'your heart belongs to Zenocrate, remember.'

Alleyn's face dropped and he hauled off his helmet, shaking his hair free. 'Which would be sheer delight,' he said, 'until you remember that Zenocrate is actually a cloth-footed fifteen-year-old baker's roundsman with shoulders like cypress chests and pustules like the Pestilence.'

'Ah.' Marlowe nodded. 'An actor's lot, Ned, an actor's lot.'

'I hope you aren't casting aspersions on the honourable art of boy players, Master Alleyn.' Thomas came through the door, panting a little from the stairs, with his arms full of timbers to carve them into Babylon, or at least his approximation of it. 'I was one myself once.' He looked around him, distracted. 'Has anyone seen my chisel?' he asked the two men.

Marlowe shrugged. 'Sorry, Thomas. I am happy to say I wouldn't know a chisel if it bit me on the leg, but I think I have the general gist and there are no tools up here that I can see. Why have you hauled all that timber up here anyway?'

'Master Henslowe is arguing about money down on the stage and I didn't think he would want me to overhear.'

'You are too sensitive for this job, Tom,' Marlowe said. 'We'll come down in a minute and drown him out with a rehearsal or two. How would that be?'

'Thank you, Kit.' Thomas Sledd shouldered his timber again and began his slow and careful descent back on to the stage.

Marlowe drained his cup and made to follow him, but Alleyn stopped him, pulling at his sleeve.

'I knew Thomas when he was with Ned Sledd's company, but I never saw him perform, only rehearse. Was he any good?'

'His performance in Cambridge when I saw him a year or so ago was as good as you would expect. Sledd's company was going up in the world when I saw it next, but Tom's voice had gone before I had a chance to see him.'

Alleyn preened. 'Well, I like to think that I could have raised the tone of the company, given time,' he said. 'Sadly, business called me away before . . .'

'Yes,' Marlowe said drily. 'Your business was stealing my *Dido* and trying to pass it off as your own, as I recall.'

Alleyn laughed, an actor's laugh, head thrown back and hands on hips. He said, as he did whenever he had to make it clear to the furthermost groundling that he was amused. 'Ha. Ha. Ha.' Then he straightened up with no preamble. 'Good days, Kit. Good days. But seriously, I never realized that Thomas was Ned Sledd's son.'

Marlowe turned his back on the stair's head and lowered his voice. 'He isn't,' he said. 'But he used to say that old Ned was the only father he knew. His mother was, I believe, a Winchester goose and his father –' he looked at Alleyn without a glimmer of a smile this time – 'some feckless actor, I expect, born to the wild road and the taverns. Ned brought up young Thomas when his mother dumped him on the company, made him the man he is today. Only natural he should take his name.' He turned to go down to the stage. 'Come on, Master Alleyn. We must help Master Sledd out of his predicament.'

Alleyn frowned, staring hard at the poet. 'How old are you, Marlowe?' he asked.

'Twenty-three,' he told him.

'Hmm. Twenty-three going on sixty,' Alleyn grunted. 'Well, then, Methuselah, give me your words of wisdom on *my* predicament.'

'If it's Cupid's measles, I understand Bucklersbury is the street you need. There are more apothecaries there than . . .'

'It's not the pox, Christopher.' Alleyn pouted. 'Thank you for caring. No, this woman is untouchable – a goddess.'

'Married?'

'No,' Alleyn enthused now, pacing the floor as Marlowe waited patiently by the door. 'No, that's the very Devil of it.' He unbuckled his epaulettes and gratefully slipped out of the breast and backplates of his armour. 'No, she's available. But I can't touch her.' He was standing next to Marlowe now and gripped his arm, shaking him gently to emphasize his words.

Marlowe frowned. He tapped Alleyn's codpiece with his knuckles. 'Something amiss?'

'Certainly not!' Alleyn sprang away, striking a manly pose, the great lover once again, if not yet the scourge of God. 'No.' His magnificent voice fell to a whisper. 'It's Shakespeare.'

'What is?'

'Oh, I'm sorry, Kit. I'm not making much sense, am I? You know Will Shakespeare's playing Theridamas, King of Argier?'

'Yes, I know who Theridamas is; I wrote the bloody play, remember? No, I didn't know Shakespeare was playing him. It was what's his name, that youngish chap with the funny walk, when I heard last.'

'I forgot you hadn't heard. Well, the funny walk turned out to be rather serious. Some kind of trouble . . .' Alleyn waved a hand vaguely behind him. 'We had to recast.'

'I see. So, Shakespeare is playing Theridamas . . .'

'Yes. Well, he's taken a room in Blackfriars. Water Lane.'

'And?'

'His landlady is Eleanor Merchant.'

Marlowe waited. Surely, that couldn't be it.

'She has a sister.'

'Ah.'

'You know my reputation, Kit. If all the whores Ned Alleyn has had, all the morts and trulls . . .'

'Not to mention the titled ladies,' Marlowe reminded him.

'Those too. If they were all laid down end to end I wouldn't be at all surprised.'

'But Mistress Merchant is not among them?'

'Not Merchant. Shakespeare's landlady is a widow. My belov-ed's name is—'

'Perhaps I had best not know. What if I met her and let her know, by word or look, that we have been discussing her?'

'A good point, Kit. But no, she is certainly not among them. I can't describe it. Her eyes, her brow, her lips, the way she talks, the way she moves. I can't sleep for thinking of her. And when

I do, she's there in my dreams. You're a poet, Kit. Tell me, is this what they call love?'

It was Marlowe's turn to ask, 'How old are you, Alleyn?'

'Twenty-one,' the actor told him.

'Twenty-one going on six,' the playwright teased him. 'Why break the habit of a lifetime, Ned? Do your usual. Promise her the world, the moon, the stars. Get her into bed and get her out of your system.'

Alleyn's face crumpled. 'I thought you'd understand,' he mumbled.

Marlowe looked into his face and held his arm. 'You're serious, aren't you?' he asked.

'As God is my judge. I need your advice, Kit. I mean it.'

Kit Marlowe had never seen himself as a matchmaker, a counsellor to the lovelorn. He was a scholar, grounded in Ramus and Plato and Aristotle. He was a poet, Ovid's right-hand man and Lucan's. And he was a playwright, the genius behind *Tamburlaine* of the mighty line. And, though it was behind him now, Marlowe had dubious friends in high places, men like Francis Walsingham, the Queen's spymaster. There were some who called him Machiavel and said he supped with the Devil. Now Ned Alleyn, of all people, wanted him to help him overcome his new tongue-tiedness with a girl, the sister of Will Shaxsper's landlady.

'Can I meet the girl?' he asked Alleyn.

'Of course!' The actor jumped at the offer and, shouldering Marlowe aside, ran down the stairs on to the stage. 'We'll go now.'

Marlowe gathered up the discarded costume and followed him down. '*Now*,' he said, 'you have a rehearsal to finish. Why don't you invite your love tomorrow night? I understand Henslowe's throwing a party afterwards – first night and all. Introduce me then.'

'Done.' Alleyn grinned, shaking the poet's hand and taking his breastplate and shrugging it on. Thomas Sledd was at his elbow in an instant, buckling him in. Alleyn didn't often stand still on stage for long enough for a rehearsal and Heaven knew he needed one. He gave Marlowe a grateful look over the actor's shoulder.

Marlowe walked across the stage, then turned at the edge, his face dark and his eyes cold. '"Vile tyrant! Barbarous bloody Tamburlaine!"' he rapped out.

'"Take them away. Th . . ." Oh, bugger!' Alleyn groped for his line.

Marlowe laughed. 'As I said,' he called as he crossed the groundling's space of the Rose. 'You have a rehearsal to finish.'

As he left the dark of the theatre and paused on the steps outside, he saw Philip Henslowe, bent towards a man he thought he knew but whose name he couldn't bring to mind. He took a step towards them but then, seeing the expression on Henslowe's face, thought better of it and, raising a hand in greeting, hurried off.

For the first time in his life, Kit Marlowe, the son of a Canterbury shoemaker, had a manservant. If you'd put the playwright into one of those iron boot contraptions they used on suspected traitors in the Tower, Marlowe couldn't exactly tell you how he'd come to hire Jack Windlass. There were times when it seemed rather the other way round, as if Jack Windlass had plucked the name 'Marlowe' from the crossrow.

From what he knew of him, Windlass was a good man, but he had his foibles. Every Thursday, come Hell or the Flood, Jack Windlass served up a mighty shin of beef for supper. And woe betide the master who missed a meal like that.

And so Marlowe missed Philip Henslowe at his most patronizing.

'I know it's you, Burbage,' Henslowe was saying, following the other man across the landing.

'You mistake me,' the man said, keeping his back to the light and his shoulder turned but Henslowe was persistent and hauled him round so he could have a proper look.

'No, I don't. You are Richard Burbage, joiner.'

The joiner stood up to become half a head taller and tore off his false nose and moustache, revealing a large nose and fledgling moustache beneath. 'Allow me to correct you, sir,' he said. 'I am Richard Burbage, Actor.'

'Whatever you say.' Henslowe dismissed it with a wave of his hand, his mind already back with the calculating of whether he had enough timber. Then he stopped and turned back. 'So what *are* you doing here?'

'Looking for Cuthbert.'

'Who?'

'My brother,' Burbage explained as though to an idiot. 'You know, the actor.'

'Oh, God,' Henslowe moaned. 'Another one?'

'I was wondering if you'd cast Tamburlaine yet?'

Henslowe stood there with his mouth open. 'Cast Tamburlaine?' he repeated. 'Man, we open tomorrow. If you want to make any kind of living in this business, I think you should try and keep your ear closer to the ground.' He turned away, chuckling to himself at the arrogance of actors, when Burbage grabbed his sleeve in his turn.

'It's Alleyn, isn't it?' he said. 'Ned Alleyn's got the part.'

'So I've heard from several ladies.' Henslowe nodded.

'He's wrong,' Burbage said solemnly. 'I don't see him in the part. He's . . . such a boy!'

Henslowe looked closely into the actor-joiner's face. He was an ugly looking thing, with a great nose and a tight little mouth over a heavy chin, but he had a bloom on his cheek that could only be that of youth. 'Talking of boys, Burbage, how old are you?'

'I was twenty last January,' Burbage told him.

'Well, there you are, then.' Henslowe chuckled. 'Why not see if there's a Children's Troupe in need of an old hand. I hear the Boys of St Paul's are usually desperate.'

'Alleyn's not much older than I.' Burbage stood his ground.

'Alleyn is a world older than you, boy,' he said. 'Come back to me when you can grow a beard.'

'You haven't heard the last of this!' Burbage called after him, ever the master of the cliché. 'I have my ways. You'll see!'

Will Shakespeare, once Shaxsper, of Stratford-on-Avon, now of London, paced his tiny attic room, mouthing silent words and gesticulating wildly. He had already caught himself a nasty one on a beam and had reined himself in somewhat, but he was what he was – an actor who wanted to be a playwright, with another man's words in this throat, trying not to choke on them. Making enemies with Kit Marlowe would not be a good idea, he sensed that, and making a hash of his performance tomorrow might well turn out the easiest way to make a powerful enemy. So, oblivious to the splinters and the pain, he mouthed and gesticulated on. His one consolation as he stumbled silently through his most difficult speech was that if his memory was bad, Ned Alleyn's was infinitely worse.

A tap at the door broke his concentration and his arms fell to his side. This could only be one person. He cleared his throat, sore from the effort of not declaiming out loud. 'Come in, Mistress Merchant,' he said.

The door creaked open and a tousled head peered round it. Whilst no longer in the first flush of youth, the woman was not old by any means and if she was a little flushed and not very tidy she had every excuse: with three children and a house to run, there was scarcely a moment when she was not on her feet. But she had decided that she was due a bit of a lie down and she had also decided that she would be lying down with Will Shakespeare before the day was out, or her name was not Eleanor Merchant.

'Master Shakespeare,' she said, coming into the room and standing coquettishly in front of him, 'I could hear you pacing to and fro as I made my bed in the room below this one and I wondered if all was well.'

'Well enough, Mistress Merchant,' the actor said with a small smile. 'I am trying to remember my lines.'

She cocked her head at him, one eyebrow arched in query.

'For the play. You remember? I am to play King Theridamas of Argier in the new play at the Rose tomorrow and I need to remember my lines.'

She flapped a hand at him. Did she remember? Had he not bored the family into stupor about his play these last weeks? But she was a woman with a mission to fulfil and so she must stay pleasant. 'Oh, of course, Master Shakespeare. Well, as long as nothing is wrong.' She half turned in the doorway. 'Do you have a moment, though, to help me with a task? Since Master Merchant passed away . . .' She wiped the corner of her eye automatically with her apron; she had shed no tears when the miserly old fool had breathed his last and she wouldn't cry now. He was only good for one thing (but oh, how good he had been!) and she could get that again with a little effort. As a provider he had been worse than useless. She felt that Master Shakespeare could probably fill his shoes and more with not too much persuasion. 'Since Master Merchant passed away, there are just a few things I need help with.' She went out of the door and halfway down the stairs.

Shakespeare stood still where she had left him, feeling rather confused. He heard her pattens clatter back up the steps.

'It's downstairs,' she said, poking her head back round the door. 'I need help with turning my mattress. It has gone flat.' She looked at him and tossed her curls. 'Just on the one side, you understand.'

Shakespeare jumped to attention and crossed the room to her. 'I am so sorry, Mistress Merchant. Of course I can help you. It will probably do me good to have a rest from my labours.'

'It will,' she assured him. 'A change is indeed as good as a rest. It's in here.' She led the way into her bedroom, which was at least three times the size of Shakespeare's own room under the eaves and also much bigger than the room he shared with his wife back in Warwickshire. The room, though large, was dominated by the bed, a huge affair with carvings and swagged curtains, looking rather sorry for itself with the goose feather mattress half on the floor and no sheets or coverlet.

'You see,' she said, 'it needs a good shake and then putting square back on the stringing. I had it tightened last season.' She bounced on the bare strings to demonstrate. 'But without the mattress is shaken out, I hardly get a wink of sleep.'

Shakespeare was a man who had always done his share in the house and he was an expert at shaking out a mattress so it was like sleeping on a cloud. He went to the far side and grabbed two corners and waited expectantly.

'I like to see a man who knows what's needed in the bedroom,' she simpered at him, then ducked her head. 'What will you think of me, Master Shakespeare, speaking so boldly?'

Shakespeare had been running his cues through his head and hadn't heard a word. 'Of course you are not bold, Mistress Merchant,' he said politely. 'Are you ready to shake this bed?' He braced himself.

Master Merchant had been dead a while now and whilst his widow had enjoyed a short tumble with her next-door neighbour but one and the boy who brought the laundry, she was no longer in the mood for small talk. Before Shakespeare could react, she had reached across the bed and dragged him into the middle of the tumbled goose down mattress. Her voice had dropped to a growl. 'I'm ready to shake this bed, Master Shakespeare,' she agreed, fumbling down to where his codpiece was laced. 'Let's see what actors are made of, shall we?'

Shakespeare always considered himself more of a scholar than a man of action, so his back somersault took him somewhat by surprise. He shook himself down and tossed back his hair. 'I think you have misunderstood me, Mistress Merchant,' he said, catching his breath. 'I am a married man.'

She narrowed her eyes at him and knelt up on the bed. 'A man married to a woman over a hundred miles away is not that married, Master Shakespeare, if you don't mind my mentioning it,' she said frostily.

'But I am married, nonetheless,' Shakespeare said, edging round the bed making sure to keep her in his sights. The woman could move as fast as a striking adder. He felt surreptitiously down to his codpiece to make sure the laces were still secure. As he looked up to judge his path to the door and his chances of making it in one piece, he met the startled eyes of his landlady's sister, Constance, who was standing in the doorway, looking aghast.

'Eleanor,' she cried at last. 'What is this man doing to you?'

Shakespeare held his breath. An accusation of rape now would not only save Mistress Merchant's face but would also end his life. He could only hope that she was inclined to be generous. He looked at her over his shoulder and she looked back, her head thrown back. Then she came to a decision.

'When will you learn, Constance,' she said, climbing down off the bed, 'that not everything that happens in a bedroom is a matter of the man doing things to a woman? Mother really should have told you a few bits and pieces before she died. Master Shakespeare and I were just changing the bed, weren't we, Master Shakespeare?'

'Indeed we were, Mistress Constance,' Shakespeare was quick to agree.

'And while we were changing the bed,' the landlady added, almost as an afterthought, 'Master Shakespeare kindly agreed to double his rent, now that he is an actor and everything.' She smiled brightly at the King of Argier. 'Wasn't that kind of him?'

Constance clapped her hands and ran into the room, to hug the actor and then her sister. 'Very kind,' she said. 'I can have my new cloak, now, sister, can I not?'

Eleanor Merchant sighed and hugged the girl. As lovely as the day but essentially she didn't have a brain in her head. 'Of course you can.' She smiled. 'But only after next rent day.' She smiled over the girl's ebony head at Shakespeare. 'Unless Master Shakespeare can give us an advance?' She winked at him. 'No? Then you'll have to wait, lovely. Now –' she let the girl go – 'help me with this bed. Master Shakespeare has to learn his lines.'

In the relative quiet of the London night, with the river lapping gently against the jetty, the tap on the door sounded at first like a branch against a window. Then it came again and the woman stirred, turned over in bed and nudged the man at her side with a sharp elbow.

'Door,' she muttered. 'Somebody at the door.'

Without speaking, he swung his legs out from under the coverlet and shrugged into his breeches, tucking his shirt in as he made towards the landing.

The woman snuggled down under the covers and pulled them right up over her ears. These taps in the night were getting more frequent, but she preferred to know no more about them than that they disturbed her sleep. Ignorance, if not exactly bliss, was preferable to knowledge. Soon, she was snoring again.

In the hall, the soft tapping was louder and more insistent. Easing the door open just a finger's width, he could see an anxious face, white in the moonlight, which ducked into shadow whenever anyone walked past. The occasional itinerant knocking on doors was not uncommon in this street of well-to-do houses and you couldn't be too careful. But no beggar ever dressed like this. Even so, better safe than sorry. The man put his lips to the crack and whispered, 'Yes?'

'I am here to see Master—'

'Ssshh,' the man said. 'Not so loud. You'll wake the house. What is it about?'

'I. . .' The man outside was stuck for an answer. Embarrassment had stilled his tongue. He dropped his voice lower and brought his mouth up to the crack. 'I need to borrow some money.'

The door flew open and a hand shot out, closed around his arm and pulled him in. The door closed behind him, hurriedly but with scarcely a sound. He had been dragged in too fast to see that the jamb and the door's edge were both lined with flannel.

'Then you've come to the right place,' he was assured in a whisper. 'Come, let's go into my study, where we can speak more clearly.'

He led the way across the hall and through a small door in the corner. With the ease of long practice, he lit a candle, but kept it well away from his face, so the visitor could only see shadows above a crumpled linen shirt.

'Do you have an amount in mind, Master . . .?'

'Do you *have* to know my name?'

The anonymous man shrugged. 'Not necessarily. Do you *have* to borrow money?'

There was a pause. 'I see. Yes, yes I do. I am Sir Avery Ambrose. I have estates in Kent and a few interests in the City.'

'Yes, Sir Avery, I have heard of you. With estates in Kent and interests in the City, why do you have need of me?'

The man slumped down on a hard chair near the window and buried his head in his hands. For a moment he couldn't speak, then, with an effort, he raised his head. 'I . . . er . . . I lent some money to a friend,' he said.

'Ah.' The man with the candle put it down on the desk and moved away into the shadows. 'And he can't pay you back? Perhaps I can help you . . . persuade him.'

'No, sadly, no one can. He is dead.'

'Ah. In that case, I can't help you in that way. But . . . how much is it that you need?'

'Forty pounds.'

'Forty pounds? That is a rather larger sum than I usually advance, Sir Avery. Very much larger. I don't have such a sum in the house.'

'I need at least twenty pounds, but if I had forty . . .'

'Ah, we all need that little bit extra, Sir Avery, don't we?' The man leaned forward a little, so that just a cheek and a gimlet eye glowed in the shadow. 'But, as I said, forty pounds . . . Wait, though. I may have the answer.' The cheek bunched as the man smiled. 'It would mean your coming back tomorrow, though.'

'No, please!' Sir Avery sprang to his feet. 'I need the money tonight. I have a mortgage due on the Home Farm tomorrow. If I can't pay . . . I have my son's inheritance to think of. He can't be left the estate with the Home Farm in strangers' hands . . .'

'Hmm . . . well, if it is that important. Let me explain. I don't have the money in the house – too dangerous, as I am sure you agree – but I do have some items of value, one in particular, which I could sell you for a promissory note. In the case of one item, a silver jug, I know someone who wants it for their collection and who has often made me an offer for it. If we were to take it to them tonight . . . well, they may have that kind of money to hand.' There was a tiny chuckle from above the candlelight. 'Not everyone is as prudent as we are, eh, Sir Avery?'

'If you could arrange it, Master . . .?' Sir Avery waited but there was no reply. 'If you could arrange it, that would be wonderful. And the promissory note?'

'Will come due in one hundred days. Time enough for you to get some rents in, that kind of thing.'

The Knight of the Shire closed his eyes and appeared to be adding on his fingers. His host sighed; with arithmetical prowess at this low level, no wonder he was knocking on dubious doors at midnight and past.

'Well?' How long could a simple calculation take?

'That is acceptable,' the man said, with a sigh. 'That takes us past the next quarter day and I will be able to repay you then. I am so grateful to you, Master . . .?' But again, there was silence. 'I will write the note right now. Oh, before I do, may I see the merchandise that is worth forty pounds?'

'Well, thirty-five pounds, shall we say. A man must live, Sir Avery. I will fetch it while you write the note,' the man said. 'Oh, don't worry. You needn't sign until you have seen it.' He indicated parchment and ink on the desk. 'You know the wording, I expect.' He pre-empted the next question. 'And just leave a space for my name. I will fill it in later.' Leaving the candle behind, he left the room.

Left on his own, Sir Avery dipped the quill in the ink and began to write: '*I, Sir Avery Ambrose, promise to pay –*' he left a long space, not knowing what name might have to fit in it – '*the sum of forty pounds, not more than one hundred days from the date below.*' He waited for the merchandise to be brought in before signing. He may be profligate, but he wasn't born yesterday.

His host returned on silent feet, carrying a silver jug, with gargoyle heads at each corner and some rather unsettling engravings on its sides. He looked for long enough to establish its quality, then said, 'It's an ugly great thing, isn't it? Who would want to buy it for forty pounds?'

'Er . . . thirty-five, but I see your point. But fortunately for you, one man's ugly old jug is another man's prized possession. Have you signed?' Sir Avery shook his head. 'Do so, I beg of you. Or it will be too late. Even I baulk at knocking people up at gone one in the morning. London is crawling with footpads, you know.'

The man signed, dated and added his address to the note, which the moneylender snatched as soon as he lifted the quill and locked away in a drawer of the desk. In his absence to fetch the jug he had added stockings, shoes and a doublet to the shirt and breeches and now he reached down a cloak from behind the door, pulling the hood well down before he turned again to the beleaguered borrower. He tucked the jug under his arm.

'Shall we?' he said, ushering the man out with a flourish. 'It isn't far.'

On the brisk walk through streets which still saw the occasional passerby, both men kept to the shadows, one through prudence, one through shame. There was no conversation; what was there to say? After a few twists and turns which Sir Avery could have never reproduced, they arrived at a house in a row, all of which had seen better days. The moneylender rapped on the door, in what seemed like a random pattern but which was in fact a complex code. After a pause, the door creaked open just a hairsbreadth.

'Yes?'

It was hard to identify, but to Sir Avery it sounded like a woman. Surely, this transaction would be a man's work. His companion put his mouth to the crack and whispered something. The word 'jug' could just be made out, but nothing more. The door opened enough for them both to squeeze through and they found themselves in a hall, shadowy and cavernous in the light of a small taper burning in a chamber stick, held in the hand of a woman in bedgown and a shawl. Her face was shaded by the frill of her nightcap, but not for subterfuge, just the vagaries of fashion.

'You have something to sell, Sir Avery?' she asked. 'I am a collector of . . .' She glanced at the other man. 'Jugs? Yes, jugs. May I see the piece?'

The moneylender extracted it from beneath his cloak and handed it to her.

'Oh, yes,' she said. 'Just the thing. But, sadly, I was offered one just this afternoon for only fifteen pounds. I have committed to buy it, I am afraid, Sir Avery. Thank you for troubling to bring it to me, but . . .'

The landowner had gone white. He glanced at his companion and licked his lips, which were suddenly dry. 'But . . . I was assured that . . . Can you not . . .?'

She looked up into his face and her face fell into an expression of compassion. 'You poor man,' she said. 'I had no idea that the situation was so desperate.' She patted his arm. 'I am a fool to myself, but I will offer you twenty pounds. It is all I have in the house. I am sure the other seller will understand. It is a very desirable piece and he will find another buyer easily enough.' She looked at him again, shaking his arm in sympathy. 'Come now? Will you take twenty?'

Sir Avery hung his head, then nodded, slowly.

'There, now,' she said, bustling off with her taper and leaving them in the dark while she ferreted for something in another room, just off the hall. Both men heard the chink of coins in a bag. Then she was back, with her light and, best of all, a chamois leather purse, heavy with gold. 'I'm sure you'll want to count it.' He shook his head. 'What a gentleman,' she said happily. Then, to the moneylender, 'Will you put it on the shelf?' He reached up and put the jug on a corner cabinet near the door. 'I would love to talk more to you both,' she said, 'but the hour is *very* late, and I can't wake my maidservant at this hour.' She already had the door open and ushered them out. 'Goodnight.' She pushed on the heavy oak, but stopped before it was quite closed. A hand came through and dropped four angels into her outstretched palm. With a wave of the fingers, it withdrew and she shut the door behind it. She leaned against the planks for a moment, catching her breath. It wasn't something she enjoyed, but ten per cent was ten per cent, no matter how you looked at it. The twenty pounds would come with the messenger sent for the jug in a day or so. And then it would just be a matter of waiting until the next time. Because there was always a next time.

THREE

The man Robert Greene was looking for had reinvented himself since leaving Cambridge. Gabriel Harvey, Fellow of Pembroke Hall, had been all set to take over the running of Corpus Christi. He even had plans to re-christen it Harvey College, but it was not to be. Now he was telling everybody that he had come to London to take his rightful place in society as the patron of the poet Edmund Spenser, the most dazzling wordsmith of this or any other age. Harvey had made the man what he was, since Spenser himself could hardly carry a rhyme in a bucket and he wanted to make sure everyone knew that. Not bad for a lad from Saffron Walden whose dad made ropes for a living.

Even so, knowing all this, Robert Greene was not prepared for the apparition sitting alone in Mrs Robertson's Ordinary along Lombard Street that night. His ruff was so huge he could barely reach his mouth with his fork and his Venetians spread wide along the bench he sat on. Greene caught the man's eye and doffed his cap, squeezing past the tables in the smoke-filled supper room.

'The last time I saw you, Greene,' Harvey said, leaning back to sip his wine, 'I kicked you out of my college.'

Greene remembered. In an age of patronage, he had once hitched his wagon to Harvey's star, but in the cutthroat world of literary endeavour, all that seemed a long time ago. '*Your* college, Professor?' In that cutthroat world, Greene could fence with the best of them.

Harvey paused, the goblet still at his lips. Then he put it down and wiped his fingers on his napkin. 'I let Copcott have it,' he said. 'I'd tired of Cambridge. Decided that my rightful place is here.'

'May I join you?' Greene asked, unbuckling his rapier and hooking it on the wall.

Harvey was about to say it was a free country, but neither man believed that. Gloriana sat like a vengeful harpy on her throne. She had had her own cousin executed and no one's life was worth more than the entrance fee to see a play.

'You know *Tamburlaine* opens tomorrow, don't you?' Greene asked. 'Part Two.'

Harvey laughed. 'So that's it. I wondered what would make you swallow your pride after our last encounter. Of course; it had to be. Your insane, irrational hatred of Kit Marlowe. Oh, malicious envy! Greene by name and green by nature.'

The would-be playwright sat down heavily, clicking his fingers for service. No one came. 'Don't pretend you don't hate him too.'

'I don't have a pretentious bone in my body,' Harvey said, arranging his stomacher and crimping his ruff. 'Unlike you, Greene, I know genius when I see it. Marlowe has that quality – what do people call it? His mighty line? It's just the man I can't stand.'

'You'll go tomorrow?' Greene asked him.

'To see *Tamburlaine* at the Rose? Assuredly.'

'So will I. As a gallery commoner. I don't want the smug bastard seeing my face on stage.'

'You think he'll be there?' Harvey asked.

'Oh, he'll be there.' Greene was still looking this way and that, trying to attract a waiter's attention. He became confidential, leaning in to his man, resting on his elbows. 'I may have a surprise for him.'

'Well, well.' Harvey clicked his fingers and a serving man was hovering at his side in seconds. 'Let it be a surprise for us all, then,' he said. 'Master Greene is about to place an order. Add my reckoning to his, would you?' And in a swirl of silk and satin, Dr Gabriel Harvey was gone.

The dead man bobbed his way down stream, rolling with the dark waters past Paul's Wharf. If he had still had his senses, he would have recoiled at the stink of Billingsgate where the corpses of gutted fish floated, like his, on the ebb tide. He was making for the sea in that casual, unhurried way that dead men will. If he once had promises to keep and places to be, he was past all that now. Time was the river's, as it had always been between those banks. The tall houses of Elizabeth's London leaned their gables over to watch him glide between them. He dallied for a while at Queenshithe, rubbing shoulders with the tarred ropes that held the merchantmen at their wharves. He

half turned to the blind alleys that ran up from the mud to
the Ropery and to Ratcliffe. His clouded dead eyes saw, with the
second sight of the dead, the spars black against the fleeting
clouds and the cold crescent of the moon beyond them. He
saw sailors and their trulls rolling home from the taverns that
lined the north bank, their calls and curses and laughter like
a half-forgotten dream.

The current turned him again, as it turned boats on this
stretch of the river too. Ahead loomed the rickety arches of
the Bridge, its stanchions knee deep in the wild, foaming water.
Lights tumbled here and there from the jumbled houses above
and to his right the heads of traitors rotted on their pikes, a
reminder to all of the risks of crossing Her Majesty the
Queen and those who served her. He was hurrying now, his
arms lifting out of the frothing current, rushing towards the
confines of the archways. His head came up, as though checking
his way in that deathly flood. And, buffeted on the slime-green
stone, he hurtled into the foam and shot past the Bridge for
one last time.

The rain was drifting across the city the next morning, driving
away the mist that wreathed the river. A knot of men stood up
to their ankles in the mud alongside Custom House Quay where
the *St John of Lubeck* rode the tide, her cargo laden and waiting
for the wind.

'How long will this take, Master Thynne?' a fat official called
from the greasy planking of the quay, keen to keep his expensive
pattens out of the clawing mud.

'How long is a giraffe's pizzle?' Thynne threw back at him.
If there was anything Hugh Thynne didn't suffer gladly, it was
fools, especially fools who wore the livery of Her Majesty's
Custom House. Because Hugh Thynne was the High Constable
of London and he routinely ate Justices of the Peace for breakfast.
Officials of Custom House Quay were just sweet-meat snacks to
assuage the hunger pangs of the day.

Thynne was squatting in the mud, hooking up his robe so that
it didn't drag in the water and testing the solidity of the ground
with his ivory-handled cane. He was looking at the dead body
caught up on the *St John*'s anchor ropes.

'Who found him?' he asked the men of the Watch standing around him.

'I did, my lord.' A waterman hauled off his cap and waited. Hugh Thynne wasn't a lord. He was a member of the Worshipful Company of Skinners and under his official robes he still wore the stitched badge of his calling, the three crowns and the field of ermine. But if garbage like watermen chose to see him as such, well, that served a purpose too.

'You found him here?'

'Yes, sir. Just as you see him. All tangled up in them ropes. We get it all the time.'

'Do we?' Thynne stood up. 'How so?'

'Suicides, my lord,' the waterman told him. 'They're drawn to the river like moths to a flame. Most of 'em jump off of the Bridge. This one . . .'

'Yes?' Thynne narrowed his eyes as the rain drove harder, bouncing off the carvel planks of the *St John* and spattering on furled canvas. Two or three crewmen in their capes and wide leather hats lolled on the ship's rail watching the morning's entertainment.

'Well, it's hard to say, sir.' The waterman rubbed his stubbled chin. While he was talking to his lordship here he wasn't getting a fare – and time, after all, was money.

Thynne turned to get his bearings. He recognized the tallest tower above the jumble of rooftops behind him. 'St Dunstan's in the East,' he said. 'Whose parish is that?'

'Mine, sir.' One of the constables saluted.

'Oh, good day, Williams. I didn't see you there. This is your patch, is it?'

'Indeed it is, sir.'

'Pay the man, Williams. You can put it down to expenses for the next quarter.'

Williams' face fell, but he rummaged in his purse and threw a couple of coins to the waterman who caught both expertly, bit them and slipped them into the leather pouch at his belt.

'I'd say he went in upstream, sir; somewhere near the Fleet, maybe, or the Bridewell.'

'What makes you say that?' Thynne asked.

'Current's tricky along that stretch. It'd take him along St

Paul's Wharf. See those marks?' The waterman pointed to the body's left arm. Thynne nodded.

'Tar. The biggest cluster of ships on the river at this time of year is Paul's Wharf. It's the hay and firewood wherries from Essex, they put in there mostly. He'd have got caught up there for a while, then the ebb tide would have sent him wide, probably midstream and once under the arches, he'd end up here.'

Thynne was impressed. You didn't need a local constable or his Watch when you had an expert like the waterman. He looked at the dead man's head, half submerged in the black water. 'What did that, would you say?' He was pointing to the back of the corpse's skull, shattered and matted with blood, kept liquid by the action of the water. 'The Bridge?'

'Could be the Bridge, my lord,' the waterman said. 'Could be an Apprentice's club.'

'Indeed it could. Constable Williams?'

'Sir?'

'Lift that head up. I want to see his face.'

Williams waded out, his boots making grotesque sucking noises as he reached the floating body. He grabbed a handful of the black hair and hauled the head upwards. Thynne took in the pale features, the eyes black with bruising, the mouth open in a snarl.

'How long would you say, Waterman, he's been in the water?'

'Not long, sir. Half a day; may be a little longer.'

'Why?'

'Look at his skin, my lord. No washerwoman's hands. The water makes the skin wrinkle, see, afore it comes away from the flesh altogether. And the rats haven't got to him yet, neither. Mind you, stuck as he is, that'd only be a matter of time.'

'Williams.' Thynne smiled. 'Whatever you just paid this man, double it. He's earned his crossing today ten times over. Waterman, give your name to the constable here. You're First Finder. You'll need to give evidence at the Inquest. Where are we?' Thynne looked to his left to where the church of All Hallows sat squat and dwarfed by the grim portals of the Tower. 'Within the Verge,' he muttered half to himself. 'That'll be Coroner Danby. Well, well. You men.' He straightened in the river mud. 'Lend a hand there and get this to dry land. I want to find out who this man was and how he came to pay his respects here at the Custom House.'

'Lot of riff-raff in today, Thomas.' George Beaumont tried to make himself heard above the row. 'Those bloody groundlings will be trying to look up my skirt again!'

'They should be so lucky,' Sledd grunted. All morning he had been wrestling with problems of his own, especially how to hoist the Governor of Babylon on his own walls in Act Five, Scene One. Anything before that was the actors' problem. Still, young Sledd had a soft spot for the boy actors. It hadn't been so long since he'd worn the farthingale himself and he knew how tricky it could be. Balance and deportment was all and then, of course, you had to be prepared to have leading men slobbering all over you. No, Thomas Sledd didn't envy George Beaumont at all.

This afternoon, George Beaumont was Zenocrate, wife and love of Tamburlaine, the scourge of God, who had been circling the wooden O earlier signing autographs while the band tuned up. The boy checked his white makeup in the foxed mirror for the last time and the trumpets announced that the play was about to start. Not that that reduced the noise among the groundlings at all. The day-labourers and the journeymen had queued all morning for this, watching for the flag to rise over the Rose, praying that the early-morning rain would not come back and jostling good-naturedly with the ribbon and mask sellers and the Winchester geese who waggled their breasts at them.

Ned Alleyn stood apart from his cast now, as was his custom. He wasn't on until Scene Four but he must be pitch-perfect the first time the crowd saw him in action. He stood in the Tiring Room, mastering his deep breaths and working his lips to twist around the mighty lines of the legendary Marlowe.

Because Marlowe was already a legend wherever players and playgoers gathered. His *Dido* had enraptured the city and his first part of *Tamburlaine* had brought grown men to tears and turned Puritans Papist. One woman was so enravelled by the Scythian Tamburlaine and his conquering sword that she had gone into labour near the orchestra space and a child was born among the flats of Persian tents. Philip Henslowe had nearly died of worry, but the child was healthy and his doting mother called him

Tamburlaine Marlowe in honour of the moment. Alleyn was furious that his name appeared nowhere.

The legend that was Marlowe was peering out between the slats above the star-canopied heaven. The place was virtually full – all two thousand seats and standing spaces occupied by faces pale in the limelight; all of them to see Alleyn and to hear the magic words that Marlowe gave him. Marlowe smiled; he could almost hear Henslowe crowing with delight, piling up the clay money boxes for the reckoning the next day.

'What about tomorrow, though?' The impresario was suddenly at his elbow, muttering, reading the man's mind, it seemed.

Marlowe looked at him. 'See this,' he said, holding up a goblet, 'that's half full, Philip. Not half empty. And if no one comes tomorrow, no one at all, you'll still have made your pile today.'

'I don't know.' Henslowe scowled, peering through the slats to see the crowd.

'Relax, Philip,' Marlowe said. 'You don't give refunds, so even if they hate it . . .'

'Why would they hate it?' Henslowe demanded, clutching convulsively at Marlowe's sleeve. What did the man know that he didn't?

'They won't hate it, Philip,' the playwright said, lowering his voice and hoping that Henslowe would do the same. 'Trust me. Well, well, well . . .' He was looking up in the gods where a shadowy figure moved to his seat, lesser beings standing up to let him pass. He would know those dark, sharp eyes anywhere, even at that distance.

'The Spymaster's here,' he said, half to himself.

'Who?' Henslowe was reduced to biting his nails now.

'Er . . . nobody.' Marlowe smiled. 'A trick of the light.'

But Jack Windlass wasn't a trick of the light. He was dressed like a poor man's roisterer and he was taking his place with the gallery commoners. There was no doubt about it; Marlowe was paying the man too much.

Something had gone wrong stageside. It was more than time for the third fanfare, and yet all they could hear was laughter and a very slow handclap, giving way to boos. The curtain in the doorway was flung aside and the shawm player burst through, clutching his throat.

'Water,' he croaked. 'Water, for God's sake.'

Thomas Sledd passed him a jug from a table and he gulped from it greedily. He coughed and spat, then wiped his mouth on his sleeve. 'Fly,' he gasped, and cleared his throat again. 'I inhaled a fly. Sorry.' He went out through the curtain again, to ironic applause.

So, finally, the third fanfare sounded and the Prologue strode out to the centre of the O, his pattens clattering on the planking. He swirled his Collyweston over his shoulder and held up his right hand, booming out over the groundlings' heads. 'The general welcome Tamburlaine received when he arrived last upon our stage . . .'

'Speak up!' somebody yelled to general laughter, but the Prologue was the warm-up man of the Rose and he'd heard it all before. He didn't miss a beat. 'Have made our poet . . .' He pointed both hands to the Arras to his left. Marlowe duly stepped out on cue and bowed with a flourish. The crowd went wild, chanting 'Marlowe! Marlowe!' The man looked up to where Walsingham sat, face invisible. He sat as he always did, his hands curled round the head of his cane, the tip, silver-shod, firmly planted between his feet. Everyone else lounged about as part of an audience out to make merry. Walsingham sat as though giving an audience, the nearest he ever came to relaxation. Marlowe bowed to the Prologue, who winked and carried on. 'Have made our poet pen his Second Part, Where death cuts off the progress of his pomp, And murderous Fates throw all his triumphs down.'

There was general booing and shouts of 'You bastard, Tamburlaine', but it was difficult to pick out words in that hulla-baloo. 'But . . .' The Prologue could pause for England and he did so now, waiting for the crowd to subside, playing with his audience like a cat with a mouse. 'What became of fair Zenocrate?'

A fond sigh broke from the throats of hundreds, turning into a general 'Ah' before some strident harpy among the groundlings echoed the sentiment, 'Quite so,' she shrilled. 'What indeed?' And she was laughed to scorn.

Marlowe nudged George Beaumont. 'Get out there, lad, or we won't get to Scene Four.' He nodded in Alleyn's direction, where the greatest actor of his age was buckling on his helmet. 'And that would never do, would it?'

George curtsied deeply and when he brought up his rouge-painted cheeks, it was to obscene gestures and thrusts from the groundlings' front row. He blew a fart through his lips and swirled away, powder flying in all directions.

'And so it begins,' Harvey muttered to Greene in their seats in the gallery. 'Did you see Part the First?'

'Of *Tamburlaine*?' Greene yawned. 'I really can't remember.'

'Liar!' Harvey chuckled. 'That show brought the house down, as I suspect this one will. Let's face it, Greene, like it or not – and I'll be the first to admit, I don't – Marlowe is the Muses' darling. No one will touch him in a hundred years. What have you got to offer against that – *Alphonsus, King of Aragon*?'

Greene was startled. 'What do you know of that?' The thing was unfinished, locked safely away – or so he thought – in his lodgings near the Vintry.

'Enough to know that a hundred years from now, no one will have heard of it – or you, Dominus Greene.' Harvey's face hardened as he watched the actors go through their paces. 'Whereas Marlowe . . . They'll still be performing this *five* hundred years from now.' And he hated himself for saying it out loud.

'Well.' Greene was at his most petulant this afternoon. 'I'll not stay here to be insulted.' And he swept away as bravely as he could, stumbling his way past knees and laps, tipping his hat and mumbling apologies as he went.

It was raining again in the Bear Garden that afternoon. Master Sackerson stretched, yawned and turned his beady little eyes up to the heavens.

'Looks almost human, doesn't he, Ing?' Nicholas Skeres was sheltering under the awning that covered the Bear Pit's entrance way. 'You wouldn't think one swipe of that paw could rip half your face away.'

'Seen him in action?' Ingram Frizer was checking the papers in the satchel slung over his shoulder, to make sure they hadn't got too wet.

'I have.' Skeres nodded. 'I owe that old gentleman a few groats, in fact. Many's the cur he's crippled with my blessing.'

'I heard Henslowe took his teeth out – loses less dogs that way.' Master Sackerson yawned again, giving Frizer the full extent of his ivory incisors. 'Looks like I heard wrong.' The man's bonhomie vanished at the sight. 'Where's he from, Nick?'

'Russia,' Skeres told him. 'The land called Muscovy. They say Henslowe spends more money on him then he does on that bloody theatre – aye up, Nick; customers.'

A young couple were jumping the puddles on their way to the Rose, hurrying past the Bear Garden with its menagerie's sights and smells.

'Let me stop you there.' Skeres stood like an ox in the furrow, barring their way. 'Play's started, you know. You're too late.'

'Too late?' The gentleman frowned, spreading his cloak over the head of the lady with him. 'Don't be ridiculous. We can go in at any time.'

'Full,' Skeres insisted.

'Full?' The gentleman stopped sheltering the girl now and stood to his full height, hand on his sword hilt. 'Man, there are two thousand seats in the Rose. They can't *all* be taken.'

'Sir.' Skeres feigned outrage. 'This is *Tamburlaine* by Christopher Marlowe, starring Ned Alleyn. Given that combination, could they be anything else?'

'Well . . .'

'Can I help you?' Ingram Frizer appeared as if from nowhere as Master Sackerson sprawled on his rock, watching events unfold. 'Is there a problem?'

'This . . . fellow,' the gentleman said, 'says the theatre is full.'

'I fear it is, sir.' Frizer nodded. 'Until tomorrow.'

'Tomorrow?' The gentleman frowned.

Frizer became confidential. 'It's actually full for the next week. Master Henslowe is considering running extra performances at night, but you know how it is, sir – the Master of the Revels himself would have to be consulted.'

The gentleman became confidential too. 'Look, I've promised . . . this lady that she should see Ned Alleyn. Can't we come to some arrangement?'

Frizer looked the lady up and down. A whore if ever he saw one, a Winchester goose, albeit one only recently plucked. He motioned the pair away from Skeres, who stood resolutely staring into the middle distance, to where the great black bear stretched and rolled in the wet mud.

'I shouldn't really do this,' Frizer whispered, 'but Philip . . . Master Henslowe, you know . . . Philip gives me a few of these.' He hauled out papers from his satchel. 'Tickets – for tomorrow's performance.'

'How much?' the gentleman asked.

'A half angel – each.'

The gentleman swallowed hard.

'And of course, for an extra half angel . . .'

'Each?' snapped the gentleman.

Frizer shrugged and smiled. 'Good lord, no, sir. A half angel for the two. For the tour. Chance to meet the cast. But, of course, if you would rather not spend . . .'

The gentleman looked down the dress of the girl at his side and sighed. 'I don't think it is a matter of rather not . . .'

The goose at his elbow snuggled closer and looked up at his ruff. 'Go on, Dickie,' she murmured. 'You know I've got a thing for actors.'

He looked down at her again. He knew exactly where that thing was. 'Oh, all right.' He ferreted in his purse. 'Here.' He thrust the coins into Frizer's hand and snatched the tickets. 'Tomorrow afternoon.' He nodded and whisked the girl away.

Skeres wandered to Frizer's side. 'Tomorrow afternoon, Ing?' he said.

His friend smiled at him. 'I thought the Cranes, Nick,' he said, jingling the money. 'The drinks are on that gentleman. Not to mention their finest brain pies.' And they trotted away in the rain, chuckling as they went.

Master Sackerson turned to watch them go, scratching thoughtfully under his belly with a fearsome claw.

'Now, bright Zenocrate,' Alleyn boomed, 'the world's fair eye . . .'

'Don't you bother with her!' a voice called from the groundlings' centre. 'I'll give you one in the eye you won't forget in a hurry!'

The woman's call was greeted with cheers and whistles. Alleyn was used to this and went on regardless although at times his voice was totally inaudible. The audience settled down after a while, in the usual style of the Rose's patrons. They needed to get a few ideas off their chest and then they were usually quiet, especially in plays with a little something for everyone – fights, kissing, fights, kissing – all the things the crowd loved best.

Alleyn reached out to Zenocrate and bent her backwards, breathing words of love into her ear.

'Watch out,' George whispered. 'My wig is loose.'

'You should use more pins,' Alleyn answered through gritted teeth. 'Why is your hair so short?'

'Ringworm,' George confided, relaxing into the actor's grip like a woman far gone in ecstasy.

Alleyn made a mental note to kick the lad from here to Kingdom come when the play was over, but for now settled for pulling back slightly from his embrace.

'Phwoar! That's the stuff!' a woman called. 'That's the way to do it!'

There was a scuffle in the crowd and two burly men were seen to be carrying out a struggling woman, her grey hair being no bar to being thrown out for the sake of the other patrons. Philip Henslowe took his responsibilities towards the paying public very seriously. Jack Windlass watched it all a little bemused. He liked to keep abreast of what his gentlemen did for a living. His last charge had been a rising star in the Guinea Company; hardly a walk on the wild side. He was enjoying this rather more.

One of the actors not on stage was Richard Burbage. He'd die rather than admit he was there to learn from the great Alleyn, so to that end he had come as an apothecary. His curls were swept up under an academic cap and his usual roisterer's satin was replaced by brown fustian, authentically stained with nameless liquids at the cuffs. The costume was authentic because he had lifted it from an actual apothecary who had temporarily laid his aside whilst entertaining himself with a Winchester goose along Maiden Lane. Every time he went there, Richard Burbage chuckled at the irony of the name.

Bugger, but Alleyn was good! Alleyn was, blast his eyes, very good. And those words! Burbage slipped a piece of parchment and an inkpot out of his purse and began scribbling in the dull light afforded him by the leaden Southwark sky.

'And I will teach thee how to charge the foe,' Tamburlaine was telling his son, 'And harmless run among the deadly pikes. If thou wilt love the wars and follow me . . .'

And half the audience who had once been sitting were on their feet, all set to do the same.

Up in the gallery, Eleanor Merchant turned to her sister and pulled her closer so she could speak. 'When does Master Shakespeare come on stage?' she asked.

Constance didn't turn her head; her eyes were full of Ned Alleyn, strutting and fretting his hour upon the stage. 'Hmm?'

'Master Shakespeare. When does his part begin?'

Constance turned to her now. 'I thought Master Shakespeare was just lodging with us,' she said tartly. She had not been fooled by her sister's performance the day before.

'He is, indeed he is,' Eleanor said. 'But he kindly gave us these tickets and it is only polite to at least see him when he comes on stage.'

Constance held her gaze for a few seconds longer, then turned away, convinced that she was right. 'I have no idea,' she said. 'I don't know what part he plays.'

The man in front of her turned round. 'Do you mind?' he asked. 'I am here to listen to Master Marlowe's masterful prose, not two gossiping women.'

Constance dropped her eyes demurely and then looked up from under her lashes. She had found this seldom failed, no matter how tense the situation. 'I beg your pardon, sir,' she said. 'My sister and I know some of the actors and we didn't want to miss their entrance.'

The man looked her up and down and then did the same to Eleanor. 'You do not surprise me that you . . . know actors,' he said, the tiny pause speaking volumes. 'But can you know them a little more quietly in future?' He turned back to watch the stage, the back of his neck showing outrage better than many people could do with a written ten-page declaration.

'I think we had better be quiet, Constance,' Eleanor said loudly. 'We wouldn't want to annoy anyone!'

'Madam,' said a black-clothed man to Eleanor's right in strident tones. 'Do not worry that you are interrupting this masque of the Devil. We should all lift up our voices and proclaim our hatred of this mumming and blasphemy, with boys dressed as women, and men—' He was cut off short as the burly men who had removed the bawdy woman appeared at his shoulder.

'Would you like to come along with us, sir?' one of them said, grabbing an arm.

'No, I have paid my penny and I intend to stay!' the man said, trying and failing to cross his arms.

'We have Master Henslowe's instructions to refund your penny, sir,' said the other man, wondering if anybody realized the extreme unlikeliness of what he had just said. He leaned round and pressed the man's jaw hard between finger and thumb. When his mouth popped open against his will, the first bouncer put a penny in it and then clamped it shut until he swallowed.

'Refund complete, Zachariah?' asked the second bouncer.

'Complete,' his colleague answered and, taking an elbow each, they walked the black-clad zealot backwards and flung him out into the street.

Constance and Eleanor had been staring transfixed as the little play within a play had unfolded, but Constance was the first to recover.

'Eleanor,' she said, 'sweet sister, I think that I will never be able to understand this play if I stay in this spot. I can see a quieter part of the crowd over there and if I can make my way there, I will. I will meet you outside by the Bear Garden when the play is over and we can go home together.'

Eleanor nodded and turned back to the stage. It was very true what they said; Master Alleyn had a well-turned calf and if he ever took the armour off, he might display a well-turned manhood, too. Why Constance was being so coy, she would never understand. She let herself drift off on a daydream of the deceased Master Merchant and his one talent, as Marlowe's mighty lines spun and twisted in the air above her oblivious head.

'You pleased with it, Kit?' Thomas Sledd was waving to his man who dutifully trooped out on to the stage with a placard round his neck that read, 'Act Five, Scene One'. 'He'll have to go,' he muttered to the playwright. 'Deaf *and* illiterate. Not the right part for him at all.'

'Relax, Thomas.' Marlowe smiled. 'It's going well. Will? You look a bit put out.'

Shakespeare was edging his way behind the Arras that screened the orchestra. 'It's this bloody gun,' he mumbled. 'I hate the things.'

Sledd snatched the arquebus out of the actor's hand. 'I've told him, Kit, a hundred times. The thing's as safe as houses. So are all the others.' He pointed across the stage to the far wings where the others in the scene shouldered their weapons. 'This fuse will burn for ever but it won't do anything. You'll get a flash and a pop and the clapper will do the rest. The Governor will scream – though, please God, not like he did in rehearsals – and you'll get a round of applause. You'll like that, Will, won't you?' And he stuffed the gun back into Shakespeare's grasp before pirouetting away into darkness.

'He'll have to go,' the Warwickshire man muttered to Marlowe. 'Jumped-up stage hand! What does he know about the Muse?'

'The Muse, Will?' Marlowe chuckled. 'Young Sledd has been making the Muse dance and sigh since I was singing at the High Altar at Canterbury and you were creeping unwillingly to school. Trust him. If he says the gun is safe, the gun is safe.'

'I care not,' the Governor of Babylon was bellowing from the ramparts below the heavens' canopy, 'nor the town will never yield As long as any life is in my breast.'

'Oh, shit, that's me!' Shakespeare stumbled out into the limelight, colliding with Techelles and his guard before straightening and getting into his role.

'Thou desperate governor of Babylon,' he cried out, cradling the arquebus in his arms. 'To save thy life, and us a little labour . . .' He paused for Techelles to chuckle in reaction, but the dolt missed his cue and Shakespeare stormed on, 'Yield speedily the city to our hands. Or else be sure thou shalt be forc'd with pains More exquisite than ever traitor felt.'

Kit Marlowe peered through the slats and sought out the face of Sir Francis Walsingham. He knew more about the pains meted out to traitors than anyone in the Rose that day but the face was as immobile and unreadable as ever.

The orchestra shattered the air and there were mixed cheers and boos as Ned Alleyn came on, drawn by half the cast in chains, their jaws strapped with leather and hauling the chariot Philip Henslowe had mortgaged Master Sackerson's Bear Garden to buy. The action went on and Marlowe could see what the audience could not. Thomas Sledd and his number two had slipped iron bracelets over the wrists of the Governor of Babylon and hauled him upwards so that he hung from his own walls. The pain in his wrists, arms and legs was appalling and he growled in agony.

'That's good,' Marlowe muttered to cast members nearby. 'Did he do that in rehearsals?'

'Your feet!' Thomas Sledd hissed through the canvas and wood flat. 'Put your feet on the ledge, you stupid bastard!'

With gratitude, the Governor found the ledge and the feeling flowed back into his wrists and hands.

'See now, my lord.' Amyras was Tamburlaine's son, although John Meres was actually a year older than Ned Alleyn. 'How brave the captain hangs.'

Alleyn gave another of his cruel, cynical laughs. ''Tis brave indeed, my boy: well done!' He turned to Shakespeare, already fumbling with his wheel-lock. 'Shoot first, my lord,' Alleyn ordered, 'and then the rest shall follow.' Six guns came up to the carry as the cast became a firing squad.

'Then have at him,' the Warwickshire man shouted, 'to begin withal.' And he levelled the arquebus, before bringing it up to point at the Governor's chest. There was a flash and a puff of black smoke. Shakespeare stumbled backwards with the thud of the explosion, momentarily blinded and with an appalling pain in his right shoulder. There was a scream and Eleanor Merchant fell back in the gallery, a gaping hole in her throat.

On his wall, the Governor jumped, jarring his wrists anew and he all but slipped off his perch. That wasn't supposed to happen. 'You save my life,' he said, trying to keep things going, even though the groundlings were screaming and shouting, swaying now towards Eleanor Merchant's box, now away from it, 'and let this wound appease the natural fury of great Tamburlaine!'

Great Tamburlaine was striding across the stage. Shakespeare was standing in shock, the murder weapon still in his hand, the harmless wick still smoking. Thomas Sledd was there seconds later, easing the gun out of the actor's cold hands while Philip Henslowe, as bewildered as everyone else, ran on to the stage and begged for order.

'A doctor here!' someone shouted. 'For the love of God!'

And the screaming started again.

FOUR

The wind whipped along Bankside that night, driving people to their beds and the stinging rain to the west. A handful of men, cloaked against the weather, splashed their way to the entrance of the Rose, dark and silent now that the crowds had gone and the place had ceased to resemble Bedlam.

A single church candle burned in the centre of the stage and the cast of *Tamburlaine* sat disconsolately around it, their faces flickering in the flame. They'd talked themselves hoarse over the bizarre events of the afternoon and Philip Henslowe had gone into a nervous decline. He had had to give some people their money back and he had never actually done that before. He was still feeling a bit queasy.

The doors crashed back and the group of men arrived, torches guttering in their faces, throwing lurid shadows around the empty galleries. Their pattens clattered on the boards and thudded on the groundlings' mud, churned by the rain and panic of the afternoon. The man at their head stood alone for a moment, half-resting on a cane, then raised his torch higher. 'I am Hugh Thynne,' he told the company, 'High Constable of London. Who's in charge here?'

Four men were on their feet: Philip Henslowe, Ned Alleyn, Thomas Sledd and Kit Marlowe.

'That's all I need,' Thynne grunted. 'A committee.' He turned to his constables of the Watch. 'Find the doors. Nobody leaves. Which of you is Henslowe?'

'I am,' the impresario said. He had never met Hugh Thynne before but he knew his reputation; he'd be lucky to have a theatre at all by midnight.

'Do I assume, Master Henslowe,' Thynne said as he climbed the steps to the stage, 'that these people are your company?'

'They are, sir,' Henslowe said. A fine-tuner of conversation was Philip Henslowe. If a man was your social inferior you called him sirrah and metaphorically shat all over him. If a man was the High Constable of London you grovelled for England.

Thynne looked him up and down. 'You own this place?' he sneered, wiping a finger along the edge of the stage.

'I do, sir,' Henslowe told him.

'Who are you?' Thynne half-turned to the next man.

'Christopher Marlowe.' There was no 'sir' this time.

'What do you do here?' Thynne asked.

'Here?' Marlowe looked around. 'I watch my plays being enacted.'

'Oh, a playwright.' Thynne was dismissive. 'I've met people like you before. Watson, was it? Nashe, I believe. There aren't many people I don't know.'

Marlowe chuckled. 'You must have misheard me, Constable. I said I was a playwright.'

Such bonhomie as Thynne showed in his face vanished in an instant and he closed in on Marlowe so that their noses almost touched. 'I didn't mishear you and that's *High* Constable, by the way.'

'High Constable indeed, Master Thynne.' Ned Alleyn felt that only his lofty intervention could defuse the moment. 'You know me, of course.'

Thynne dragged his eyes away from Marlowe, committing every feature to memory, for the next time. And there would be a next time, he just knew it. He focussed on Alleyn. 'No,' he said flatly.

'Edmund Alleyn.' The actor bowed with an extravagant flourish, though it looked less dignified than it might have done because he was still wearing Tamburlaine's half-armour, unbuckled and curiously unbecoming in Thynne's torch light. The High Constable ignored him. 'Let's have more light in here!' he shouted to no one in particular and Thomas Sledd obliged, clapping his hands and sending his stage hands skipping to find and light candles.

'Careful, Thomas,' Henslowe hissed. 'Naked flame. Straw. Timber. I don't have to paint you a picture.' And he stared at the constables' torches with undisguised panic.

'Er . . . yes.' Alleyn couldn't let it go at that. 'I am currently on loan to Master Henslowe, as it were, from the Lord Admiral's Men. The Lord Admiral—'

'I know who the Lord Admiral is,' Thynne stopped him short.

'One of too many rich gentlemen with troupes of actors as toys. Well, let me tell you – all of you – while I've got you here, you and your triple-damned theatres give me and my lads more grief than all the other low-life of London put together. You!' He pointed his cane at Sledd, now back in the seated circle. 'You're the factotum here?'

'Master Sledd is my Stage Manager,' Henslowe volunteered.

'Mute, is he?' Thynne asked.

'No, I ain't!' Sledd stood up to his full height and barely reached Hugh Thynne's nose.

The High Constable smiled. 'Then you're the one I want to see. Where's the gun?'

'Backstage,' Sledd told him.

'And the body?'

'The Tiring Room.'

'Right. One thing more. Where was the victim when she was shot?'

'Over there.' Sledd pointed to a gallery to the left of the stage, half-hidden in darkness now.

Thynne took it in, turned and walked to the stage's edge. Then he turned back. 'Who fired the fatal shot?'

There was a silence in which eyes flicked from right to left and back again. After what seemed an eternity, a balding actor got to his feet. 'I did,' he said, looking Thynne squarely in the face.

'Name?' the High Constable asked.

'Shakespeare . . . er . . . Shaxsper.'

Thynne walked slowly towards the man. 'Well, which is it?' he asked.

The Warwickshire man stood his ground. 'Shakespeare,' he said.

Thynne tucked the cane under his arm, reached out and took the actor's right hand. He held it close to his eyes and proceeded to sniff his fingers, until Shakespeare pulled it away.

'Powder,' Thynne said. 'You've fired a gun all right, and recently. Just checking you aren't covering for another of your number. You know what they say . . . thick as thieves.'

'That's outrageous,' Alleyn began, but Thynne was probably the only man in London capable of stopping the greatest actor since the time of Jesus from holding forth and it worked, with one flick of his hand.

'Shakespeare. Sledd. You will come with me.' And he marched towards the Arras at the back of the stage, the pair trooping behind him. Marlowe joined him. So did Henslowe and Alleyn. 'Not you,' Thynne growled. 'Nor you. Nor you.'

'These men were working under my auspices, Master Thynne,' Marlowe said in level tones. 'I owe them my support.'

'Support?' Thynne chuckled. 'They're going to need more than that.' He paused for a moment, then relented. 'All right,' he said. 'But just you, Marlowe. And the rest of you,' he yelled to the still sitting cast. 'My men are at every door, every gate and there are others outside. If anyone attempts to leave . . . well, don't attempt to leave.'

Sledd led the way behind the Arras, making sure Thynne's flames didn't catch the sparkling velvet and he led them down a small flight of stairs to the Tiring Room. Props lay everywhere here, wigs, dresses, shackles and all the panoply of ancient Persia, all of it made a few weeks ago by the sweated labour of Spitalfields. What had looked like gold and costly vestments to the groundlings was shown here in its true tawdriness as paint, plaster and a sprinkling of glamour, which was all lost in the harsh light of the Constable's torch.

On a table in the centre lay the body of Eleanor Merchant. Her cap and cowl had gone and her bodice had been ripped open in a frantic attempt to save her life. Somebody had closed her eyes, but her mouth was still open with the shock and impact of the musket ball that had hit her in the throat and blown her backwards off her seat.

'Anybody know who she was?' Thynne asked, peering at the gaping wound, almost black now with congealed blood.

'Eleanor Merchant,' Marlowe said.

'My landlady.' Shakespeare's voice was almost inaudible.

Thynne's head came up slowly. 'Indeed?' he murmured. 'So you knew her well?'

'Tolerably.' Shakespeare shrugged.

'Intimately?' Thynne was watching the man closely.

'I said "tolerably",' Shakespeare repeated, louder this time.

'Yes.' Thynne smiled coldly. 'I heard what you said. Where's the gun, Factotum?'

Thomas Sledd crossed the room and handed the arquebus to

Thynne, who swapped it for his torch. He sniffed the lock, cocked it, reversed it in his hand and looked down the bore. 'It was supposed to have been empty,' Sledd said. 'They all were.'

'Who set the charge?' Thynne asked.

'I did,' the stage manager told him.

'When?'

Sledd was on his best behaviour, so he kept his voice level in the face of the endless questions rapped out by the High Constable. He owed it to Philip Henslowe not to annoy this man who could ruin him in the bat of an eye. 'Half an hour, perhaps more . . . Before the play began, I know that. I don't have time later.'

'And when – in whatever play this was – did Master Shakespeare here kill this woman?'

Shakespeare raised a hand to protest, to have it knocked down again by Marlowe.

'Act Five, Scene One,' Marlowe explained.

'In the real world.' Thynne tried to be patient. 'How long elapsed between the loading of the gun and the shooting?'

'An hour and a half, perhaps a little more.'

'Thank you. Now, that wasn't too difficult, was it?' The High Constable weighted the arquebus and brought the butt to the floor with a thud. 'And who handled it in that hour and a half or a little more?'

'Anyone could have,' Marlowe said.

'That's right!' Sledd clicked his fingers as he realized, his face oddly pale under the torch's guttering light.

'And did that "anyone" include you, Master Shakespeare?' the High Constable asked.

'Yes,' the actor said.

'Good enough. You will come with me. Consider yourself under arrest.'

'On what charge?' Marlowe asked.

Thynne frowned at him before taking his torch back from Sledd. He tucked the gun under his free arm. 'I thought you told me you were a playwright,' he said. 'You work it out.' He saw Shakespeare hesitating. 'Now, you *are* going to come quietly, aren't you, Master Shakespeare? I know my hands are full at the moment, but it's surprising what a mess a flaming brand can make of a face. And like most of you vain bastards, I expect your face is your fortune, isn't it?' He peered closer at the pasty cheeks, the receding hair, the slightly petulant mouth. 'Although possibly not so much in your particular case.'

'I'll come quietly,' Shakespeare said sulkily. 'I didn't do anything. You can't keep me locked up if I didn't do anything.'

At least two men in that Tiring Room knew that wasn't true, but neither of them was going to debate it. In High Constable Thynne's world, *habeas corpus* was merely a serving suggestion.

'Of course not,' Thynne said, his voice flat. 'We'll let your friends know where you are when we have found a little corner for you somewhere.' And he shepherded the actor in front of him with little prods of the gun barrel and passed through the Arras, leaving Marlowe and Sledd behind in the gloom.

After a moment or two, Thomas Sledd spoke. 'Old Will, eh? That was a surprise.'

'Yes,' Marlowe said. 'To Master Shakespeare as well as to you, Tom, I think. We have work to do, but we'll let the dust settle a bit, first. All may yet be well.' Although for the life of him, he couldn't see how.

The sun filtering through the grimy window was weak, but even so it seemed to have a knack for lingering on every cobweb, every worn seat, every burn and ring on the oak table in the centre of the room. The chairs gathered around it were a motley bunch, some from great houses that had seen better days, others from alehouses where the owner was still trying to work out how the drinkers managed to steal things even when they were nailed down. The room seemed to be holding its breath. Despite overlooking Rose Alley the cries from below and the rumbling of wheels seemed muffled by atmosphere and the only sound that was noticeable to the man who sat slumped in the best chair in the house at the head of the table was the soft chink of coins in the round pot he rolled from hand to hand over the ridged wood in front of him. Occasionally he added a sigh to the mix, but generally the room just waited for the next Act.

Eventually, voices were heard below and then feet on the stairs. The door crashed back and suddenly the room seemed full of people, milling about, jostling to get the most comfortable chairs, of which there were precious few.

'Good morning, Master Henslowe,' said a large man, florid in the face and with his hair combed forward in careful curls, making every strand count. 'Sad news that brings us here.' He eyed the pots on the table and weighed one in his hand. 'No refunds, then?' He smiled round at the others, shuffling into position around the board. Some chuckled. Others looked mildly shocked. Only one face did not alter its expression: Nicholas Faunt had not risen to be Spymaster Walsingham's right-hand man by wearing his heart on his cheek.

Henslowe waited, his chin supported on one weary hand. He had learned over the few years of his theatrical career that adopting a world-weary pose from the outset was always the best plan. There was no need to be too enthusiastic; the best of plays could let you down, he knew that better than anyone, and if the Master of the Revels woke up dyspeptic some morning, he could close you down just for the fun of it. Then again, the Plague could come calling and business could come to a dead stop. So he kept his thoughts to himself. Finally, all the shuffling and muted greetings from the men around the table subsided and he cleared his throat to speak.

'As you must know, gentlemen, a very sad and shocking occurrence took place at the play yesterday afternoon. A member of the audience was shot and killed during the execution scene and a member of the cast has been taken by the High Constable to the Clink.'

'A member of the cast?' The florid man was aghast. 'Not Ned Alleyn, surely?'

Murmurs ran round the table again. None of the men present had any grounding in theatre, but they all knew box-office gold when they saw it posturing before them.

'No, no, Master Alleyn is not implicated,' Henslowe said hurriedly – adding, in his head, *for once*. 'It was Master Shaxsper – Shakespeare he calls himself now – from Stratford.'

'A local man, then?' someone checked.

'Er . . . local? No. Stratford-on-Avon. It is . . .' Henslowe waved a vague hand above his head. Money was his talent, not geography.

'It is near to Oxford, gentlemen,' Faunt supplied. He knew every corner of the realm; madmen intent on harm didn't just come from London and it paid to keep your eyes everywhere.

He looked at Henslowe. 'I understood Master Shaxsper to be a playwright, Master Henslowe, not a player.'

'You are very knowledgeable, Master . . . er . . .' Henslowe looked at Faunt with an eyebrow raised, waiting for his name, but nothing came. 'It is true that Master Shaxsper does . . . dabble. But we have Master Marlowe as our playwright here, and need no other.'

Faunt smiled his secret, closed smile and said nothing.

Henslowe began to feel he was losing his momentum. He cleared his throat and continued. 'Master Shaxsper's role was not large, so he can be replaced, but I wonder whether we might perhaps do best to cancel the performances. At least for a while.' The men around the table were all looking at him aghast. At least one of them had made very big plans for the money which would pour in and several had spent it already.

The florid man was a pork butcher by trade, and money ran in his veins, alongside the lard. 'We can't close down Master Marlowe's *Tamburlaine* just because some jade is dead!' he cried. There were protests this time from every side. He blustered a little and some of his curls began to unravel. 'You say this woman was shot. That's not what I heard. I heard she was . . . well, shall we say she took on more than she could manage and she died of it.'

'I heard she was stabbed,' said a man from the bottom of the board. He was dried up, desiccated, and could only be a lawyer.

'No, I heard what Walter here said, that she took a client while she was watching the play and she . . .'

Henslowe rapped on the table with the money box, which split and rolled its pennies across the table. The sight of the money collected their wits together again and they were quiet. 'Gentlemen, please! I don't care what you heard. I saw it and I know she was shot.' He looked down for a moment to collect himself. He had seen some sights, God knew, but the mess the woman had been in was something he never wanted to see again. He swallowed hard, to force the bile back down his throat. 'She was shot and Master Shakespeare's gun seems to have been the guilty weapon. It was a sad event, brought about, as I understand it, because of some lovers' tiff. So from that respect alone, it won't happen again. We are also replacing the blank firing mechanism in the arquebuses in the execution scene with . . . Apparently the orchestra are coming up with something. I doubt it will be so effective, but . . . well, there are obvious advantages.' He tried a wry smile. 'But even so, we will not be putting on this play for at least . . .'

The dried-up lawyer licked his lips and spoke. His voice was as dry as he was, but he spoke for almost every man around the table and so they all listened. 'You are closing the play down? Are you mad?'

'Pardon?' Henslowe was as keen for a penny as the next man, but there was a limit and he had reached it.

'We could never buy publicity like this,' the lawyer said. 'Have the family been in touch? The dead woman's, I mean.'

'No. I understand Master Alleyn knows the sister . . .'

There was coarse laughter from the pork butcher's direction. 'Ned Alleyn knows everyone's sister,' he said.

Henslowe waited a second more for the man's bulk to stop shaking, then continued: 'Knows the sister of the deceased. He hasn't managed to speak to her yet; apparently she is prostrated with grief at present.'

'Well off?' the lawyer asked.

Henslowe raised his hands. 'I really don't know,' he said. 'I understand that Mistress Merchant was a widow in comfortable circumstances. I can't speak for her sister.'

Faunt leaned forward. 'Shall I try and find out for you, Master Henslowe? I think what our friend Master Spenlove is getting at is – correct me if I am wrong – that we need to know what kind of payment Mistress Merchant's family may require.'

'Payment?' The voice came from right next to Henslowe's right elbow and made him jump. The man had sat there since the beginning and had hardly uttered a word. In fact, he had been so still that Henslowe had begun to wonder if he had dropped off to sleep. 'Payment? Whatever for?'

Faunt blinked and exchanged startled glances with Henslowe. 'Well, the woman is dead . . .'

All eyes turned to the man on Henslowe's right. He was well dressed but not flashy, and sported a little beard which was years too young for him. He had been part of Henslowe's little coterie of investors since the theatre had been built, but no one had heard him speak before.

'She paid her money to come in, didn't she? Just like all the others? She knew the risks. Paying to come in implies that there is no blame to be attached to the theatre whatever happens. Surely?' He looked round for others to agree with him. Slowly, the heads around the table began to nod.

The lawyer coughed gently. 'I think, Master Bancroft, that buying a ticket to a play does not imply that you expect to be shot,' he said. 'Although it is true the law is silent on this issue. Theatres are, after all, new, and the law is old.'

'Look here, Spenlove.' The pork butcher pointed down the table with a meaty finger. 'Master Bancroft has a good point. She knew there are guns in this play. She took the risk when she bought her ticket.'

'There is a slight complication, gentlemen,' Henslowe said quietly.

'What, another?' spat Bancroft.

'Mistress Merchant and her sister did not pay to come in . . .'

'Aha!' The pork butcher's finger was in the air now. 'That's done them in then, as far as money from us goes. They crept in without paying.'

A weaselly man opposite the butcher piped up. He was one who had already spent his dividend and he felt his heart descend from his throat for the first time since he had heard of the shooting. 'Can't we sue her in Chancery, then?' he said.

'She *is* dead,' Faunt said, reasonably.

'Her estate, then?' the weasel said. 'For . . . distress. Loss of income.'

The nods were even more enthusiastic now, but Henslowe felt it incumbent upon him to ruin their relief. He usually went through as many somersaults as were needed to keep his investors happy, but he was not in the business of robbing orphans, even so. 'There are two things that make that a really bad idea,' he told the money men. 'The first is that her estate comprises a house and some money which she has left to her small children and her young sister. All very vulnerable and the children about to be made wards of the courts, so that is unlikely to work. We will have the full weight of the law against us, begging your pardon, of course, Master Spenlove. And secondly, I have to tell you that they didn't pay because they were in the audience as guests of Master Shakespeare.'

The silence that met that piece of news was absolute and the dust swirling in the weak sunbeams was the only thing moving in the room. As always, the pork butcher was the first to break the silence.

'Bugger.'

'Bugger indeed, Master Preston,' Spenlove said. 'Perhaps we can put aside talk of money and this . . . tragedy for the moment and concentrate on how we should proceed with whether this play goes on or not.' There was something about the pause around the word 'tragedy' that made it hard to tell whether he was talking about his fellow investors or the woman stiff and stark in a coroner's court.

The weaselly man swivelled his eyes to the counting pots on the table. 'Do we know the total, Master Henslowe? For yesterday?'

Henslowe poked the pots and set them rolling. 'As you see, Master Corkerdale,' he said, 'they have not been broken yet. I believe that we had a full house, though, so we have done well. We will count them into the chest later. I need to know what I should do about—'

Preston's fist came down on the table and made the pots jump. 'All those in favour of going on with the play, say Aye.'

The table roared back, 'Aye.'

Preston turned a greasy eye in Henslowe's direction. 'All those against going ahead with the play and ruining us all, causing our wives and children to live out their lives in poverty and disgrace, say Nay.'

Henslowe set his mouth. The play was indeed the thing, but his conscience was troubling him all the same. A woman was dead. A man was in prison and likely to die there. There was something not quite right in his little world within the wooden O. He pushed himself back from the table.

'As you wish, gentlemen. I will let Thomas Sledd know to tell the actors and stage men. Meanwhile, I think I'm going to have a little chat with my bear.' He left the room with what dignity he could muster. What no one heard was his final sally as he clattered down the stairs. 'At least you can get some sense out of Master Sackerson.'

Thaddeus Bancroft was picking his way carefully down Rose Lane when he became aware of a noise behind him. He knew who it was, so didn't panic, but it struck him it was not a noise one would wish to hear coming from inside the linen press in a bedroom on a cold dark winter's night. It sounded as though Master Sackerson, struck down with catarrh, was breathing down a trumpet whilst eating a very soggy pie. Bancroft was being chased by Preston, the pork butcher.

'Master Preston,' he said, without turning round.

'Master Bancroft,' the butcher wheezed. 'I wonder, could we sit down? I find walking and talking together somewhat of a trial these days.'

Bancroft looked at him dispassionately and couldn't help but wonder how long 'these days' were. That amount of lard around the middle didn't happen overnight. And were the man's eyes simply extraordinarily like the animals he cosseted then slaughtered, or were they ordinary eyes, but very deeply sunk in fat? He settled on a combination of the two.

Bancroft steered him to a low wall and the man lowered himself on to it, gratefully. The wall was very low and getting up would be a challenge, but it was better than walking, any day. Bancroft stayed standing, his eye straying down the street to where Henslowe leaned over the wall into Master Sackerson's Pit, talking earnestly, throwing his arms around as excitably as any actor and, worryingly for anyone who had money invested in the man's enterprise, apparently waiting now and then for a reply.

'Did you chase after me for a reason, Master Preston, or is this a social call?' Bancroft was a busy man. His business didn't run itself. Unlike Preston he didn't have a family of burly sons who could do the work three times as well and twice as fast.

Preston took offence. 'I just thought I might have a word, Master Bancroft, that's all. I wouldn't trust that lawyer further than I could throw my prize pig and as for Corkerdale, he'd murder his mother for fivepence.'

'What about the new man. Flaunt, was it? I didn't catch his name properly. Is he a new investor?'

'That was one thing I was going to ask you,' the butcher wheezed, his lungs sounding like a bagpipe with moths. 'Can we afford new investors? My dividend was very small last Lady Day.'

'Marlowe's plays will make us all rich men,' Bancroft said.

'I can't remember the last time I went home with lines from a play ringing through my head.'

Preston was aghast. 'You've been to one of his plays?' He tried to get up by rocking back and forth, but gave it up as a bad job. 'I didn't have you down for an arty type, Bancroft. I had you down as a hard-nosed money man.'

Bancroft sighed. The man was, indeed, a pig. 'I invest in the theatre because I love poetry and beauty,' he said. 'If occasionally we have to back plays about rude mechanicals hitting each other with bladders, then so be it. But even then, I attend. I think it only fair.' He paused. 'Why do you invest in the theatre?'

'Why, to make money, of course!' Preston was as amazed as he was disgusted. That he had been about to ask financial advice from some primping poetry-spouting prig . . . He was aghast. 'I invest in all kinds of things. I've got money in . . .' He raised one fat finger after another, listing his interests: 'Pigs – well, that goes without saying. The pig will never go out of fashion. Hides. Candlemaking – the rendering side of things, of course. Er . . . I have some interests in a printer in Paternoster Row, but I think he's gone a bit religious. Not reliable, so I may remove my patronage there. Er . . .' He waggled his thumb as he tried to remember his other money-making ventures.

'A very mixed lot of interests,' Bancroft said. 'I just invest in my business and the theatre. The two things keep me busy enough.'

The butcher leaned over and took a pinch of Bancroft's doublet between his finger and thumb. Looking down, Bancroft could hardly believe how like a trotter it looked. 'Nice bit of stuff, Master Bancroft. The wife is always on at me to smarten myself up. Who is your tailor?'

Bancroft conjured up a picture of the man who made his clothes, a gentle-eyed man with a soft voice and agile hands. Going to be fitted for a new shirt or doublet was a little piece of Eden in the middle of Pandemonium and he wouldn't share his name with this porcine bully. 'Er . . . my cousin's wife arranges all that. I don't know the man's name. I am sorry, Master Preston.'

Preston started rocking again, holding his arms out to Bancroft for help. Bancroft looked down at him and smiled ruefully, then put his hands in the small of his back. 'I'd love to help you, Master Preston,' he said, 'but my apothecary says I really mustn't.

I have to dash now. Give my regards to Mistress Preston and the boys.' And he was gone, picking his way through the mud as though Preston didn't exist.

As he turned the corner, he stopped an urchin who was running with almost everyone else in earshot to see what the noise was about. 'If you help that fat man off that wall,' he told him, 'he will give you a penny.'

The child's eyes lit up and he turned to go.

'Make sure you get it up front,' Bancroft advised, and went on his way, a smile playing on his thin lips above his fashionable beard.

On his way to commune with Master Sackerson, Henslowe had been waylaid by Richard Burbage again. He was leaning against the oak beams of the Rose, making small talk with a girl and when he saw Henslowe, he broke away and pounded over to the theatre owner.

'Master Henslowe.' He doffed his cap with a theatricality that might have rivalled the incomparable Alleyn, assuming Burbage could act at all. 'I just heard of the tragedy.'

'Just heard of it, Burbage? You were there, man. You heard it at the time. And saw it. Good day. I have a bear to see to.'

'No, no.' Burbage was insistent. 'Not the woman. Oh, that was . . . dreadful, of course, quite dreadful. No, no, I mean Master Shakespeare. What a loss to the theatre.'

'We'll manage,' Henslowe grunted.

'I don't see how,' Burbage said, too loudly and too quickly. Then, more cajolingly, 'I mean, you have a vacancy. Who could possibly play the King of Argier?'

Henslowe frowned. 'Almost anybody,' he said.

'But I . . .'

'*You*,' Henslowe said, prodding the man's chest, 'are not even of my company. Or indeed, any company.' He looked at the boy's large nose and straw-stubbled chin. 'Come back when you can grow a beard.'

From his point of view, the conversation was over, so he crossed to the low wall above the Bear Pit, smiling broadly. 'How's my little dumpling?' he cooed to the four-hundredweight mass of fur, sinew and bone snoring gently on his rock.

FIVE

Because Eleanor Merchant had died in the Rose Theatre and because the Rose lay within the verge, within twelve miles of where Her Majesty lay at Placentia, it was Sir William Danby, the Coroner Royal, who presided over the proceedings.

He had every reason to be pleased with himself. After years of slogging it out at the Bar, from the Inns of Court to the heights of the Queen's favour, he had become, at last, Coroner Royal and he sat that morning in his outer office in the great Palace of Whitehall, the glittering chain around his neck. There were some unkind souls who said he wore it in the bath.

Hugh Thynne was not one of those. As he waited to be shown into the presence, looking out of the window at the Queen's guard marching and counter-marching in the mud of the tilt yard, he reflected on his lot in life. He would never see forty again, but the round of a skinner's assistant had never really appealed and one day he had hung up his scraping knife forever and offered his services to the parish. However, he kept his yearly subscription to the Worshipful Company of Skinners just in case crime began to pall.

The door opened and a liveried flunkey ushered Thynne into the chamber.

'Thynne.' Danby was sitting cross-legged at his desk, its surface buried in scrolls. 'I expected you at the inquest.'

'Sir William?'

'The dead man in the Thames.'

'I thought it was time Constable Williams won his spurs, sir. How was he?'

'Perfectly good.' Danby rolled up a paper and slid it aside. 'Perfectly good. I don't suppose we know who he was, the dead man?'

'We are still making our enquiries, Sir William,' Thynne told him. 'Now, to the other matter—'

There was a sharp rap at the door. 'Begging your pardon, Sir William,' said the flunkey standing there with a letter in his hand. 'This came just now, sir. It carries the seal of Lord Burghley.'

Danby frowned. 'Does it now? Er . . . later, Hugh . . .'

'Are we still for supper on Wednesday night?' Thynne asked. 'My wife is so looking forward . . .'

'Ah, I've a problem there, Hugh,' Danby said, slitting the wax seal with his knife. He read Burghley's missive quickly. 'Er . . . I'll let you know. Can you see yourself out?' He waved the letter. 'Affairs of State. You understand.'

Three days had passed since William Shakespeare had been unceremoniously frogmarched to the grim, low granite of the Clink in the Liberty of the See of Winchester and there they threw away the key. It was not until the next day that Kit Marlowe jumped the puddles of Bankside in another London downpour. Windlass had argued he should go with him, but Marlowe had hired, he reminded him, a manservant, not a nursemaid. Windlass was to stay put – hadn't he got some pewter to polish? Marlowe tapped with his rapier hilt on the solid oak door. A grille slid sideways and a face peered out, one or two brown teeth still clinging desperately to their gums. 'Yes?'

'I wish to see a prisoner, newly brought.'

'Name?'

'William Shakespeare.'

'Who wants him?' the face beyond the grille asked.

'I do,' Marlowe told him.

'You'll need a pass,' the gaoler grunted, narrow-eyed.

Marlowe slid the sword away into its hanger and flashed a silver groat. The gaoler smiled. 'The very one,' he said and the grille slammed shut. There was a growl of locks and a rattle of chains and a wicket door creaked open. Marlowe stepped inside. He was standing in a yard surrounded on all sides by ramshackle buildings that had once been inns. Prisoners wandered everywhere, some ignoring each other, others in whispered conversations out of the corners of their mouths. On a hay mound in the far corner, a large man was lying on top of a trollop, jerking up and down. Her legs were spread wide but other than that she appeared to be totally unmoved by the whole experience and was in fact carrying on a desultory conversation with a woman who sat on the ground alongside, suckling a child.

'The pass?' The gaoler held Marlowe's sleeve. He flipped the coin to him.

'Where will I find Master Shakespeare?'

'What's he in for?' the gaoler asked.

'He's accused of murder,' Marlowe told him.

'Oh.' The gaoler's face lit up. '*That* Master Shakespeare. You'd better leave that sword here, sir. There's people in this building would kill you for that.'

'They can always try,' Marlowe told him, his hand on the weapon's hilt.

'Suit yourself.' The gaoler slid back the wicket bolts before lighting a lantern and trudging across the yard. 'We don't have many murderers here, as it happens. Harlots, fornicators, pretty boys, night-wanderers. Oh . . . and over there –' he pointed to the corner with the copulating couple – 'recusants. Go on, my son,' he bellowed to the thrusting man. 'Give her one from me.' He leaned closer to Marlowe, his dreadful teeth bared in a grin. 'Not that I'd go nearer than a bargeman's pole to her,' he assured him. 'Your Master Shakespeare has a whole room to himself; Master Side's what we call it here.' He fumbled with a huge key in another lock and then stopped short. ''Ere.' He looked hard at Marlowe and his weapons, having noted that the man was also carrying a dagger at his back. 'You 'aven't come to kill him, have you? Only, I've got a reputation to uphold.'

'No.' Marlowe smiled. 'He's a friend of mine.'

'Oh,' the gaoler sneered. 'Pretty boy, eh? Well, it takes all sorts. Just remember –' he pressed his face close again – 'there *are* laws against that sort of thing, you know.' He kicked open what had once been an inn door and held up the lantern so that Marlowe could see his way in the room's grim interior. A whole family of rats had made their home in the crumbled wainscoting and the floor was slippery with urine-soaked straw. A pale, balding man was crouched on a rough stool in one corner. He peered at him as the light from the outside hurt his eyes.

'Thank you, gaoler,' Marlowe said. 'Leave the lantern, will you?'

'I'll have to lock you in,' the man grunted. 'Bang on the door when you're ready.' And he trudged off, turning the key behind him.

Marlowe squatted in front of the actor, placing the lantern carefully on the floor. There was no possible chance that the straw would catch fire, wet as it was, but he wanted to keep the glare from the man's eyes. He leaned forward. 'Will?' he said, gently. 'How are you?'

'Kit?' Shakespeare got up suddenly, nearly bowling the playwright over. 'Kit. I thought everyone had forgotten me.'

'It's been three days, that's all. I got here as soon as I could.'

'They've had the inquest, then?'

'They have, yes.'

'What was the verdict?' Shakespeare looked anxiously into Marlowe's face. 'What was the verdict? Was it murder?'

Marlowe looked at the man. He may not be the greatest poet in the business, nor the greatest playwright, but he had not taken him to be as stupid as all that. 'Of course it was murder, Master Shakespeare,' he said, formality returning now he was reassured that the man was still alive and kicking. 'Eleanor Merchant was killed by a ball through the throat. There are not many ways of having that happen other than murder.' Marlowe had sent Windlass to the Coroner's court where Sir William Danby and his sixteen men and true had decided on the course of events and the value of the arquebus's deodand.

'Accident!' Shakespeare shouted. 'Accident, that was what it was.'

'Are you saying you shot her, then?' Marlowe asked. 'Be careful how you answer that question, especially if anyone else asks it.'

Shakespeare turned away and punched the wall. In any other room he would have hurt his hand. Here, it just made a dent in the rotting wattle and daub. 'I don't see how I can have done. I wasn't directly facing her or anything close. But . . .' He leant his head on the plaster and put his hands flat on the wall on either side. His voice was low and muffled. 'But . . . how could it be otherwise?'

'I saw the gun kick in your hand, so I know it was loaded. But I was watching you, not the others, so I don't know if they had shot in their guns too,' Marlowe said. 'But I have to tell you, Will, that I don't see that there would have been time for anyone to load all of the arquebuses without being seen.'

Shakespeare didn't answer for a while and when he did it was just to murmur, 'I know. It had to have been me.'

'Did you give Eleanor Merchant a ticket?'

'Yes,' Shakespeare said, turning round and facing Marlowe and drawing a shuddering sigh. 'Yes. Her and her sister.'

'I've heard a little about her sister,' Marlowe told him.

'Constance? Have you? Who from? No, don't tell me. Ned Alleyn.'

'Yes. Have you seen him around the house?'

'No, but I have heard of his . . . interest.'

'Is she a pretty girl, Will?'

'Beautiful, I'd say.' Shakespeare looked rather serious. 'Eleanor was a handsome enough woman too, I suppose.' He gave the ghost of a smile. 'Most men in London are lodging with uglier women, I would venture.'

Marlowe was quiet, thinking. 'So . . . you and Eleanor were . . .?'

'No!' Shakespeare drew himself up. 'I am a married man, Master Marlowe. There was no such behaviour going on . . .'

Marlowe heard the pause and read it. 'But she would have liked there to be, perhaps?'

'She did make overtures, from time to time. The last time on the day before she . . . before she . . .'

Marlowe clapped a friendly hand on the man's shoulder. 'Don't upset yourself. You weren't to know. But perhaps we should keep this between ourselves.'

The actor nodded. 'Mmm.'

Marlowe couldn't read this silence so well. 'If there is more, Will, would you like to tell me?'

The man from Stratford drew a huge sigh and let everything out in a rush. 'There was something going on in the house, that's certain. There would be comings and goings, whispering at night. Sometimes there would be a knock, a strange knock, a code if you know what I mean?' Marlowe nodded. He knew all about strange knocks and codes in the dead of night. 'Eleanor would always go down to answer it, not Constance.'

'How do you know?'

A flush crept up Shakespeare's parchment cheek.

'Don't tell me you spied on them?' Marlowe said, and then, when the answer was a shake of the head, he added, 'You know because . . . you were in bed with Eleanor when the knock came.' A shake of the head. 'Constance! You were in bed with Constance! Does Alleyn know?'

'No. Constance has kept Master Alleyn at arm's length. She . . . well, she says she loves me.' Even Shakespeare found this unlikely, Marlowe could tell.

'I thought you were a married man,' Marlowe reminded him.

'I *am*. I *am* a married man. But . . . well, my wife and I . . . we don't get on. And . . . Constance was here and so was I and . . . she surprised me one night as I was washing myself and . . . well . . .' Shakespeare was now so fiery red that Marlowe could almost feel the heat.

'One thing led to another. I see.' Marlowe tapped his chin with his fingertips.

Shakespeare nodded. 'Yes. Not one thing, so much as . . .'

'Two things?'

'I haven't kept count. Many things, let's say.'

Marlowe looked at him solemnly. 'Did Eleanor know?'

'No. No, she thinks – thought – that Constance was still a maid. She often teased her about it, but I don't think she would like to think she was not.'

'And if she found out?'

'She would have thrown *me* out, for certain. And probably Constance, as well. Although perhaps not that, because the house belongs to them both. Their father was quite wealthy, I gather, and left them properties all over London. Master Merchant had a go at speculation, or so I understand, but was no good at it and now they only have the house in Water Lane. I suppose she could have gone somewhere else to live . . .'

'I am trying to find a motive for your killing Eleanor Merchant,' Marlowe reminded him, 'and you have given me one, though weak. Is there anything else I should know?'

'No. Except to say that there were shady doings in that house.'

'Did she keep a bawdy house, perhaps?'

'I don't *think* so. She only had just the one maid and herself.'

'And Constance . . . but of course, you can account for Constance. May I ask . . . was she . . .? Did she seem to know what she was doing?'

'She was quite . . . worldly,' Shakespeare had to concede.

'Perhaps that's it, then. Although why she would let Constance cease her duties seems a little strange . . . Did she think she was with child, perhaps?'

Shakespeare looked fit to explode.

'Will! Surely not?'

The poet shrugged. 'I am very potent, Master Marlowe,' he said. 'Ask my wife. Ask . . . not anyone, but sundry persons, yes.'

'Another motive, then,' Marlowe sighed. 'Thynne will now say that you hit Eleanor when aiming at Constance.'

'But Constance was not near Eleanor. I could see her in the gallery. She was on the other side.'

'That is a relief at least. But the fact that you could see your landlady in the crowd, that is a strike against you. It would have been better if you hadn't known where she was.' Marlowe looked at Shakespeare solemnly. 'I must say this, Master Shaxsper,' he said, 'I have had to rethink my view of you this day and no mistake. Stay here.'

Shakespeare couldn't help himself. 'I have little option, Master Marlowe,' he pointed out.

Marlowe shrugged. 'I will go and see the gaoler. A groat got me in. Let's see how much it will take to get you out.' He banged on the door and as it opened, he slid through it, already addressing the gaoler in wheedling tones.

The crowds had gone home again the next day and Philip Henslowe was sitting in his counting house, running the coins through his fingers like a man who had died and gone to Heaven. That wasn't Kit Marlowe's concern, not directly, anyway. What concerned him was that Eleanor Merchant had really died. Had she gone to Heaven? Who knew? Not Kit Marlowe, who had created the atheist Tamburlaine and was standing alone on the dimly lit stage as another damp spring day gave way to evening. The arc of a rainbow lay briefly over Southwark before the clouds eclipsed it, but the poet missed it. He had watched from the gods today, especially Act Five, Scene One, and noted in his mind where everybody had been standing. The Governor had been hauled up by his wrists on to his precarious perch on the far flat that doubled as Babylon's gate, courtesy of Thomas Sledd's brushwork and carpentry. The stage had been quite full. Ned Alleyn stood centre stage, a position Marlowe noticed the man hardly ever left, with his son Amyras to his left. Spear-bearers had just lashed Orcanes, King of Natolia and the King of Jerusalem to Tamburlaine's chariot. Theridamus had come on stage right, behind Amyras, Shakespeare's part being played since his arrest by an eternally grateful Walter Hodgett, who had only ever had one line in his life before this. Hodgett had stood where Marlowe stood now, lining up an invisible arquebus, to shoot the dangling Governor. There was no more risk-taking with shot and charges, for all most of today's crowd had turned up to see it. They may have hoped to see the Governor riddled with shot and jerking like a marionette at the end of his chains but all they got was a rattle of a thunder board and they had to imagine the rest.

Marlowe cursed and shook his head. He couldn't work out a damned thing without props. And the prop in question, the gun that had killed Eleanor Merchant, was now officially deemed the deodand, part of the estate of her murderer and no one except Sir William Danby was ever likely to see that again. Still, any gun would do and Marlowe went in search of one.

'Kit?' Thomas Sledd was in the Tiring Room, his mouth full of twine as he patched Zenocrate's gown.

'Thomas.' Marlowe had assumed he was alone. 'Got a gun?'

'Yes,' the stage manager said slowly. He and Kit Marlowe went back a while, and he knew this man. He was Machiavel; he was quicksilver – for all he knew, he was the Devil himself. What was he up to now?

'Come with me.' The two of them, the arquebus in Marlowe's hand, strode back out on to the stage. 'Get your ladder up there,' Marlowe told him and Sledd obliged. 'Up you go.'

'What are you going to do?' Sledd asked, hesitating on the first rung.

'Keep Will Shakespeare out of gaol. He didn't like the decor very much. Show me where the ledge is, the one where the Governor puts his feet. I can't see it from down here.'

'That's the general idea,' Sledd told him. 'Tamburlaine's not much of a scourge of God, is he, if he lets his enemies have a little rest before he has them shot?'

'Clever, Thomas,' Marlowe said. 'I knew there had to *be* a reason Henslowe kept you on.'

'Oh, ha.' Sledd was halfway up the ladder now. 'Ow. Shit.'

'Problem?' Marlowe called.

'Splinter.' Sledd winced. 'Right down the quick of my nail.' He sucked at his thumb. 'Never mind, all in a day's work. Now what?'

'Your feet are at the level of the ledge are they?'

'Yes.'

'Stop there, then.' Marlowe brought the arquebus up to the level, the ornate butt hard against his shoulder and his eyes narrowing along the barrel to the sight. 'I've never fired one of these. What happens, to the shot, I mean?'

'All depends,' Sledd said. 'They're all different, of course. Some dip, others rise. Still others skew right or left.'

'Don't any of them actually hit their target?'

Sledd laughed. 'That's where the skill of the shooter comes in,' he said. 'You've got to make allowances, see. Even note the wind if you're shooting in the open, as you usually would be. One thing's certain, though, they've all got a kick like a bloody ass. No wonder Will's shot went wide.'

'But did it, Thomas?' Marlowe was half talking to himself. 'Did it?' He lowered the gun. 'Run your fingers over the wall. There, about shoulder height. No, to the right.'

Sledd did as he was told, wondering what the point was in . . . 'Hello?'

'Something?' Marlowe crossed to the ladder. He saw Sledd rubbing the flat with his fingers, then reach for his knife and start attacking the woodwork.

'Bugger me!' Sledd said. 'It's a lead ball.'

'Show me.' Marlowe caught it as Sledd let go and he held it up to the little light he had. 'Dented to one side,' he murmured.

'Where it hit the frame,' Sledd said, slapping the timber to show its sturdy construction.

'Where it came from Shaxsper's gun,' Marlowe said.

'What?' Sledd did the old stage manager's trick and slid down the ladder's uprights as though the rungs weren't there. He took the lead ball. 'But it can't be, Kit.' He frowned. 'Will's shot hit Eleanor Merchant.'

'See that ledge up there?' Marlowe waved his hand in the air.

'Yes,' Sledd said.

Marlowe turned to face him. 'Can you, Thomas? Can you really see it? Or do you know it's there because you put it there?'

'Er . . .'

'It's all part of the illusion, Thomas,' Marlowe said softly to the boy. 'You said so yourself. "That's the general idea", you said. It's all part of the smoke and mirrors of the theatre. Will Shaxsper fires a gun and somebody dies. *Igitur* . . . Will Shaxsper killed that somebody. Actually, he didn't. Oh, he could have killed the Governor of Babylon, but the shot went wild and the man lives to this day, to take his bow with the great Ned Alleyn.'

'Then how?'

'Get us two candles, Thomas.' Marlowe looked up to the lowering night sky that frowned on the groundlings' yard. 'And I'll show you how this particular trick was pulled off.'

He looked behind him. He looked again to the box where Eleanor Merchant had sat. He crouched and dropped to one knee, taking Tom Sledd's proffered candle.

'Back there,' he said, after a moment. 'The shot came from there. Everybody in the theatre had their eyes on Will Shakespeare at that moment. Would he pull the trigger or wouldn't he? One or two might have anticipated that he would and they would have been watching the Governor for his reaction. But nobody, *nobody* would have been looking in *that* direction.'

He stood up, raising the candle high and crossing the stage again. He asked, 'And who sits here, Thomas, in this most shadowy corner of Henslowe's Rose?'

'The orchestra!' Sledd shouted. 'The bloody orchestra!'

'Bring your candle, Tom.' Marlowe was striding across the wooden O. 'We struck lucky once. I wonder if . . .'

He dropped off the edge of the stage and crossed to where the gallery seats began. 'Where was Eleanor Merchant sitting? Exactly, I mean.'

'Next level up,' the stage manager told him. 'And over to your left.'

Marlowe dashed up the steps and worked his way along the benches. 'Here?' he called back to Sledd.

'Next alcove. There.'

Marlowe looked back and crouched. Behind him the timbers of the upright were splintered and he held the line in his mind, sighting it with where Sledd stood in front of the orchestra's space. He drew his dagger, holding the candle to give him more light and eased its tip into the hole he found there. He felt it strike something and angled it out. *Another* lead shot, but different from Shakespeare's. And this one was brown with the blood of a theatre-goer.

There weren't enough fields for Shakespeare. As a boy, he'd chased pheasants in the orchards at Charlecote, run wild in the forest of Arden with the brambles ripping at his legs. Here it was all smoke and tanneries and the clanging and banging of a great city, as old priories came down and secular replacements went up, the cloisters turning into counting houses.

Norton Folgate, it was true, was on the edge of all this. It was on the edge of everything, in fact, being a Liberty outside the jurisdiction of the City of London, a fact that Shakespeare had grasped with both hands when Marlowe told him of it, until he realized that it made absolutely no difference to his status of wanted man on the run. Not being subject to petty bye-laws was one thing; being a man indicted by an inquest jury for murder was another. Escaping this was not as simple as walking down Hog Lane. But at least Hog Lane gave him a view of green. At its northern end it gave on to a vista of fields and trees and if he kept his back to the tanneries and breweries and could ignore the smells, he felt he could be back in Warwickshire.

With his eyes slits and a hand over his nose, he could concentrate on the drovers from the country, bringing their flocks into the city down the great artery of Ermine Street, heading for Smithfield. The honking of the geese greeted the dawn and the bells of lowing cattle rang him to his bed. But if he missed the pheasants, and the sleepy hollows of Arden, if he missed Anne and the children, he missed Constance Tyler more.

He had been wary when Marlowe had offered him room in his lodgings. Back in Blackfriars, Eleanor Merchant had been a constant presence in his room, listening on the stairs, peering out of the casement whenever he left the house. A landlady outside the door would not make hiding easy; Shakespeare had gone straight from his father's house to his wife's and had no idea that landladies in general, although quite keen to prevent their lodgers from stealing the fixtures and fittings, nevertheless usually left them well alone, except on rent day.

Marlowe's house had come as a revelation. Although once far grander than it now was, it still was a much more substantial building than the one he had roomed in with Eleanor and Constance. It was not hemmed in between its neighbours, all leaning on each other for support. Although Hog Lane was scarcely a wide thoroughfare, it would not have been possible to shake hands across it from the upstairs windows; no neighbours would be able to see in from across the way. The windows were large and airy, with wide sills on the inside that made excellent seats for a poetically minded young man to sit brooding, with his fevered brow against the cool pane. And not only that; Marlowe did not live in one poky garret room with a hard and narrow bed. He had two rooms, both well furnished, aired and clean; the rushes on the floor still smelt sweetly of river grass and the mattress on the bed was soft goose down, with not even a hint of prickly straw. Jack Windlass had an eye for such things. And a nose. All in all, for all his sour looks, he was one in a million.

Shakespeare hid his disappointment well when Marlowe opened a cupboard in the corner, revealing the foot of a ladder leading up into the attic above his rooms. A truckle bed in the corner looked comfortable enough and the cobwebbed window in the gable end gave light enough to see by.

'If you want to have a candle burning,' Marlowe had told him, 'come down into my room, but only when I am here. Otherwise, you will have to sit in the dark, I'm afraid. No one must know you are here, and if they see a light from the attic, they will be suspicious. More than that, they may fear that there is a fire and then the whole street will be in on the action, buckets every which way, poles to tear down the roof.'

Shakespeare looked mulish, but Marlowe ignored him. It had been almost an automatic action to bribe the gaoler, to bring Shakespeare back here to his rooms, but already a thread of doubt had begun to stitch itself through his brain. Shakespeare wasn't stupid, he knew, but for all that he could sometimes be so simple in his thinking that Marlowe thought that being locked up for his own good would perhaps be the best way forward. He would wait and see and meanwhile he would work out how to secure the cupboard door to lock him in; one prison exchanged for another. Windlass had not been keen on the whole enterprise; Marlowe had sensed that. Here was another mouth to feed, another chamber pot to empty.

Shakespeare sat hour after hour in his garret room, writing Constance sonnets that she would never read, that no one would ever read. More often than not he would tear them up or screw them into tight balls of frustration, flinging them around what little space he had like the arrows of outrageous fortune and watching them bounce and settle in the dust. Apart from his bed, hard and small but at least not in the dank walls of the Clink, the room was used for storage. At one end, lengths of lumber and some old shutters, spongy and green with damp and mould, were leaning against the chimney piece. Boxes of God-knew-what were stacked around the eaves and he had dragged one over to his bed to act as a table for his scribbling.

It was just as the sun was setting and his evening vigil alone with his thoughts was just beginning that he heard it. It was the time when, as a boy, the Shaxspers would kneel at home in prayer, each one in turn watching the street through a window for the prying eyes of the Puritans. But this wasn't the whispered Mass or the gentle chant of the psalms. It was a tapping, muffled but getting nearer. It sounded hesitant, like an old blind man feeling his way with a stick in a strange and darkened world.

Shakespeare closed his own eyes to focus on the sound. It was downstairs, two floors below. The floor where there should have been no one at that hour. This was Kit Marlowe's place. And Kit Marlowe was at the Rose again tonight, talking to Henslowe as the man cracked open his money pots and discovered yet again that he was richer than God. The servant Windlass was out too, lying with some whore in the Vintry or fleecing some poor paralytic sod at Primero where the Kings and Queens and Knaves tumbled like confetti. 'On no account, Will –' Shakespeare could hear Marlowe's voice in his head – 'on no account play cards with this man.'

Will Shakespeare wasn't in the mood to play cards with anybody tonight. His acting days at the Rose were over. Christ, his life was over, if he wasn't careful. Unless some miracle could save him. And the Shaxspers didn't believe in miracles any more. They had vanished with the Mass and the Rood and the certainty of the Holy Father. Even the Muse seemed to have deserted him but the tap-tap-tapping wouldn't go away. And it was getting nearer.

Shakespeare couldn't wait any longer. He'd pawned his spare coat when he'd first reached London and bought himself a sword. It was an old weapon, heavy, broad-bladed, the sort of steel old soldiers kept when they retired, to chop wood at home. And Will Shakespeare was no swordsman, especially in the half dark as the night of London closed in on him. He crept down the ladder, sliding the bolts as noiselessly as he could and eased the door open.

Shit! He cursed in his head as the hinges creaked. It was like being back in the Clink again. Ahead of him the landing stretched bare and dark, lit barely by the window at the far end. He stepped out, one pace, two, holding the door to the garret with a trailing hand in case it creaked again as it closed. He squatted, trying to make himself invisible, trying to blend with the darkness. The tapping had stopped. He felt his lips parchment-dry and his tongue thick with fear in his mouth.

There was a bang and he jumped, dropping the sword which thudded on to the boards. His heart was pounding as he picked it up, rising now before he lost all feeling in his legs. The taps had started again, getting nearer, getting louder. He squeezed through the doorway on to the gallery, leaning over to get a better view of the stairs. That was where the sounds came from but there was no one there. He edged forward, the blade point ahead of him like a dancer in the dark.

'Will!'

The name was hissed behind him, like an inrush of breath or the drawing of steel. He spun round, slashing the clumsy broadsword in a wide arc that flashed in the half light. It rang on other steel, slimmer, faster, more deadly, and he felt the hilt fly from his hand as the sword twirled in a high circle to clatter and bounce on the stairs below. Not that Shakespeare saw it fall because his head was held upright in a painful lock, a rapier point squarely between the collars of his shirt and tickling his throat.

'Now, what did I tell you about leaving your room?' a familiar voice said as Kit Marlowe slid out of the darkness. He dropped the sword point and Shakespeare's head flopped forward, his shoulders sagging as he breathed for the first time in what felt like years.

'You absolute bastard!' the Warwickshire man shouted and Marlowe sheathed his rapier before wagging a finger at him.

'I shall tell my dad,' he said. 'And my dad's bigger than yours.'

'I thought . . .'

Marlowe took the man by the arm and led him down the stairs. 'You thought I was at the Rose. You thought Windlass was out on the town. You thought you heard a cane tapping its way upstairs.'

On the first landing, Marlowe raised a finger and Windlass stood there in his leather jerkin, operating a couple of levers which reached across to the stairwell. He pulled one, then the other and the ends of the levers clacked on the wood. 'Wrong, wrong and wrong. I *was* at the Rose, but I've been back for an hour. Windlass *was* out on the town . . . How much did you make today, Jack?'

'Enough, Master Marlowe, thank you.' Windlass smiled, his auburn moustaches curling at their ends.

Marlowe leaned in to whisper to Shakespeare. 'He's a deep one.' He chuckled. 'Never a straight answer.' He pointed at the levers on the stairs. 'As far as the cane goes, a little gadget that a friend of mine uses from time to time. Just to scare people. Nicholas Faunt – I would ask if you had met him, but men don't always know when they have. He is a tricksy one and no mistake.'

Shakespeare shook his head.

'Well, just pray you never do,' Marlowe said. 'All right, Jack,' he called down the stairs. 'That's enough nonsense for one day. Will and I will dine through here. When you've got a moment?'

Windlass stopped playing with Faunt's gadget and wandered off into the scullery, muttering. Marlowe threw himself down in the chair by the empty grate. 'Just a little lesson, Will,' he said, looking at Shakespeare who stood, still quietly fuming, in front of him.

'I don't care for your games, Kit,' the Warwickshire man said. 'There's a price on my head.'

'And mine,' Marlowe reminded him, 'as the person who sprung you.'

Shakespeare sat down. 'Look.' He raised both hands in an attempt to explain his predicament. 'I'm grateful to you and all that. Really, I am. It's just this . . . this endless waiting around. Not knowing what's going on. I'd have done better going home.'

Marlowe sat back in the chair, unhooking the rapier and its hanger and easing the sheathed dagger from the small of his back. 'The door's open,' he said, with an extravagant flourish of his arm. 'Your road's to the north. They probably won't stop and search you at Bishopsgate and at this time of the year, the Hackney Brook shouldn't be too brimming in its banks, so you probably won't drown. Of course, I've heard there are ruffians between Shoreditch and Finsbury Fields who like nothing better than to welcome a gentleman from London with a reasonably sized purse, even if his sword isn't up to much.'

Shakespeare sat upright. 'I *can* find my way home, you know,' he said. 'I'm not a child.'

'Of course you can.' Marlowe nodded. He smiled, giving the Warwickshire man time to picture the scene. 'So you've returned home. You're back in . . . what's that place called, your wife's place?'

'Shottery.'

'You're back in Shottery. All homecomings and welcomes and "Daddy! Daddy!".' Marlowe leaned forward. 'Then what? "Isn't it about time you got back to work, Will?"' For a man who had never met Anne Shakespeare, he did a rattling impression of her. 'So there you have it; Will Shaxsper the glover is back at his trade again, his mind numbing, his senses dying. You'll never see a play again, still less act in one. Man, the only book you'll ever read will be the Bible – and we all know how that one ends.'

Shakespeare leapt to his feet and slammed his hand on to the mantel shelf, staring into the blackness of the grate. He knew Marlowe was right. And he hated him for it.

'Will.' Marlowe's voice was soft like sin. 'I've seen you out there on that stage. I've read your poetry – it's really come a long way since . . .'

'What?' Shakespeare spun to face him.

'I'm sorry.' Marlowe's hands were in the air now. 'They were lying on your bed and I couldn't help myself. Not bad. Not bad at all.'

'You had no right,' Shakespeare snarled.

'And you have no right to conceal the truth,' Marlowe sat back again. 'The truth is in your blood, Will Shaxsper, just as surely as it is in mine. You can write your poetry anywhere, I concede that point. But plays, Will? Treading the boards? Making the Muse dance to your tune? That . . . well, that can only be done here, in London. That's why you won't go home. And that's why we have to get you out of this little difficulty of yours.'

Shakespeare subsided again. The man was right. Damn him to Hell, Kit Marlowe was always right.

SIX

Mary Bancroft huddled close to her cousin as they waited in the ante room of the High Constable. Outside a feeble March sun shone on the comings and goings in Candlewick Street. Costers wheeled their carts along its twisting length and men and women roared out their street cries in pale imitation of Cheapside bustling and roaring to the north.

Here, though, the light and sound hardly carried at all and the oak-panelled walls were dark and foreboding. A clerk, Sam Renton, sat in a corner on a high stool scratching at vellum with his quill, doing his best to ignore the worried woman sobbing occasionally into her kerchief.

Hugh Thynne clattered into the stillness, his cane tapping on the stairs and the strewn floor. He took in the couple before him. He knew faces. Never forgot a face. It didn't pay in his line of work. But he didn't know these two. The man was a Johannes-come-lately, all new satins and cheap fur. His beard was rather too curled for his liking and his cheeks too closely shaved. And he had a smell about him that Thynne recognized but couldn't place.

The woman was a little older, careworn, pale and distraught, her fingers twisting endlessly in her kerchief, her eyes red with crying. Although her face was lined and her hair greying at the brow, her clothes too were new and gaudy. They sat on her body harshly, not worn into the creases and folds of her elbows and waist as good clothes, handed down and cared for by the impoverished gentry were. They were a good attempt at the clothes of a gentlewoman, but the extraneous bows and ribbons, the fluttering of laces let her down. Combined with her sodden cheeks and hand clenched round her lace-trimmed kerchief, they looked almost laughable. Like a costume she consciously wore for the world, not for herself.

'I understand,' the man said as he rose to meet the High Constable, 'that you have a body.'

Thynne saw the woman shudder. 'Perhaps,' he said.

'Let me explain,' the man said. 'I am Thaddeus Bancroft, tobacconist.'

Thynne smiled. So *that* was the smell he couldn't place. 'This is my cousin, Mary.'

Thynne nodded. He had been closeted with the mayor all morning and that never put him in the best of moods. And as to bodies, he came across them all the time, the flotsam of London. It was easy to forget that to someone they had once been as dear as life itself. And Hugh Thynne had forgotten it a long, long time ago.

'Simon Bancroft is my cousin, the husband of this good lady. He has been . . . missing for a while.'

'What sort of while?' Thynne wanted to know.

'A week ago yesterday,' Mary Bancroft said. 'That's when I saw him last.'

'What does he do, your husband?' The High Constable crossed to the fire, still smouldering in the grate for all it was spring outside. He was not much of a fashion plate himself, and he took little notice of what others wore, except when the clothes were so clearly at odds with the person within. Besides, this was Elizabeth's England. Clothes marked the man, the gallant from the counterfeit crank, the queer-cuffin magistrate from the queer-bird serving his time. There used to be laws about such things. It didn't take a perfumer to smell the tobacco on Thaddeus Bancroft nor to smell new money on his cousin's wife.

'He is a tobacconist too, sir,' she told him. 'He carries on his business in Fish Street, hard by the Bell.'

Thynne nodded. That explained the new money smell. Fish Street lay to the north of the Steelyards along the river. A man bent on self-slaughter only had a short walk to take. Alternatively . . .

'How is your husband's business, madam?' Thynne asked.

Mary looked confused as if the High Constable were speaking Greek. 'I don't know,' she mumbled. 'I don't know . . .'

'Look about you, High Constable,' Bancroft said. 'Anyone who is anyone in this great city of ours drinks smoke these days. The business is thriving.'

Thynne nodded. That was all to the good. 'Tell me, madam,'

he said, 'in the days you saw him last, did your husband seem . . . different in any way? Distracted?'

Mary blinked. 'I don't know what you mean,' she said, screwing up her kerchief in one hand. She looked up at Bancroft and clutched his sleeve. 'Thaddeus . . .?'

Bancroft turned her to face him and held her shoulders gently. He bent towards her and spoke quietly, but not so quietly that Thynne couldn't hear. 'What the High Constable is trying to say,' he said softly, 'is . . . did Simon have any reason to kill himself?'

The woman's hands fluttered up to her mouth and her sob came as a guttural sigh, wrenched from her. Then she controlled herself. 'None,' she said. 'That is no solution to anything. Simon would never . . . he would never do such a thing. It is a mortal sin.'

'Indeed it is,' Thynne said. He turned back to the fire, prodding it with his cane. 'Well, then,' he said, stirring the embers. 'Enemies? Does your husband have enemies, Mistress Bancroft? You say, sir, that his business is doing well. Is it doing too well? You share his trade. You must know everyone who sells this weed. Are any of them, in your opinion, of a murderous disposition?'

'Have you found his body?' Mary shouted, unable to bear this cold man and his questions any longer.

Thynne crossed from the fire and looked down at the woman. 'I have found *a* body,' he said. 'And I should warn you, it is not pretty. It has been in the water for a day, perhaps more. Since then . . . well, you shall see for yourself.'

The High Constable took his broad-brimmed hat from the stand and hoisted his cane aloft. He nodded at the clerk and ushered the Bancrofts from the room. He led them down the stairs that wound down to the street. Here, people melted away. Those who could avoid his gaze did so, the scurrying multitude scurrying elsewhere, *anywhere* away from Hugh Thynne. One or two touched their caps to him. No one offered him their wares. And since the Bancrofts were clearly with the High Constable, no one bothered them either. He suddenly ducked to his left, into a dark alley and rapped the heavy end of his cane on the little oak door that seemed to crouch, half-buried in ancient stone. This was the church of St Mary Aldermary and this was where Hugh Thynne habitually took his corpses.

The door creaked open and an old man stood there, bare-headed and wearing a long, leather apron.

'The Reverend isn't here, sir,' he croaked with an ingratiating smile.

'Did I ask you that?' Thynne batted him aside. 'The river body? Which one?'

There were four corpses in the low-vaulted cellar of the church, each one wrapped in a shroud, bound above the head and below the feet, crossed at the ankles. The old man led his visitors to the far corner, where a solitary candle burned. 'Give us more light, man,' Thynne barked. 'Are we moles?'

The old man scuttled away, lighting more tapers as he went and placing them in a semicircle around the body. Thynne took hold of the mildewed linen, then paused. 'Are you sure?' he asked. 'Do you really want to see this? Master Bancroft, would it not be best . . .?'

But Mary Bancroft had not come down into this dank, dark hole, cold as a witch's tit and smelling of the sweet dampness of death, to turn back now. She nodded and squeezed Thaddeus Bancroft's arm. He nodded too and said, 'Let's get it over with.'

Thynne pulled the edges of the shroud apart and the candles guttered on the ghastly head inside it. The eyes were sunken back in their sockets and the lips had peeled back from the teeth as the once water-logged skin had contracted. The skin was dark blue, almost black in that half-light. Mary cried out and crossed herself, stumbling backwards and Bancroft caught her in case she fell.

'Oh, Lord!' she screamed, her voice coming out in a shrill whistle, as though there was no breath left in her body. 'Oh, thank the Lord. That dreadful thing is not my Simon.' She looked up eagerly into Bancroft's face. 'It isn't, is it, Thaddeus? Not Simon?'

Bancroft put a restraining arm around her shoulders and turned her into his chest, where she settled, weeping gently. 'Show me the hand,' he said to Thynne quietly. 'The left.'

Thynne ferreted under the linen and hauled out the limb, limp now and useless. He held the fingers, noting the discolouration of the nails. 'There may have been a ring here once,' he said, in case that helped. Not many corpses lay for more than a minute or two along the Thames without losing a ring or two. But it didn't help.

'It's not a ring I'm looking for,' Bancroft said, over his cousin's bent head. 'It's that. The scar.' Thynne peered closer. A pale line ran in a jagged pattern from knuckles to wrist. 'He got that when we were boys, falling from a tree. Lucky he didn't lose his fingers. That's him; that's Simon Bancroft.'

He wanted to get Mary away from that place, with its unburied dead. She had gone so quiet, huddled into his jerkin, clutching at the back of it with one hand, the front of his shirt with the other. She was just rolling her head back and forth and whimpering, 'No, no, no.' He wanted to get her to the light, to the air, to the life of Candlewick Street, to reassure her that the whole world did not live in a dripping, foul-smelling tomb. He started to edge around the corpse, towards the door, but Hugh Thynne stepped into his path.

'A token, if you will,' he said firmly, jerking his head in the direction of the old man. Bancroft muttered under his breath and fumbled in his purse. He slapped a silver coin into Thynne's palm. The High Constable looked at it. 'Then there's the storage of the corpse thus far,' he said. 'Not to mention the shroud. And the candles. And do you want us to see to the burial?'

This last brought a fresh storm of weeping from the widow.

Bancroft was outraged. 'We Bancrofts bury our own, sir!' he said, drawing himself up.

'Well, that is of course your prerogative,' Thynne said. 'When shall I tell the magistrate you want to have the case heard?'

'What?'

Thynne shrugged. 'Most bodies found in the river are suicides and of course, burying them in consecrated ground is . . . well, not possible, in fact. There are some clergy who will allow it – they keep a little corner, you know the kind of place . . .'

Bancroft did indeed know the kind of place. It was usually against the churchyard wall, where the ground was too hard or full of roots to dig too deep. There were no graves marked, no stones to show who rested there. Just nettles and some sad and faded nosegays for a child born dead, a man hanged, a woman drowned. And after a time, grey bones bobbing to the surface to be ploughed back with the next crop. Mary deserved to be kept from ever having to visit a place such as that. He sighed. 'Or . . .?' He let the question hang on the polluted air.

'Or we can give your cousin a decent burial, no questions asked.'

'Where will that be?' Bancroft asked.

Thynne shrugged. 'Wherever we can find room,' he said. 'London's churchyards are . . . filling up, as you know. But it will be decent.'

'A funeral it is, then,' Bancroft sighed, reaching for his purse again. His sense of family honour surfaced for one last time and he snapped, 'Would you like something for a Requiem to be sung as well?'

Thynne smiled, thin-lipped as always, sardonic. 'Now, Master Bancroft,' he said. 'We both know that would be against the law, don't we?' He watched the pair haul open the door and disappear gratefully into the light of the street. Then he half turned to the old man, pointing the tip of his cane downwards. 'There are four groats there,' he said. 'Pauper's burial. And tell the vicar he still owes me for the last one.' He slipped Thaddeus Bancroft's silver into his purse and left.

Kit Marlowe didn't mind having guests. In fact, he was only just getting used to being able to have guests, the rooms in Corpus Christi not being built for much carousing and entertaining. But he knew the old adage that was attributed to the Chinese but which was as true in Norton Folgate as it was in the Forbidden City: that guests and fish both stink after three days. If only Shaxsper would stay in the attic, writing poems comparing his mistress to a summer's day or something equally unlikely, things wouldn't be so bad. Windlass could feed him and make sure his chamber pot was emptied and in a while the hue and cry would die down, the man could be got out of London and no harm done. But the man would just not stay put and if he wandered out of doors, then he and Marlowe were both for that pleasant little contraption called Skeffington's Gyves that they kept in the Tower, the innocent-looking machine that punctured lungs and snapped spines. It was true that Marlowe knew people in some very high places, but aiding and abetting a murderer might be a misdemeanour too far, even for Sir Francis Walsingham to put right.

And it wasn't as though he didn't have plenty to do. Avoiding Nicholas Faunt was taking up much of his time as it was. Marlowe had seen him at the Rose, meeting with Henslowe and his money men; but investing in plays was not Nicholas Faunt's style. He had surely been there for some other, darker reason and Marlowe had a sneaky feeling, like a worm in his guts, that said such a reason would involve him, sooner or later. So, the sooner he could move Shakespeare on, out of his garret and back to Stratford, the better. Then he could concentrate on his next play, which, if all went according to plan, would mean that he could retire somewhere that Faunt and his feelers, like the threads of an invading fungus, could not find him. Somewhere he could write, read and laze away his days, with just the fresh air and a few like-minded men for company.

His thoughts had accompanied him in his walk through the dark to the door of Shakespeare's erstwhile lodging in Water Lane and he raised his hand to knock. But his knuckle had scarcely grazed the wood when the door was flung inwards and a lovely woman stood there, red in the face and with her hair down around her shoulders.

'Oh!' she said, hitching up the shoulders of her gown and pulling her hair back from her breasts and trying to tuck it into the combs at the back of her head. 'Oh! Who are you?' She peered at him with beautiful, short-sighted eyes. 'I know you! You're Kit Marlowe. Will pointed you out one day.'

Marlowe nodded his head pleasantly. 'I am indeed Christopher Marlowe,' he said. 'At your service, madam. And you, I assume, are Mistress Constance Tyler.'

'Yes,' she said, giving up the uneven struggle with her hair. 'I'm sorry to answer the door to you like this. Our maidservant has given notice. Well, not so much given notice as gone home to her mother. She didn't like—' Her voice broke. 'She didn't like it that there was murder in the house.'

'A sensitive soul, was she?' Marlowe asked, pushing the girl back gently and stepping in, closing the door behind him. With the clamour of the street shut out, he dropped his voice. 'I can't think of many maidservants who would give up service in a pleasant household like this just because her mistress died. And elsewhere, too. It wasn't as though the murder happened here.'

'True.' Constance chewed her lip, thinking. 'And it isn't as though this house was easy before Eleanor died. The children alone would drive you demented, with their constant crying and want, want, want. And the comings and goings at night were like nobody's business . . .' She raised her eyes to Marlowe's and put a soft, white hand on his chest. 'And now there's only me and the old nurse, and the maid has gone. Back to mother, she says, though I don't think she is any better than she should be.'

'Her mother?' Marlowe was almost disappointed that this was proving to be so easy. This girl was like a fountain trickling from a wall; all he needed to do was to sit beside it and he would hear all he needed to know.

She stroked gently down his chest and tucked one finger into his belt. He removed it and held her hand, for good measure. He remembered Shakespeare's admission that she seemed to know her way about a man. 'No, Master Marlowe,' she said, in a voice like a sucking dove, as Shakespeare would doubtless have it. 'No, the *maid* is not better than she should be.'

'Oh, I see. So, you think that she was the cause of all this coming and going, do you?'

'Well, it wasn't me, and old nurse is past that kind of thing. And of course, Eleanor is – was – a widow, a very respectable widow. She wouldn't be up at all hours, with the door opening and closing all night long.'

Marlowe decided to play her at her own game and took a tendril of her ebony hair and twisted it round his finger. 'Not you, Mistress Constance? Surely you are a woman who could well cause a bit of door opening and closing?'

'Master Marlowe,' she said, leaning in to his hand, 'I am a maid.'

He twisted the hair once more round his finger and she winced, putting up her hand to free it but finding he had her fast. 'Not a maid, as such, Mistress Constance, surely,' he said, still in the same friendly tone. He reached with his other hand and patted her belly, which was tight as a drum behind her stomacher. 'Or should I perhaps inform the Archbishop of Canterbury that we have a virgin birth to look forward to?'

She twisted away, but took his hand with her. He was pulling her hair quite frankly now, there was no caress left in the gesture. 'Let me go. You're hurting me. I will tell the Constable.'

'Will you? I believe that philandery is a felony, Mistress Constance. You have a lovely house here, no doubt with lovely things in it. What a difference some of this would make to the life of poor Mistress Shaxsper, bringing up three children all alone in Stratford.'

Constance stopped pulling against his restraining hand. 'Mistress Shaxsper?' she asked, smiling. 'What has she to do with anything?'

'Criminal conversation, Mistress. With William Shakespeare, as he calls himself in London.'

'I would hardly call it a conversation, Master Marlowe, if I were to be honest. We had a chat now and again, to that I will attest. Anything lasting less than three minutes is not a conversation. But, you are right . . .' She tossed her head again. 'Can you let go of my hair? I will tell you all I can, but it is a little painful.'

He twirled his finger to release the curl and she stepped back, combing her fingers through her hair gratefully. She twisted it up behind her head, away from temptation and secured it quickly with her combs.

'I am right?' he prompted her.

'You are right, I am with child. But it isn't Master Shakespeare's child. I was already with child when I came to him. He must not know much if he thinks it is his – and yet you tell me he has three children?'

'He does. Two girls and a boy, if memory serves.'

'Well, his wife must keep her counsel.' She smiled wryly. 'No, my child belongs to someone else entirely and –' she held up a finger – 'do not ask who, because I don't know.'

Marlowe was secretly disappointed. He had hoped not to find that Eleanor Merchant was keeping a common bawdy house, and yet it seemed to be the case. 'A . . . customer?'

'No. I am not a whore, Master Marlowe, no matter what you think of me. After the father of my child, Master Shakespeare is the only man with whom I have lain.' Her navy-blue eyes looked into his and, although he knew he had often been fooled before, he felt inclined to believe her. 'I was asleep in my bed some four

months since and I was awoken by the noise of a strange knock
on the door. I heard my sister go down to answer it and then
footsteps on the stairs. Then, before they reached the second
landing, where my sister sleeps with the children, there was another
knock, a hammering this time, not the gentle knock there had been
before. I heard my sister speak, sharply, to whoever was with her
and the light that had been shining under my door went out. She
went downstairs and I heard her talking again. This time, she took
whoever it was into the kitchen, at the back of the house.'

She sat down suddenly on an oak chair in the hall and crouched
over with her hands across her stomach.

'I was frightened. I didn't know what was going on. I was too
afraid to go to sleep, but could see nothing in the dark. Then,
my door opened. I saw the figure of a man outlined against the
faint light from the landing and then the door closed again. I
held my breath. I didn't know who it was.'

'But surely, your sister would not have taken a stranger upstairs,
to where her children slept?' Marlowe was still ready to bet his
purse on the bawdy house.

'I didn't know what to do. I lay as still as I could as the man
backed into the room. When the backs of his legs hit the bed,
he sat down and I gasped, or cried out, because he whispered,
"Who's there?" and twisted round to find my throat. I felt his
fingers closing, then he said again, really softly, "A girl? How
old are you?" I told him eighteen and he took his hand away.
He told me to be quiet, for his sake if not my own, then asked
if he could hide in my room, that he was a friend of my sister.
I was still afraid, but said he could and eventually, I went back
to sleep, although I know that sounds strange.'

Marlowe knew what she meant. Often, in moments of extreme
danger, he had felt a lassitude creep over him. It was nature's
way of cutting the fear, of sending you to sleep, to a better place.
'No, Mistress. I understand. And he took advantage of you?'

She smiled then, and looked up under her lashes at him. 'No,
Master Marlowe, by no means. I woke up in the early dawn and
he was sleeping beside me. He wasn't much older than I
was, handsome but tired looking and wearing poor clothes.
I watched him sleep and saw that he was . . . stirring. I think you
take my meaning?'

Marlowe nodded.

'I have only a sister, Master Marlowe, and although I lived with her while her husband lived, I was never privy to . . . any of their private ways, if you understand me. I was curious. I unlaced his breeches, just to see what he kept in there. I was admiring his possessions when I heard a sound and realized that he had woken up. Then . . . well, who took advantage of who is still a mystery to me. I slept . . . afterwards, and when I woke, he had gone. Eleanor never spoke of him, and how could I ask her? So, here I am.' She spread her arms, leaning back so that Marlowe could see the swell of her stomach. 'No husband, no lover, no sister and, since today, no maidservant. I am not even sure how much money I have. My nephew and nieces are with an aunt in the country, as wards of court. The only thing of value in the house is that old silver jug there.' She indicated it with a toss of her head. 'And I'm not even sure that is really mine. Sometimes it stands on that shelf, and sometimes it does not.'

Marlowe walked across to the little shelf across the corner. The silver jug was no ordinary piece, he could see. He hefted it in his hand. The weight of silver alone made it more valuable than most of the other fixtures in the house, if the hall was any guide. It was, as far as he could judge, Italian, with a squared-off top, each corner finished with a grotesque mask, with lolling tongue and squinting eyes. Each one was slightly different, but each one had a hole through to the jug's interior, so all could be used to pour through. The sides were heavily chased and the scenes were as grotesque as the masks. It was not a church vessel, the images made that clear. But as to its value, he wouldn't like to say.

'It frightens me.' Her voice sounded like a child's. 'In the dark, when candlelight falls on it, the people seem to run, the tongues to drool. I wish it had been away when Eleanor died. Then I wouldn't have to worry about it.'

Marlowe could see what she meant. He could almost feel the little figures squirming under his hand. 'It is valuable, Mistress Constance. I don't care to take it back to my lodgings, but I know a man who would understand this and could keep it safe for you. Until you find out to whom it belongs, at least.'

'Would you take it? Please, do. I don't like it in the house.

Where does it go when it isn't here?' Her voice was beginning to rise, and she was clasping and unclasping her hands in front of her.

'I'll take it,' he said. 'Do you have a bag, or a cloth, perhaps . . .?'

'In the kitchen. At least the maidservant washed the linen before she went.' She went through a door into a passage behind her, speaking as she did so over her shoulder. 'So . . . now you know what is happening to me, Master Marlowe. How goes it with Master Shakespeare?' She came back into the hall and passed him a piece of ironed linen, which he used to wrap the jug. She seemed happier just to see it out of sight.

'He is . . . well.' Marlowe was trying to assimilate it all. Then he had a thought. 'Master Alleyn. Is he still . . . calling on you?'

She pulled out her combs and tossed her head. 'Who do you think I was waiting for, Master Marlowe? My baby needs a father and one actor will do as well as any other, don't you think?'

Marlowe turned to the door when there was a firm knock on the other side.

'That's him,' Constance said, jumping up and loosening the shoulders of her gown. 'Go, go out the back way. I am four months gone already and don't have a moment to lose.' She pushed him down the passage towards the kitchen. 'If you go through there, you will reach the yard. You can climb over the back wall and you will be in a lane that joins this street again further down.'

The knock came again, harder this time. The knock of a man with little time to lose. Marlowe looked at her standing there, none too bright, lovely as the day. She had an actor to con. He could come back and see her again if he needed more information.

'Goodbye, Mistress Tyler,' he said, stroking her cheek. 'Good luck with Master Alleyn.' And he ran off down the corridor, chuckling at the thought of Alleyn, learning his lines through the howls of another man's bastard. What went around surely did come around.

The night suited Nicholas Faunt. It fitted him like a glove as he padded silently through sleeping Blackfriars. He saw the officers of the Watch with their staffs and horn lanterns and the Apprentice boys who should have been in bed loitering in dark corners. At his back he carried a dagger; any footpad who fancied his luck would be ready for that. They may even have been ready for the second, tucked neatly under his left armpit and thin as a needle. But no one would be expecting the third, slipped into his left buskin. That was the one that got them every time. And all the more so because the deadly blade came from nowhere, from a man to all intents and purposes unarmed.

He reached the door he wanted in Water Lane and tapped on it. He heard voices from inside, a female one, shrill and insistent, a man's voice, not saying much and fading from even Faunt's almost miraculous hearing. But no one came to the door. He tapped again, rather harder this time. He may be under cover, but he was after all on the Queen's business. This time, after a brief pause, the door swung open about halfway and a girl's face peered round it, coquettishly. Her face was a perfect oval, with startled and startling navy-blue eyes reflecting back the light from the torches in the street. Her hair, so black it was almost blue, hung loose about her shoulders, one tendril curling on to a milk-white breast. One hand held a candle aloft and the shadows did such wonderful things for her bone structure that Faunt could not believe that it was accidental.

She stared into his face and her own face fell.

'My apologies, madam,' Faunt said, sweeping off his hat and sweeping into the hall in one fluid movement. 'I believe you may have been expecting someone else.'

She looked hurriedly round the door before she closed it. 'Do you know what chime was last heard?' she said anxiously.

He smiled to see someone so innocent that she didn't ask who he was, but took steps first to find out how late her lover was; because it was clearly a man she was waiting for and he was very late. Faunt had no idea just how late; a little matter of four months. 'I believe I heard it strike the quarter to seven as I passed St Katharine Trinity,' he said. Then he bent to her. 'Mistress Tyler?' he said. 'My condolences, madam.'

'Do I know you?' she asked.

'We have met,' Faunt said, taking her hand and kissing it gallantly. 'From time to time.'

There was a faint flicker of recognition in her eyes. 'You are Eleanor's friend,' she remembered. 'You came here sometimes.'

'More a friend of Master Merchant, perhaps, in the early years. But after his . . . demise, your sister's friend also, I hope. I remember when I met you first, you were just a little girl. You played the dulcimer for me. You were very good.'

'I was terrible,' she said with a smile. 'I can't remember your name, though.'

Faunt seemed not to have heard. He was admiring the black drapes, proper for a house in mourning. He walked around the hall, taking in such details as were visible in the light of her single candle. Then he turned to her again. 'I believe you also know Master Shakespeare,' he said, as though making conversation over dinner.

She looked at him frostily. 'Of course I do,' she said. 'He was our lodger and he killed my sister. I will remember Master Shakespeare if I live to be a hundred.'

'He is in the Clink, I believe.'

'So I understand,' she said. Then she furrowed her brow. 'May I ask why you are here, Master . . .?'

'Oh, just to pay my respects and to make sure that you are well. How are the children? Are they here?' He looked about him as though they might be playing blind man's buff in a corner.

'The children are to be wards of court. They are with their aunt, my sister's husband's sister, so nothing to me. I am not considered old enough to look after them and I am happy enough with that, so long may they live in Moorfields. I live here because the house is to be mine and there seems to be no hurry to make any other arrangements.'

'The servants? Are they behaving well? They must be made aware that you are their mistress now.'

'The servants have all gone, save for the old nurse who is up in the garret, no doubt waiting for her bread and milk. I am her servant now, if she is not to starve. She hasn't left the room she sleeps in for a year or more now. I don't know why my sister kept her here.' She looked sulky and he was amused to see that it made her no less beautiful. She would certainly not be all alone for long.

'I believe I remember your old nurse,' Faunt said. 'She was good to you as a child. Perhaps your sister just kept her out of kindness.'

The eyes that met his were puzzled. 'Do you think so?' she asked. 'I hadn't thought of that. I won't turn her out, you know. It's just my way of speaking.'

'Do you have a man of business?' Faunt asked, changing the subject.

'I think so. I don't know who. I am hoping that when . . .' She cast her arms out to the sides. 'When all this is settled, I will be able to live here as I did before. There will be servants who won't know about what happened to Eleanor. There must be someone in London who will come and work for me. I am not a hard mistress –' not yet, Faunt thought, but given time – 'and I will need help when the . . .'

There was a silence that seemed to ring through the house. Faunt fancied he could hear the draperies whispering the echo back to the hall from the highest attic. He coughed a small cough and waited. He was a good waiter, was Nicholas Faunt. He had found over the years that a moment's careful waiting could do the work of a thousand words.

She decided she had gone so far she might just as well go the whole way. 'When the baby comes, I shall need some help around the house. A wet nurse, that kind of thing.'

She looked so young standing there, with her great dark eyes turned on him, he almost offered to marry her himself. 'Er . . . Master Shakespeare?'

'He thinks so,' she said. 'But no. And anyway, he is married, so no help to me.'

'Won't the father marry you, then? Or can't, perhaps.'

'I don't know who he is. We only met . . . the once, and there was no time for talking.'

Faunt's ears pricked up even more than they usually were, hearing a nuance where most men would hear none. 'A stranger?' he asked, all innocence. 'In a friend's house, perhaps?' He pulled a little face, sympathy and understanding embodied in a tiny gesture. 'A handsome stable lad, something of that kind.'

She drew herself up. 'I understand that you may not think much of me . . . I still can't remember your name?' He stayed looking down at her, blandly. 'Er . . . I do not consort with stable lads, no matter how handsome. He was –' she slumped, all the fight gone out of her – 'passing through.'

Although Faunt's expression did not alter, inside he was dancing. She clearly didn't know anything about the goings-on in her sister's house. In one way, it was a nuisance because he would have to begin again. But in another way, it was excellent, because he wouldn't have to have this lovely creature silenced, with all that meant in the dark world in which he bustled.

As they both stood there, lost in thought, there was a single sharp rap on the door and before the sound had died away, a sweet and plangent voice hulloaed, 'Mistress Constance? It is Ned Alleyn, here to pay my respects. May I come in?'

Faunt allowed one eyebrow a tiny twitch, but she saw it and smiled at him.

'Master Whoever-you-are,' she said. 'I must ask you to leave through the kitchen. I believe my baby's new father is at the door.'

Nicholas Faunt unbent so far as to give her an avuncular kiss on the top of her lovely head. She wasn't really cut out for keeping secrets, but for sheer barefaced cheek, she outdid the best of his agents in the field. Bar one.

SEVEN

Enoch Harrison held court along the Shambles in the shadow of the Grey Friars. He'd long ago kicked the squatters out and sat on the ornate carved chair into which the late Cardinal Wolsey used to squeeze his haunches every Friday at eight of the clock. He made his way through the throng standing in the low room with the fan-vaulted ceiling and pressed the clove-studded orange to his nose. Not much point in clearing the squatters out if this riff-raff had replaced them. Still, *this* riff-raff was *his* riff-raff and that made all the difference.

One by one they knelt before him, the women curtseying as best they could and the men snatching off their caps. They knew that Harrison was not the man who could solve their problems; after him there was another, and then another, but they had learned not to be slow in bending the knee. They had seen what happened when anyone didn't do that quickly enough; two very large men with shaven heads and leather jerkins stood slightly behind Wolsey's chair, to jog their memories and to instil in them all the need to show respect to the Constable. One of them looked as though he hadn't a thought in his head save violence against his fellow man. One fist was tightly clenched and he bounced it in and out of the opposite palm, as though testing its weight. His eyes were blank and dead-looking and didn't focus on anything, near or far. The other only looked sentient because he was standing so near his colleague. In any other company, he would have looked as though his last brain cell had died of loneliness years before. He was considered to be the thinker of the two and he was Harrison's right-hand man.

But it was more complicated than that. Harrison kept these oafs around for effect, for an immediate response. If he was feeling *particularly* bloody-minded, he could always increase the speed and efficiency of his Under Constables, his Headboroughs. An unpaid licence here, the wrong clothes there, a piece of lead no longer on a church roof, a recusancy fine unpaid and Constable

Harrison had the power to conduct any of the people now in front of him to Newgate or the Compter, the Clink or any of the dozen other hell-holes that passed as London's prisons. Goodbye freedom, goodbye family. An appearance before a magistrate? Well that could take weeks, and weeks had a habit of turning into months.

Better not to cross Constable Harrison. Better to provide him with the trinkets he seemed to crave, the glittering things that appealed to his magpie senses, for like a magpie, he was the Devil's creature. That way, he might just leave them alone.

The Constable looked at the wares they placed before him, trinkets of pewter, silver plate and Venetian glass. Much of it was the loot of the churches, still doing the rounds after all these years since the Dissolution. Once or twice he beckoned a suppli-cant forward and looked more closely at their offerings, fixing an enlarging glass into his eye-socket and nodding silently. He flicked his fingers right and left and his minions placed certain goods to one side, on a table draped with blackest velvet. These were the choicest goods and the clerk, Sam Renton, wrote them down in his ledger. Every so often, Harrison raised a hand. 'Not that one, Sam,' he said with a smile, tapping the side of his nose. 'That one's special.' The clerk's quill rested in his hand, going nowhere near ink or parchment. The payment for every piece was one penny – just enough for its recipient to go to watch Christopher Marlowe's new play at the Rose. Renton passed it solemnly over, as if he were delivering the sacrament.

A woman curtseyed to Harrison, letting two short brass candle-sticks tumble from her apron. He took in the curve of her cheek and the rise and fall of her breasts. 'Are you married, madam?' he asked.

'I am, sir,' she answered, not quite able to look the Constable in the face.

'What is your husband?' he asked her. 'His calling?'

'He is a carpenter, sir.'

'And now he has a new calling,' he said. 'He is a cuckold.' The minions at his elbows chuckled. So did Renton. 'I trust he can make his own horns.' He beckoned her closer and she half rose from her knees. 'I would normally pay you a penny for this tat, mistress,' he said.

'They are worth four groats at least, sir,' she told him, her eyes fierce, her mouth set firm. She knew the chance she was taking.

'You know that,' he said, leaning back again. '*I* know that. But the shortfall is more than made up by the fact that you shall share my bed tonight.'

'I shall, sir?' Her eyes were wider now.

'You shall.' He nodded and jerked his head. A minion swept the woman up as if she were a doll and whisked her away. 'See that she is bathed,' he called after the retreating pair. 'I must be careful not to get splinters.'

A man was hauled in front of the Constable. He was offering no trinkets, just his life.

'Who is this?' Harrison asked.

Harrison's right-hand man threw him down and continued to hold the man with his arm twisted painfully up behind his back. 'This is Jack Wheeler, sir.' He leaned closer and spoke quietly out of the corner of his mouth. 'Gatekeeper at the Clink.'

The Constable looked closely at the man, who was as white as whey and was showing his fear with a line of dank sweat across his brow and upper lip. 'Get rid of these people,' he said to his guard, with a dismissive wave at the small group that remained. 'Another day, another day will do.' Renton closed his ledger and inkwell and sat back to enjoy whatever show Harrison was about to put on. The Constable then forgot they were even there and turned to the trembling gatekeeper.

'Master Wheeler, yes. We have been waiting to have a word with you.' He flicked his hand and the lout let Wheeler go. The man stayed on his knees, always the best place to be in the presence of Harrison and his men, in his experience. Come to think of it, the *very* best place was a hundred miles away, but the dusty floor of his impromptu court would have to do.

'What can you tell me about Master Shakespeare?' Harrison asked.

'Who, sir?'

He felt the lout's steel-shod boot crunch into his ribs and his forehead hit the floor with a dull thud.

The Constable leaned forward. He'd earned his blood money already tonight and he had a nice warm woman waiting upstairs. 'Gaoler,' he said, 'I am not inclined to be patient. William

Shakespeare was entrusted recently to your care and when I sent
Master Peach here – Master Peach, by the way, is the one intent
on breaking your ribs; I don't suppose he introduced himself –
when I sent Master Peach to interview him, lo and behold, he
had gone. Vanished like a conjuror's monkey.'

'I know nothing . . .'

'Quite probably, Gaoler. But in this case . . . What is it of the
clock, Master Peach?'

The lout half-turned to check the candle guttering on the side
table. 'Nearly ten of the clock, sir,' he told him.

'Hmm, not fair to bother Master Topcliffe at this hour. No
doubt he's had a long and busy day.'

'Master Topcliffe?' Wheeler mouthed.

'Yes,' Harrison said, as though they were discussing the
weather. 'You do know what Master Topcliffe's calling is, don't
you, Wheeler?'

'Y . . . yes, sir.' The gaoler's lips were trembling, his eyes
flicking from side to side.

'Tell me,' the Constable said with the affability of a kindly
old schoolmaster testing one of his pupils.

'He . . . he's a rackmaster, sir.' The gaoler swallowed with
difficulty the bile that was rising in his throat.

Harrison frowned. 'Not *a* rackmaster, Wheeler. *The* Rackmaster.
The Queen's, in fact. Why, he can do things with a length of
rope that would make your eyes water.' He leaned forward. 'And
I mean that.' He leaned back. 'But we can't bother a busy man
like that, not tonight. Besides, Master Topcliffe is used to more
elegant customers than you – seditious noblemen, Papist priests.
I doubt he'd want to dirty his equipment. So . . .' A look of
concern spread over the Constable's face. 'Such a glum face,
Master Gaoler,' he said. 'We can't have that. We can provide a
useful service here without bothering the important gentlemen
at the Tower. Master Peach.'

The lout grabbed both Wheeler's arms and forced him to kneel
upright with his arms pulled taut behind him and Peach's boot
in the small of his back. Harrison stood and slowly drew the
silver dagger from the small of his back. He let the blade glint
in the candlelight and looked at Wheeler's face, the working lips,
the tear-filled eyes, and shook his head. 'No,' the Constable said,

'we need a smile. Perhaps –' he pricked the man's right cheek so that Wheeler gasped and drew back – 'from there to –' he jabbed the same point on his left cheek – 'there.'

Wheeler screamed as he felt the blood trickle down both sides of his face.

'Let me see,' Harrison frowned and put his head on one side, as though working out how best to carve a joint of game, 'if I can join those dots.'

'He made me do it, sir. I had no choice.'

Harrison was ignoring him, still deciding how best to make the cut as Wheeler struggled against the vice-like grip of Master Peach. 'Hmm?' he asked casually. 'Who made you do what?'

'The man, sir.' Wheeler was gabbling for his life now. 'The popinjay who sprung Shakespeare. He threatened me, sir. My wife. My wife and dear children. Said he'd kill them if I didn't let Shakespeare go. Kill 'em slow, he would, like . . .'

'Like I am going to kill you?' Harrison smiled, then a thought appeared to come to him. 'Mr Peach,' he said, 'do you know Mrs Wheeler and all the little Wheelers, with their bright eyes and downy cheeks?'

Peach grunted and gave an extra tug on Wheeler's arms, making him wince. 'Who'd have him? Only a beast would make the beast with two backs with him.'

Harrison chuckled and leaned forward again to the helpless gaoler. 'Well, Master Liar, it seems you and I have something in common after all, but apart from our single state, I can think of nothing else. You have one more chance to save yourself and one only. This popinjay, did he give you a name?'

'Yes, sir,' Wheeler gabbled and nodded. 'Oh, yes, he did, sir. I insisted on it. Greene. Robert Greene. Said he was a playwright.'

Harrison looked at Peach and raised an eyebrow. 'I don't know whether we know a Robert Greene, do we, Peach?'

'I have heard the name, sir,' Peach said. 'I can't place the face, though.'

'Never mind for now. I'm sure a playwright is easily enough found.' He turned back to Wheeler. 'And how much did he pay you, this playwright?'

'An angel, sir.'

'An angel?' Harrison's eyebrows almost disappeared into his

hairline. 'An angel? Master Peach, take this man back to the Clink. He is to resume his duties there.'

'Sir.' Peach removed his foot from the small of the gaoler's back and hauled the quivering wreck to his feet, dragging him by the sleeve towards the door.

'Thank you, sir,' babbled Wheeler. 'Oh, thank you.'

'Oh, Peach,' Harrison said, 'I will need to have this decision sealed by my superiors but I have no reason to suppose they will argue with it. My arithmetic may be at fault, but since Master Wheeler is in receipt of an angel and being aware, as I am, of his daily wage, the next payment he will receive will be in the year of our Lord 1618. Give or take.'

'Give or take, sir,' Peach agreed and dragged the man away.

It was late that night that Robert Greene found Gabriel Harvey. The man sat with his back to an oak-panelled wall and he had a quill in one hand and a parchment in the other. Candles shone all round him giving him the look of a plaster saint such as Greene remembered from his childhood, the sort men still knelt to in the capitals of Europe he had visited; the sort no man in England dared kneel to any more.

'I just heard the news,' the would-be playwright blurted out.

'What news would that be, Greene?' Harvey held a finger aloft while he drew a correcting line with his quill in the other hand.

'The Rose. That actor . . . what's his name? Shakespeare?'

'Indeed.' Harvey nodded. 'An interesting diversion. At first I thought Marlowe had engineered it.'

'Marlowe?' Greene shook the rain from his hat and found a hook to hang his cloak. Harvey's face fell. It looked as though the man was planning to stay. 'I definitely heard Shakespeare.'

'Shakespeare, Marlowe. Marlowe, Shakespeare. Two buttocks of the one arse, Greene.'

'In terms of writing, you mean? I'd heard Shakespeare fancied himself as something of a scribbler.'

'Not in terms of writing, man, in terms of their enormous arrogance. You saw how Marlowe preened when the Prologue announced him. Nauseating.'

'Precisely.' Greene looked with a certain envy at the bread, grapes and cheese on Harvey's platter. 'That's why I left. They'll be closing it down, of course.'

'Will they?' Harvey laid the quill down and poured himself some wine. There was no goblet for Greene.

'Well, of course.' Greene unhooked his rapier and smoothed down his doublet. He had run all the way from the Vintry and his feet, sodden in their doeskin boots, were letting him know it. It was hard to be a man of action and a slave to fashion, especially while it rained so relentlessly. 'Stands to reason. Marlowe's finished.'

'You haven't seen the queues, then?'

'What queues?' Greene watched intently as Harvey broke off a hunk of cheese and popped it in whole.

'The queues around the Rose.'

'*Around* the Rose?' Greene knew what he had heard, but felt compelled to check.

'Dominus Greene.' Harvey thought it was about time he set out his stall and he carefully checked his scanty locks in a hand mirror on the table before he began. 'I am a Professor of Cambridge University; noted literary critic; the founder of that select circle of literati called Areopagitica; friend and patron of Edmund Spenser . . . I could go on, but it would embarrass us both. If I say "around", I mean around. Indeed, I am short-changing the word. The groundlings stretched along Maiden Lane and round the Bear Garden. The watermen have calluses from rowing them all across.'

'You mean, *since* the incident?'

'I do.'

Greene thought for a moment. 'Well, then,' he shrugged, 'nothing to do with Marlowe. It's just the prurience of the multitude. Bread and circuses. Henslowe hires out his rubbish tip for prize fights every other Wednesday, not to mention his bear-baiting on the side. Nothing to do with Marlowe.'

'I can't help thinking, Dominus Greene,' Harvey delighted in giving the man his old university title; it brought out the academic gap between them perfectly, 'that you are missing the point. Whether it's Marlowe or not, the mindless mob are fighting each other to get in to watch his play. And he and Henslowe are getting richer than God as a result.'

Greene had no answer to that and slumped into a chair, easing his wet feet. He would have dearly loved to take off his boots but they were so tight he needed help both to remove and replace them and he instinctively felt that asking Harvey for a hand with his buskins would not go well. 'So what actually happened?' He sighed. 'At the Rose, I mean?'

It was Harvey's turn to shrug as he took another swig of wine. 'It was an accident as far as I could tell,' he said. 'Shakespeare's gun got away from him. The man's a glover or some such mechanical. What people like that are doing on the stage, I'll never know.'

There was a silence.

'Have you heard the other news?' Greene asked.

'Other news?' Harvey selected a grape and peeled it carefully. 'What other news?'

'From Cambridge?'

Harvey yawned extravagantly and rocked his chair back on its rear legs, leaning against the wall. 'Cambridge was so six months ago, Greene,' he said. He was so patronizing that Greene could feel the metaphorical pat on the head.

'That may be so,' Greene said, nastily. He knew that this news would hit Harvey like Sisyphus' rock right between the eyes and he mended his pace, to give the words their full impact. 'But it's more news on Marlowe. They've given him his Master's Degree.'

Harvey's chair crashed back to earth and the goblet hit the table so that the grapes bounced and the quill, balanced on the inkwell, jumped in the air, over the edge of the table and disappeared, mingled with the rushes on the floor. 'The Devil you say,' Harvey snarled. Then, collecting himself, he sneered, 'That'll be Copcott's doing. He and Marlowe were always thick as thieves.'

'Not this time,' said Greene, whose university contact had never let him down. 'This time it's from the top. Lord Burghley himself.'

'Burghley?' Harvey repeated, frowning.

'Wrote to Copcott, was how I heard it. Threatened them all with fire and brimstone if they didn't give the degenerate his degree. They caved in.'

'Of course they did,' Harvey muttered. 'Of course they did. Robyn –' Greene didn't like it these days when Harvey used his given name. The oiliness of the man's voice repelled him. But even so – 'tell me, when you heard that news, did it occur to you to ask yourself what the Queen's Chief Secretary has to do with a common playwright . . . oh, saving your presence, of course.'

'Well . . . yes, of course,' Greene bluffed. It wasn't true, but he sensed the old vituperative Gabriel Harvey was about to make a new entrance.

'I think we've got to investigate this, Robyn,' Harvey said. There was a look in his eyes that made Greene's hair crawl. The man had murder in him. 'What's today?'

'Er . . . Thursday.'

'Right. Tomorrow morning, get yourself round to Paul's Cross.'

Greene's face fell. 'I can't stand all that Puritan ranting, Gabriel,' he said.

'You're not going for the sermon, man. The crowd. Watch the crowd. St Paul's is crawling with likely lads who'd cut their own gammer's throat for a piece of silver. Find one – no, better – find two. I'd like them to do us a little favour in the case of Master Marlowe.'

Christopher Marlowe had never been much of a man for sleeping and yet again he had reason to be grateful that he didn't need nine hours between the sheets. Like Nicholas Faunt, night became him; he could see as well as any cat and was as soft on his feet as one. He had left Constance Tyler's house in a thoughtful mood and had walked along Goose Street to where he had left his horse in the care of an urchin. That the urchin and horse, complete with all the saddle accoutrements and bridle, were still there was a testimony to Marlowe's personality. Usually, leaving a horse in Blackfriars was the best way of giving it away to the needy, as the horse thieves, the priggers of prancers, liked to think of themselves. He had given the child a coin which made his eyes water and had ambled away, thinking. The jug was an odd thing to find in a respectable household. And why did it come and go? Did Eleanor use it as some kind of ready money, to be taken to the moneylenders when times were hard? But that kind of moneylending was not legal and anyway, how did she get the money to get it back? It was a mystery that he knew he may never solve. But he knew a man who could tell him all there was to know about the jug, and that was where he turned his horse's head.

Kit Marlowe had a map in his head of his life so far and his life yet to come. His life with his family, in cloistered Canterbury, enduring his father's financial ups and downs with every tap of his shoemaker's awl, was far away, over a hill and in the misty distance. His years in cobbled Cambridge were closer, in a dark, shadowy wood, with some parts in such deep shade that even he, who had lived it, could no longer tell what was where. The Devil merged with the Eagle and Child and the Brazen Head and the swirling, terrible waters of Paradise. Some parts of his life landscape were a welter of blood and he could smell it when he was upwind.

But one part was always lit by gentle candlelight and perfumed with amber and lavender. Under that gentle glow were two heads, the grey and the golden, John Dee and his beautiful wife, Helene, Nell, now dead and gone. But John Dee, the Queen's Magus, was back in London, Marlowe had heard, in another house now that his magickal manor at Mortlake had burned down. He had heard he was at Whitehall; he had heard he was staying out in Richmond, in the country, where his explosions and fires could do no damage. If he wasn't there, he could be anywhere on the globe, so Marlowe crossed his fingers and rode on, it being better to travel hopefully, possibly, than arrive.

He hardly knew why his spine kept thrilling and the skin on his arms kept springing into goose flesh, but ever since the lead ball had shattered Eleanor Merchant's throat, he had been waiting for the other boot to fall. Nemesis was waiting round a corner, with a cosh in her hand, and it was Marlowe's principle to always be ready for whatever Fate might have in store. When it came to reading the future, John Dee was your man; but for the far more useful insight that he could give you into the past, then he had no peer. So Marlowe rode down to Whitehall, with a lead ball in his purse and a silver jug on the pommel of his saddle, all ready to see old friends, or so he hoped. He would reach the Royal Palace by midnight. At any other house he would have the dogs set on him, but he knew that Sam Bowes, Dee's general factotum and all-round moaner, would still be up. He kept his master's hours, and they were clock-round.

The turrets of Whitehall stood square before him against the London sky. This was the finest palace in Europe, and the biggest. Marlowe had never been here before and he had no idea if the

Queen's Magus was at home. The rumour had it that the Queen did nothing without consulting the mercurial Dr Dee. And that Dee did nothing without gazing long and hard with those reflective eyes, like a viper's, into that black scrying mirror of his.

The playwright reined in his horse at the gateway to the tiltyard and dismounted. A sergeant of the Queen's Guard marched towards him, the light from the torch he carried flickering on helmet and breastplate, throwing off shards of light so that he almost seemed to be covered with St Elmo's fire.

'Your name and your business,' he barked. There were men at his back, bristling with arms and ready to use them.

'Christopher Marlowe. To see Dr Dee.'

'Marlowe?' The sergeant cocked an eyebrow under the helmet brim. The Muse's Darling meant nothing to him. 'What is your calling?'

'Scholar,' Marlowe said, hoping that was more of an entrée to the great magus than 'playwright'.

The sergeant looked him up and down. The man was dressed like no scholar he had ever seen. Where was the academic robe? The string of books? The parchment and quill? He glanced at the horse. Large. Expensive. Flemish, if he knew his horseflesh.

'Kit?' A voice rang across the parade ground, pale under a fitful moon. 'Kit Marlowe!'

'Dr Dee.' Marlowe bowed low with a flourish and Dee hugged him.

'Dolt!' the old man muttered to the sergeant. 'Since when do you stop my friends at my gate?'

The sergeant was about to point out that this was actually the Queen's gate, as all twenty-three acres of the place were the Queen's, but he checked himself. After all, John Dee had the ear of the Queen. After all, John Dee turned men to stone, to toads and to little piles of smoking sulphur. He slapped his sword hilt and stood to attention.

'You men, there,' Dee snapped at his lackeys. 'Tend to this man's horse. Have you eaten, Kit? Bowes has a capon coming to the boil somewhere. Man, it's been months. Years, even. How have you been? I hear great things of your plays. I must come to see one, one of these days.'

Marlowe looked into those blank eyes and decided to risk it. 'But surely, Doctor, I saw you one afternoon, at the Rose, sitting at the back. My first *Tamburlaine*, I think it was.' He smiled. 'A Tuesday, if memory serves. You should have asked me. I could have got you a much better seat.'

Dee patted his arm. 'You were mistaken, Kit,' he said. 'But had I visited your play house, it would have been a Wednesday. Much more propitious. Come, come in and have some food. Sam will be so pleased to see you. Tell me what you have been doing with yourself.'

'Don't you know?' Marlowe laughed. 'I have often felt your scrying mirror shining on the back of my neck.'

'I don't spy on my friends, Kit,' the old magician said, his long white beard wagging as the pair clattered along the Queen's corridor. 'But my spies tell me you are doing well. Quite the coming man these days. Smart rooms, a manservant, no less.'

'Windlass is no more my servant than Bowes is yours,' Marlowe told him. 'Like Sam, he chooses to keep company with me, in exchange for a small stipend. I like him. He has no . . . side. When you are with actors a lot, you have to find reality where you can.'

A voice in his ear was both familiar and welcome and it wafted to him on a gust of boiled fowl. 'So, you pay your Windlass, do you?' it said. 'Master Dee has not yet grasped that principle.'

Marlowe turned and hugged the man who had crept up so silently behind him. 'Sam!' he said. 'I'm so glad to find you here.' Dee's factotum was like a kind deed in a naughty world. Like his master, he risked the shifting opprobrium of that world from day to day. It was like that with prophecies; get it right and you're wined and dined, sought out by the superstitious and guaranteed a grave in Westminster Abbey. Get it wrong and you weren't guaranteed a grave at all.

Bowes gave a lowering look at Dee, who looked away. Marlowe caught the look.

'What?' He stopped and folded his arms.

'He's off, isn't he,' Bowes blurted out, 'with that Kelley? Looking to raise some angel, or some such nonsense. For a clever man, Master Marlowe, I am afraid my master is a fool.'

Dee drew himself up and glared at Bowes from his basilisk

eyes. 'Back to the kitchen, Samuel Bowes,' he cried, 'or I will turn you into a toad. Not a difficult task, seeing as you are already halfway there, you loathsome thing.'

Without a backward glance, Bowes shambled off to the kitchen, muttering under his breath. Dee turned to Marlowe and smiled. 'So, Kit, as you see, nothing changes here.' He ushered him into a room to their right, with a bright fire burning and rich draperies drawn against the night outside. The Queen's *Semper Eadem* glittered on the cloth of gold fittings.

'Are you really going away?' Marlowe asked. 'And with Edward Kelley, of all people? I don't hear much about him that is good.'

'Edward is . . . Well, you're right, Kit,' Dee said, ruefully. 'But I must give one more chance to my work on contacting angels and Edward does seem to have a knack. Perhaps it is all trickery, I don't know . . . Things aren't the same since Nell died. I don't seem to have the interest . . .'

Marlowe was unaccountably sad. He was very fond of the old magus and was suddenly aware that he hadn't visited him, had had no thought of him, even, for months. Even when he saw him in the theatre, with a hat pulled down over his eyes and a cloak to disguise him, even then he had not gone up into the gallery to renew his old acquaintance, to relive old times. But it had been good to know he was there.

'When are you off?'

'It could be tomorrow,' the magus said. 'It could be next week, next year or never. I can plan the tides and the winds, but one never knows with Edward. But enough of plans. Tell me what you have been doing. I have tried scrying, I will tell you truthfully, but can't often find you. This isle is full of noises . . .'

'You should have come to speak to me that Tuesday,' Marlowe said with a small, sad smile. This visit had a lot of the goodbye in it.

'Wednesday,' Dee said. 'Let's not be sad, though, Kit. It's good to see you and let that be an end to it.' He peered at the playwright by the light of the candles and flickering flame. 'What's in the parcel?'

'The reason for my late visit,' Marlowe said. 'It was given into my safe keeping tonight and I wanted to know what it is.

And when I want to know what something is, naturally the first place I think of is wherever you are.'

'Let me see,' Dee said. 'You are keeping it close by you, I notice. Even sitting in my room, before my fire, you keep it in your lap. Is it very precious?'

'Either very precious or totally worthless,' Marlowe said. 'I can't decide.'

He handed his linen-wrapped parcel across to Dee and the old magus took it eagerly. He pulled over a small table, placed the jug in its shroud on it and unwrapped it carefully. Just before the last layer came away he looked up at Marlowe. 'It isn't alive, is it?'

Marlowe shook his head, hoping he was right. Those dancing engravings had shaken him more than he cared to admit.

The magician checked again. 'Nor has it been alive? I have seen too many things in my life, Kit, to be easily revolted, but it is late in the night to have a limb suddenly unwrapped on my favourite table.'

'No.' This time Marlowe smiled a little. 'No, no limbs, no rats, nothing severed or trapped. Unwrap the linen and see for yourself.'

Dee let the final layer fall away and the jug was revealed in the glow of the guttering candles and the fire. He sat back in his chair and looked at it, cocking his head as a blackbird does to get a bead on a worm. He foraged in his gown and brought out his spectacles, which he pinched on to his nose, then he leaned forward again. He moved the jug so he could see all sides, but Marlowe noticed that he did it by pulling on the linen, not by touching the jug itself. After what seemed like a lifetime, the alchemist spoke.

'Where did you get this?' he asked, almost in a whisper.

'Hmm,' Marlowe said. 'Now you've asked me. I *got* it in a house in Blackfriars, but whether it belongs there or not is a moot point. Not even the lady of the house was sure. Apparently, it comes and goes.'

'Comes and goes?' Dee unpinched his spectacles and rubbed his eyes. 'What, by itself?'

'Its . . . owner, as I suppose we must call her now, didn't seem to know. She has only just come to her inheritance and, as she remembers it, sometimes the jug is on its shelf, sometimes it is not. But as for it moving by itself, I should tell you, before you suspect angels, that when I took it down, there were finger marks in the dust around it. Apart from that, there were rings in the dust, where it had clearly been gone, then come back, then gone again; different thicknesses of dust, building up in its absence.' He looked eagerly at Dee, who was still sitting upright, almost leaning away from the jug. 'So, what can you tell me?'

'I can tell you that your lady friend in Blackfriars should change her maidservant.'

Marlowe inclined his head with a small smile. 'About the jug. What can you tell me about the jug?'

Dee steepled his fingers and tapped his chin with the topmost spire. 'I have never seen this jug before,' he said. 'Let's establish that first. But I have seen pictures of it, although they don't do it justice by any means.'

'Pictures? Where? Do you mean it is included on someone's portrait? We can find out who it belongs to, perhaps.'

'Oh, I know who it belongs to – to whom it once belonged, at least. The Knights Templar.' Dee leaned back, content that he would have shocked Marlowe into silence and indeed he had. He leaned forward and pointed, but still seemed unwilling to touch the metal itself. 'These heads on the corners, they represent Baphomet, the Devil. The . . . images on the sides show some of the rather less acceptable rituals that we hear about in relation to the Templars.' He looked up at Marlowe. 'Do they seem to move to you? Hmm?'

Marlowe moistened his lips, which seemed to have become very dry all of a sudden. 'Yes, they do, sometimes. I thought it might be because of the candlelight. I haven't seen it in the day.'

'I think night is the natural habitat of this thing,' Dee said. He picked up the corners of the linen and, gathering them up, tied them together over the mouth of the jug. Now it looked even more like a shroud than ever. He picked it up using the loose fabric and carried it across the room to a large oaken cupboard, black with age. A coiled snake on the top had let its tail drop down across the door, as it dozed in its evening torpor. He chose a key from the bunch at his waist and unlocked it. Flicking the serpent's tail aside and without opening the door more than was necessary, he slipped it inside and then locked the door again, muttering to himself as he did so.

Marlowe had twisted in his seat to watch him. 'I'm sorry,' he
said. 'I didn't catch what you said.'

Dee sat back down again and settled his robes. 'Just a little
binding spell, dear boy. Nothing to worry yourself about. Could
you just go to the door and give Sam a call? I could do with
some brandy; would you like to join me?'

It was true that the old man did look pale and his hand shook
a little. Marlowe went to the door and opened it, to find Sam
Bowes standing outside, a flask in one hand, two glasses in the
other. Without speaking, he handed them to Marlowe and then
padded silently away. Marlowe took the drink back to the little
table and was about to put them down when Dee waved him
away, over to the larger trestle in the centre of the room.

'Call me superstitious if you like,' he said to Marlowe, 'but I
would rather we didn't use this table for a while.'

The playwright paused in the pouring of the brandy. 'That
bad?' he asked, with a raised eyebrow.

'Probably not,' Dee said. 'But sometimes I prefer to be careful.
I have attracted too much attention in the angelic spheres already.
The jug could be the undoing of years of work. As soon as it is
light tomorrow, I will be taking it to somewhere it can do no harm.'

'That could be awkward,' Marlowe said, handing him his glass.
'It doesn't belong to me . . .'

'Nor to your little friend in Blackfriars,' Dee said, waspishly.
'It isn't like you to be so easily led, Kit.'

'Easily led?' Marlowe was stung by the tone. 'By whom?'

'By some little trull who takes her fee in goods, rather than
cold, hard cash.'

'It isn't like that at all,' Marlowe said, on his dignity. 'She is
a cog in a wheel of an investigation of murder, if you must know.
I was just . . .'

'Murder, is it? I am not surprised. The person who owns that
jug is not likely to survive. Even if no one is looking for the jug,
bad luck will follow it wherever it goes.'

'Bad luck? You might say it was bad luck for its owner when
she was shot in the throat at my play.' Marlowe was not superstitious and often laughed at the actors and stage helpers at the
Rose, who were constantly crossing their fingers and indeed
themselves for the slightest reason. When a magpie had flown

in one afternoon in the early run of his first *Tamburlaine*, one of the orchestra had fainted with fright.

Dee nodded and slapped his hands down on the arms of his chair. 'So, that *is* why you are here. I said to Sam, I said you would not be able to leave that alone.'

Marlowe laughed to see Dee come out of his superstitious fright. He looked himself again. 'Will Shaxsper has been accused of the murder, and I don't believe he did it.'

'Will Shaxsper? Never heard of him.'

Marlowe shook his curls and said, with a smile, 'Don't ever let him hear you say that. He aims to be the most famous man in London one day. Or at least the most famous man in Rose Alley.'

'Well, I wish him good luck with that, anyway,' Dee said. 'But if you are investigating murder at the Rose, why were you in Blackfriars? Tell me about it.'

'Shaxsper was in the execution squad, towards the end of the play. He fired and it was a real charge, not the fake one he was expecting. I looked in the scenery and found this.' He ferreted in his purse and brought out the lead shot that Tom Sledd had prised out of the wall. 'But then, I worked out that he could not have shot the woman, not without turning to his right and firing into the crowd and, of course, everyone would have seen him do that, and no one did. So, Tom Sledd and I – Tom is the stage manager at the Rose – Tom and I worked out that the shot had come from the orchestra, and then we found this –' he held out the second ball on the palm of his hand – 'up in the gallery, where it passed through Eleanor Merchant's throat.'

Dee looked at the lead balls in Marlowe's hand. 'They are different,' he said. 'Which one went through her throat?' Marlowe pointed. 'This looks to me as though it came from . . . But it can't be, unless . . .'

'Dr Dee . . .' Marlowe sat back as patiently as he knew how. The old man always talked in riddles, and that was part of his charm, but it was also infuriating. Every hour Marlowe wasted was one that put him nearer to that scaffold, slowly twirling in the wind at the end of a rope, alongside Will Shaxsper.

The magus held up his hand, twisting the lead shot in his fingers. He held it up to the candlelight, sniffed it, bit it, threw

it into the air to catch it with a slick flourish which still
spellbound his audiences after all these years.

'How's your Flemish?' the old man asked.

Kit Marlowe had grown up with the Huguenot weavers in their
gabled houses along the Stour in his boyhood Canterbury. They
spoke it almost to the rhythm of their high warp looms and the
lilt stayed with him. 'Passable,' he said.

'*Snaphaunce*,' Dee said, chuckling as Marlowe frowned.

'Sounds like . . . like "pecking bird",' the playwright said.
'That can't be right.'

'Oh, but it can. Go to the top of the class, Dominus Marlowe.
It describes the mechanism of a new kind of gun. The cock holds
a piece of flint which is released by the trigger to strike the
frizzen, a piece of steel which sends sparks into the priming pan
and . . . there you have it. A ball – *this* ball – flies through the
air until it finds a home.'

'A new kind of gun.' Marlowe was still frowning, assimilating
it all. 'Not a wheel-lock, then?'

'Pah!' Dee threw the lead ball back to the playwright. 'By
comparison with this, wheel-locks will be as the sticks and stones
of the Ancient Britons. Believe me, Kit, there's a terrible new
age coming to the battlefield and I don't want to be around to
see it.'

'Where can I find one of these guns?'

'You can't,' Dee told him flatly. 'As far as I know there is
only one of its kind in London. In the country, even.'

'And that is?'

'The Tower, Kit,' Dee smiled. 'It's in Her Majesty's Armoury.'

'Is it now?' Marlowe was thinking. And Dee could read his
mind.

'So . . .' he said, smiling, 'you've solved your little murder.'
And he leaned forward, knowing full well that *these* walls had
ears, whispering, 'It's the Queen of England, by the grace of
God.'

Marlowe allowed the old man a little time to chuckle, then
asked, 'How do I get in to the Tower?'

'Easily enough,' Dee assured him. 'Indeed, I am amazed you
have not been there already. It is getting out that is more
difficult.'

'I mean, to see the armourer.'

'Pass me that parchment and my quill,' Dee said. 'And the ink. It should be in that upturned rat's skull, over there.'

Marlowe passed it across with a grimace. 'Any reason for the skull? It isn't even properly watertight.' Ink had dripped everywhere, across the surface of the table and had soaked into some rare-looking incunabula, piled haphazardly next to a charger on which a piece of pie and an orange had begun to fuse together with a fascinating mould.

'Just for the look of the thing, my dear boy. Just for the look of the thing.' Dee scratched at the parchment and then waved it in the air to dry it. 'This should get you in. And out.' He dripped some wax on the fold and pressed his ring on it.

Marlowe took it and put it away in his doublet. 'Do you know everyone?' he asked.

Dee thought for a moment, and then answered. 'Not everyone, just everyone who needs knowing.' He stopped speaking and looked fondly at the young man opposite. Kit Marlowe was all things to all men; when men spoke his lines, people listened. When he spoke them for himself, they listened harder. When he moved, there was almost a hint of burning tin on the air, the taste of lighting on open ground. But to John Dee, he was just a boy who, once upon a time, had sat beside his dead wife and promised to make Helene live again with his words. As if, for once, he had read the magus's mind, Marlowe spoke, low and soft.

'Helene was beautiful,' he said. '"She is fairer than the evening air, clad in the beauty of a thousand stars."'

'You remembered!' The old man looked up, with tears in his eyes.

'No one will forget her while you live,' Marlowe said, standing up and shrugging on his cloak. 'And, when I have time, I will write such a play that will mean no one will forget her, not even when we are both gone, you and I.'

Dee stood up and hugged the playwright, patting his back, reluctant to let him go. 'When you have time, Kit,' he said.

'When I have time.'

EIGHT

'And I tell you he's not here!' an exasperated Thomas Sledd was all but screaming at the High Constable who stood in the centre of the Rose's stage like an ox in the furrow.

'What's all this fuss?' Philip Henslowe clattered down the stairs from his counting house. 'High Constable.' He half bowed. 'I'm afraid we're full for this afternoon. Perhaps you could come back in August.'

The last time Philip Henslowe had met Hugh Thynne, the owner of the Rose had been more circumspect, as soon as he realized who Hugh Thynne was. But Philip Henslowe had made rather a lot of money since then and he could probably buy the High Constable three times over by now. That fact made him a little cavalier.

'I'm looking for the actor William Shakespeare,' Thynne told him flatly.

'I keep telling the High Constable.' Sledd sighed. 'He *was* of this company. Now he's in the Clink.'

'He's *not* in the Clink!' Thynne lost his temper at last, roaring at the boy-actor-turned-stage-manager. 'He was released from the Clink by one Robert Greene . . . Do you know him, either of you?'

'No,' both men chorused and, for once, it was half true. Henslowe had met the crawler once and didn't like him. To Thomas Sledd, Greene was one of those groatsworths who hung around theatres like grey miasma hung around graveyards.

'Search it,' Thynne barked to his catchpoles. 'Every nook. Every cranny. And get under this!' He thumped his right foot down on the stage so that the floorboards jumped and the dust flew.

'Just a minute . . .' Henslowe stopped them. 'Where's your warrant?'

Thynne turned to the man and fixed him with his basilisk stare. 'My warrant, apple-squire? Can you be serious?'

'Apple-squire?' Henslowe spluttered. Tom Sledd had to wander away rather than burst out laughing. 'Apple-squire?' So outraged was Henslowe that he had to repeat it.

'You *are* familiar with the term?' Thynne checked.

'Of course I am,' Henslowe fumed. 'And if you are insinuating that I am a pimp, a serving man in a bawdy house . . .'

'Well?' Thynne raised a dismissive eyebrow.

'I *own* three of them,' Henslowe roared. 'The Punk Alice along Rose Alley. The Upright Man in Maiden Lane—' Suddenly he stopped, realizing the extent to which he had incriminated himself.

An eerie sound rattled across the stage of the Rose; it was the sound of Hugh Thynne laughing. 'Don't worry, Master Henslowe,' he chuckled, 'I know the haunts you own and what goes on in them. I can close you down with a click of my fingers.' He stepped closer to Henslowe and leaned in. 'Do we have an understanding? About the warrant, I mean?'

Henslowe licked his lips and turned to Thynne's men, already dispersing in pursuit of their enquiries. 'Search away, lads. We've nothing to hide here.' He dashed across the O and hurtled behind the gates of Babylon, already in position for the afternoon's sell-out performance of *Tamburlaine*. 'Tom, Tom,' he hissed. 'He's not here, is he?'

Sledd looked at him, aghast. 'No! I told Thynne, he's in the Clink.'

Henslowe waved him away. 'Just checking, Tom, I know you don't tell me everything that goes on here.'

'But . . .' Sledd had been brought up on the road, with a troupe of vagabonds and thieves, most of whom wouldn't know the truth if it got up and hit them round the head with a spade. But, against all the odds, he was probably the most truthful man in London.

'No, no, don't tell me. Best I don't know. Just get up to my office, will you? I don't want those flat-footed boobies ferreting about in my chest.' He tutted and rolled his eyes to the Heavens. 'God's teeth! Give me an honest thief any day.'

Robert Greene, scholar of St John's College, Cambridge, went to St Paul's Cross that morning, in search of likely lads. As he watched the sun sparkling on the waters of the river, his task seemed as unlikely as something in a dream and he half expected to wake up any minute. As he turned to his left and saw the carrion kites wheeling over the bridge, swooping for their breakfast on the traitors' heads on their pikes at the far end, the dream became a nightmare.

The din of the city was already starting up, the shouts of the watermen, 'Eastward ho!' and 'Westward ho!' echoing and re-echoing in the Vintry. Greene had been in London long enough to know which areas to avoid. Even in broad daylight he'd never venture into Alsatia, the Bermudas or Damnation Alley – he'd lose a lot more than his dignity if he ventured there. He crossed the Fleet Ditch and walked on up Ludgate. As he turned the half corner the smell hit him first, then the clamour. Hands were clawing at him through the bars of the grille at the gaol. 'Alms, sir. For the love of God.'

Greene ignored them. He had places to be and the sweepings of the prison held no interest for him. On the hill ahead, St Paul's rose in its granite vastness, dwarfing the little rickety houses lying round it. Yesterday had been an execution day and the temporary scaffold still stood there, to the left of the crowd at the Cross. Judging by the ankle-deep garbage that Greene trudged through, the crowd had been sizeable. The crowd there now were standing fascinated by a preacher in black from head to foot, haranguing them. 'Beware,' he was bellowing over the clash of the city and the lowing cattle on their way to Paradise by way of Smithfield, 'for the Devil is among you.' Greene was confident he didn't mean him but as always when near a mob of the great unwashed, he kept his purse tight about him and his hand on his sword hilt.

Greene knew St Paul's Walk. Like so many gulls new to the city he had lost his gold on his first visit there. He wasn't about to make the same mistake. In the south aisle, he knew, the usurers gathered, those strange bearded Jews from Portugal, with their skull-caps and clipped way of talking. They were rarer than blackamoors, but if you found them anywhere in London it would be St Paul's Walk, where their great-great-grandfathers had spat at the man in their own Damascus. Here, too, although Greene didn't know it, Papists conversed in hurried, whispered conversations, spreading the vital news of their detested heresy. Like most vain people, Greene took little notice of anything more than an inch from the end of his nose and he would have passed the Pope himself without a second glance. The north aisle was already crawling with clerics hungry for a living and pestering anyone wearing an ecclesiastic robe just in case he was their ticket to a comfortable future.

At Duke Humphrey's tomb the beggars clustered, in assorted rags and smelling like the Fleet Ditch. He didn't linger long there, in case someone assumed he, too, was of their persuasion; although surely, no one so well dressed could be thought to dine regularly with the Duke. There was the usual crowd at the Si Quis Door, scanning the notices flapping in the breeze. Some of the more generous were reading out the job offers to those who couldn't manage the long words and Greene toyed briefly with posting a notice himself: '*If anyone wants to take down an arrogant whoreson playwright a peg or two, please apply . . .*' But then he realized he didn't have to.

A cripple was dragging himself across the sunlit floor. He was grey and bent, his rags sweeping the flags and he hobbled on a crutch, a useless stump waving to one side of it. 'The Dons took my leg, sir,' the man was saying to a gentleman who stood there, at once appalled and transfixed by the beauty and the squalor of the place, 'at those islands men call the Hesperides.'

The gentleman's lady was leaning forward, a gentle look on her face. 'You poor man,' she was saying. 'Have you no pension?'

The cripple looked at her, uncomprehendingly. 'Pension, lady? I sailed as a privateer, madam. The Queen don't pay us, because we don't fly her colours.'

'That's dreadful,' said the lady, reaching out with a kid-gloved hand, only to change her mind at the last minute. 'Ralph,' she looked up at her husband. 'Give this poor man some money.'

'Well, now, wait a minute . . .' Ralph was by no means sure he wanted to share his worldly goods, even a little of them, with this ragged privateer.

'Now, Ralph,' his lady insisted, with a small edge creeping in to her voice.

Ralph sighed and, half turning from the beggar, tugged a couple of coins from his purse.

'I said "some money", Ralph,' his wife said frostily, 'not "an insult".' And, sighing, the hapless Ralph added more to his handout.

'God bless you both,' the beggar croaked, tugging his forelock as he hobbled away. He made for the Si Quis Door and Greene followed him. Once through the throng, the cripple's dragging walk mysteriously speeded up and he vanished around a corner. Greene stopped and waited. It may be he was wasting his time, but he had a sixth sense about this man.

As he twisted around the buttress, a miracle happened. Not only was the beggar a head taller than he had been, he seemed to have shed fifteen years and grown a new leg. That was the one he was rubbing now, to bring the feeling back into it. Alongside him lay a leather harness, the one that had pinned the limb up into his tattered Venetians a moment ago. Alongside him too, another man was counting out coins, including the goodly handful just wrested from Ralph, via his soft-hearted wife.

'Bravo!' Greene cried, clapping his hands slowly. 'I've never seen it better done. But what are you, exactly? A whipjack or a ruffler?'

The beggar looked confused and decided to brazen it out. The roisterer standing there, hands on hips, wasn't a constable nor even a catchpole. No need to feel his ears burning just yet. 'I'm afraid I don't . . .'

'Beg for a living, pretending to be a soldier? Or a man who has suffered losses at sea . . . yes, you do, I've just seen you do it.'

'All right,' the ex-beggar's accomplice said flatly. 'You know thieves' cant and you've caught out my friend here. The question is . . . are you going to live to tell the tale?' Suddenly there was a knife in his hand and he was on his feet. Greene stepped backwards, his hand on his sword-hilt again.

'Gentlemen, gentlemen,' he said quickly. 'You misunderstand. I have need of your services.'

'Oh?' said the newly restored cripple. 'For what?'

Greene came as close as he dared, trying to ignore the blade inches from him. 'Does the name Christopher Marlowe mean anything to you?'

'It might,' the knife man said.

'He's a playwright,' the cripple said, still flexing his leg and fumbling behind him for his boot. 'His *Tamburlaine*'s playing at the Rose.'

'That's right.' The other one slipped his knife away in an economic movement borne of long practice. 'He's a genius, some say.'

'That's right,' his friend agreed.

'That's not right!' Greene tried to prevent his voice sounding too shrill and all but succeeded. 'The man is a purloiner of other people's creation. *I* wrote *Tamburlaine*.'

'Did you now?' said the money man, turning to his friend. 'This is the *real* genius, Ing.'

'I knew it, Nick.' The erstwhile cripple stood up and stamped around to remind himself where his toes used to be. 'Genius will always out, they say.'

'This Marlowe,' the other man said. 'What do you want done to him? And who are you, as a matter of fact? We don't do . . . jobs for just anyone.'

'I am Robert Greene,' he announced. 'Poet and playwright. And you are . . .?'

The man got up and bowed with a flourish. 'Nicholas Skeres, ruffler, whipjack, palliard and, if needs must, a prigger of prancers. My badly dressed friend here is Ingram Frizer – largely the same qualifications, but not so good.'

'Stow you!' Frizer spat. 'Well, Master Greene,' he beamed, 'I believe Nick asked which of our many skills you require. Throat-slitting comes extra.'

'It does.' Skeres nodded solemnly. 'We have our own blades, of course, but there's the cost of hiding out in the country.'

'New clothes,' Frizer added. 'You can rarely get the stains out.'

'True,' Skeres agreed. 'Sometimes, we even need a passport . . .'

'Dear God, no,' Greene said.

Frizer looked at Skeres. 'Doesn't look like a big payer, Nick,' he said.

'You're right.' Skeres nodded.

'It's not the money, gentlemen,' Greene assured them. 'It's the task. I don't want Marlowe dead. Just . . . well, done down, shall we say?'

'In what way,' Frizer asked, 'done down?'

'I'm not sure.'

Skeres raised his hands to Heaven. 'I'm not getting a good feeling about this, Ing.'

'Nor am I, Nick.'

'Can you read?' Greene asked them.

'Does Master Sackerson eat hounds for breakfast?'

'Here.' He handed Skeres a piece of parchment. The man read

it. '"Dr Gabriel Harvey. At the sign of the Coiled Serpent." Is that an apt address, Master Greene?'

'This morning, if you have time,' Greene said. 'He'll be expecting you.'

'How about the retainer?' Frizer asked, holding out his hand.

'Oh, yes,' Greene said, scowling, 'how remiss of me,' and he threw a silver coin which Skeres caught expertly.

'That will turn miraculously to gold when the job's done,' Greene said. 'As miraculously as growing a new leg.'

He turned back to the Si Quis Door and bought an oyster from a pale-faced waif standing in the Mediterranean Aisle. He would have liked to have known what Gabriel Harvey had in mind before he hired Frizer and Skeres on his behalf, but in a way, not knowing had its advantages – he could indulge his imagination all the more.

Greene was halfway down Ludgate Hill before he found his way blocked by two burly men wearing the cross and sword of the City on their breasts. They were looking intently at him.

'Master Greene?' one of them asked. The playwright spun on his pattens and strode back up the hill, only to bump into two more men, wearing the same livery, blocking his path. For a moment, he toyed with ducking into Sea Coal Lane but the alley was narrow and his chance of outrunning four of them was remote. He felt a time-honoured hand on his shoulder and he was turned again. 'I said "Master Greene?"'

The Cambridge man decided to brazen it out. By comparison with half the denizens of St Paul's behind him, he was a paragon of virtue. 'I am Greene,' he said, mustering all his poise and arrogance and shrugging off the restraining hand.

'I am Constable Harrison,' the man said, 'and you are under arrest.'

'Where is your magistrate's warrant?' Greene asked. He'd get to the charge later.

'Here!' said Harrison and he drove his fist into the playwright's face. For Greene, day became night and he slumped backwards into the arms of Harrison's catchpoles. 'Well, well,' the Constable said. 'What a coincidence. Here we are with a felon on our hands and just over there is Ludgate Gaol. Lively, now, lads. Let's get him out of the way. Last thing we want is a riot over the heavy-handed tactics of the authorities.'

And they carried Greene away, Harrison unhooking the man's expensive sword in case somebody hurt themselves.

Kit Marlowe's horse clattered under the archway and up the rise to the White Tower. The ravens fluttered and croaked across the broad sweep of the grass as a Yeoman warder took the horse's reins and let its rider pass. The seal of Dr John Dee on the parchment he carried opened doors in this bleak place that the Yeoman warder didn't even know existed.

Marlowe flashed his warrant again at the outer door and padded down the stone steps into the Armoury. Ahead of him, astride a massive wooden destrier, sat an image of the Queen's father, King Harry, in his armour for the tilt. The painted eyes behind the visor bars seemed to move as Marlowe watched them and he felt for all the world that he had stepped back into Dr Dee's study, where serpents coiled and demons lurked.

'Master Marlowe?' He turned at the sound of his name. A square, squat man with a scarred face and wearing the livery of the Queen emerged from a side door and crossed the floor to him. Marlowe took the proffered hand. 'William Waad, Lieutenant of the Tower. To what do I owe the pleasure?'

'You were expecting me, sir?' Marlowe was surprised. Even in this city of rumours, the speed astonished him. He had only left John Dee a matter of hours before.

'Look about you, sir.' Waad smiled. 'This is the White Tower, a royal residence. You were, just last night, in another one – Whitehall. All the residences have a means of communication. It's done by mirrors.' He saw the uncertainty on Marlowe's face. 'I could tell you how it's done,' he chuckled, 'but then, of course, I'd have to kill you.'

There was something about the man that made Marlowe think perhaps he wasn't joking.

'How's Francis?' Waad asked, ushering Marlowe into a side chamber.

'Francis?'

Waad looked at him. He'd heard all about Marlowe. The man was fire and air, a University wit and a ready blade. Had a mind

like a Toledo rapier . . . and yet . . . 'Francis Walsingham,' Waad
explained. 'His uncle was a predecessor of mine here at the
Tower.'

'It's a small world.' Marlowe smiled, but he had no intention
of sharing more confidences with this man than he needed to.
'Don't know him.'

Liar, thought Waad. He knew Walsingham had recruited
Marlowe at Cambridge and, once recruited by Walsingham, you
stayed recruited. But each man, Intelligencer or not, had his
reasons and found his own way in the world. If Marlowe chose
not to know the Queen's Spymaster, so be it. 'So,' Waad poured
a goblet of finest claret and passed it to his visitor, 'to your
purpose.'

'A snaphaunce,' Marlowe told him. 'Dr Dee tells me your
Armoury has the only one in England.'

'Ah,' Waad became confidential. 'Not for sale, I'm afraid.'

'I don't want to buy it,' Marlowe told him. 'Merely to look
at it. Handle it, perhaps.'

Waad sucked his teeth. 'Well,' he said slowly, 'it does come
under the *Res Novae* category.'

'*Res Novae*?' Marlowe queried.

Oh dear, thought Waad. This wasn't going well at all. Perhaps
this wasn't the real Kit Marlowe. 'New things,' he translated. 'In
Latin.'

Marlowe smiled and said, '*Nouveauté*, νέα πράγματα, *nieuwe
dingen* . . . I understand it, Sir William. I just don't know what
it means.'

'Oh, I see.' Waad beamed. 'Yes, of course. Quite. Well, here
at the Armoury we are constantly experimenting with new
gadgets. Bristle letters. Aqua Fortis.' He clapped a hand over his
own mouth. 'There!' he scolded himself. 'I've said too much
already. Please forget what I've just said. State secrets. National
treasures. That sort of thing.'

'The snaphaunce?'

'Yes.' Waad clicked his fingers, glad to be moving on. 'You'll
have to sign the book, of course.'

'Of course.' Marlowe took the proffered quill and wrote his
name in the large ledger open on Waad's desk. He quickly read
down the other names on the page, but there were none that he

recognized. Waad led him through a small door that all but disappeared in a book case and took Marlowe along a narrow, dark passageway lit by small, high barred windows and a solitary taper burning at the far end. Here was another door and Waad unlocked it before stepping inside.

'Look at nothing around the walls,' Waad warned him. 'This –' he hauled a gun from a rack – 'is the weapon you seek.'

'So this is a snaphaunce.' Marlowe weighted it, cocked it, saw at once the pecking bird of the mechanism.

'It is. They say,' Waad dropped his voice and closed in so his chin was almost on Marlowe's shoulder, 'that the Dons have a similar device they call a *miquelet*.' He stepped back and spoke more normally. 'So you see why we need to develop this as soon as we can. What is your interest, exactly?'

From what Walsingham had told Waad of Kit Marlowe, he wasn't likely to be spying for the Spaniards, but this was a dangerous, topsy-turvy, brave new world and who could be sure of anyone or anything in it?

'This gun could have been used to kill a woman in the Rose Theatre, Sir William.' Marlowe looked at the lieutenant and saw that the avid gleam that lit everyone's eye when gruesome murder was abroad was in his now. 'I see you know of it.'

'*This* gun?' Waad took it back from Marlowe. 'Impossible. It has never left the building.'

'You're sure of that?'

'Absolutely. Only a handful of people know about it. And you are only the third person to handle it.'

'You, I presume,' he said, 'are the first. Who is the second?'

'No, Marlowe,' Waad corrected him. 'I am the second. The first is the man who made it.' There was a pause. 'Of course . . .'

'Yes?' Marlowe looked the man in the face. Something was not right.

'There is a second snaphaunce.'

'There is?'

'The man who made it, in fact made two. A brace for Her Majesty.'

'And the other one?'

Waad cleared his throat and put the gun back on its rack. 'The other one was bought by private treaty, before I could prevent it.'

'By whom?' Marlowe was surprised that after all the subterfuge and secrecy, there was another gun like this, possibly, by now, dozens, on the streets of London. Not to mention in the hands of any enemy who cared to invest a little gold.

Waad shrugged. 'I don't know,' he said.

Marlowe rounded on him. 'Sir William . . .'

'As God is my judge,' Waad blurted out, not liking the look in Marlowe's eye at all. 'All I can tell you is what I heard. It's gossip, so it may be wrong.'

'Try me,' Marlowe said, coldly.

'Yes, well, when I heard this, it stuck in my mind as being rather odd. Why this man should want such a weapon, but also how he could afford it. I know that men of his profession are doing well at the moment, but . . .'

'The gossip, Master Waad, if you please.' Marlowe took a step closer and Waad put up a restraining hand.

'A tobacconist,' he said. 'He was a tobacconist.'

'The Coiled Serpent?' Ingram Frizer was not at all sure that he knew where it was. He knew most inns in the entire city of London, but not all went by the name on their sign. For all he knew, the Coiled Serpent could be one of his regular watering holes. He never looked above his head; opportunity and danger lay below, where the people were.

'Yes, Ing,' Skeres reminded him. 'It's down the Bailey. You know the one. Does meals. Lets out rooms. More of an ordinary than an inn.' Frizer shook his head. 'Landlord won't allow swearing in the place. A bit of a Bible thumper.'

The light dawned on Frizer's rather weasel-like face. 'I *do* know it, now you say that,' he said. 'I've often thought that keeping an inn was a strange calling for someone like that.'

'There's a lot of wine in the Bible, or so he says. In any event, I know where it is; are we going there now?' ·

'Why not?' Frizer said. 'The sooner we go and see this lunatic, the sooner the money is in our pockets.'

'But I still don't see what he wants us to do. "Done down" – what is that supposed to mean?'

'Did he say "gunned down", perhaps?' Frizer said. 'In that case, it could be difficult, as we don't have a gun.'

Skeres thought for a moment, then said, 'No. He definitely said "done". He wants us to be . . . unpleasant about this man, Marlowe. This playwright. I suppose we could go and say nasty things in his play.'

'We'll be shouted down. Everyone loves this play that's on. *Tamburlaine*. We'll have to do better than that.'

'Is he married? We could tell his wife he has a woman on the side.'

Frizer pulled a face. 'No,' he said. 'These are players. The surprise is when they *haven't* got a woman on the side. Ned Alleyn is a legend, they say, in the bedroom.'

Skeres shrugged. 'I don't know, then. Perhaps this Harvey will have some ideas. Come on,' he tugged at Frizer's sleeve, 'it's down here, the Coiled Serpent.' The pair jostled their way along Giltspur Street, with the old Grey Friars to their left and old Rahere's Hospital of St Bartholomew at their backs.

The inn sign swung in the morning breeze, rather faded and tattered. 'Oh.' Frizer looked up at it. 'A coiled *serpent*. I don't think I had ever noticed it before. Terrible carving.'

'What did you think it was?' Skeres asked, pushing the door open.

Frizer looked up once more and followed his colleague inside. He shook his head. 'I have no idea,' he muttered.

Skeres was asking for Harvey. The grey-faced skivvy pointed up the stairs. The two men were about halfway up before she remembered her instructions. Her shriek went through them like an ice-cold knife in the back of the neck.

'Master Harveee!' It sounded like something a farmer might use to attract his pigs. 'Master Harveeee! Two gennlemen to see yer.'

Gabriel Harvey's face around the edge of the door was as startled as theirs. 'I apologize, gentlemen,' he said in a low voice, holding his head. 'She never seems to learn. It goes right through me,' he pointed to his temple, 'here.'

Frizer nodded. 'I know what you mean,' he said. 'What a delightful girl.'

'I am only here until my own house is ready, you understand,' Harvey was quick to point out. 'It's along the Strand. Rather large. Rather imposing. But, may I ask to whom I have the pleasure of speaking?'

Skeres silently rearranged the words in his head, to see what he had just been asked. 'Ingram Frizer,' he said, pointing to the other man, 'and I am Nicholas Skeres. We met a . . . friend of yours today in St Paul's. He said you may have a . . .'

Before he could finish his sentence, Harvey had hooked a finger into the front of his doublet and pulled him inside. Frizer nipped in quickly before the door was slammed in his face.

'Please,' Harvey hissed. 'Please, be careful. No one must know what I have planned.'

Skeres gave Frizer a meaningful look. So, murder was afoot, then. All that nonsense of 'doing someone down' was all so much double talk. This was going to cost.

'I think I can make myself clear, gentlemen, in very few and succinct sentences. You look like men of the world.'

Frizer and Skeres exchanged satisfied glances. They certainly *felt* like men of the world. It was nice to have their suspicions borne out by a stranger.

'So,' Harvey continued, 'you know how annoying it is when you find that someone else in your area of endeavour is fêted when you yourself are doomed to be ignored.'

They weren't quite so clear about that, but they were being paid, so they nodded. Or should they have shaken? The strange man with the rather mad eyes and flecks of foam at the corners of his mouth seemed content with nods, so they nodded some more.

'I am so glad we understand each other. Now, do you know Master M—' He stopped himself. 'The person who is at issue here?'

'We've heard of him,' Frizer said, 'but we have never met.'

'You are fortunate in the extreme,' Harvey said. 'I have heard nothing but his name and seen nothing but his face every time I close my eyes for years. But I digress. I would like him . . . eliminated.'

'You've come to the right men, Master . . .'

'Professor.'

'Professor Harvey.' Skeres didn't miss a beat. When there was serious money to be had, the customer was always right, be they barking mad or only nor' by nor'west. 'We do elimination to order, and very discreetly.'

Harvey looked puzzled. 'Discreetly?' he asked. 'How can you do it discreetly? I want Marlowe's sins shouted from the roof tops. He must be . . .'

'Eliminated, yes.' Frizer jumped in. He had enough blood on his hands to see him in Hell, should there be one, for the rest of time, so a little more wouldn't hurt. But if he could earn money with no blood being spilled, then so much the better for his immortal soul – should he have one. A man couldn't be too careful these days. 'I just need to get your orders straight in my mind. Could you just answer "yes" or "no" so we all know what is going on?'

'Yes.' Harvey was not happy with monosyllables, but realized that needs must when the Devil drives.

'Do you want us to kill Master Marlowe?' Frizer asked.

'God, no! Sorry.' Harvey composed his face and folded his hands in his lap. 'No.'

'Do you want him to be injured at all, even slightly?' Skeres had the idea and was joining in with a will. 'Kneecaps, that kind of thing.'

'No.'

'Do you want us to –' now it was his turn again, Frizer was stuck for the phrase for a moment – 'say nasty things about him?'

Harvey brightened up. God's teeth, could it be that these idiots had got the idea at last? 'Yes!'

'That's all? No knives, no beating, no injuries of any kind?'

Harvey was a literal-minded man and was stuck for the right answer. 'Um . . . Yes, and . . . yes?' He wasn't sure that was right. 'Yes, that's all. Yes, no knives, no beating, no injuries of any kind?' He stood up sharply, looking madder than ever. 'What do you take me for?'

Now Frizer and Skeres were both stuck for answers, but eventually Frizer spoke. 'A man of the world, who doesn't resort to violence,' he said, soothingly. 'Refreshing, in our line of work.' He rubbed his hands together. 'Well, Ma—Professor Harvey. Time is money. The sooner we start the sooner we finish . . .'

'Please,' Harvey said, closing his eyes. 'Enough clichés. Here is your payment; I trust you will find it adequate for your task.' He handed them a purse, reassuringly heavy, then walked to the door and opened it for them. 'Good morning, gentlemen.'

'Er . . . good morning,' muttered Frizer.

'Shall we be in touch?' Skeres asked. 'To let you know how we get on?'

Harvey looked at him and laughed, a harsh bark. 'I shall know,' he said. 'The heavens will proclaim it when the Muses' Darling crashes to earth. I will hear the angels sing.'

Skeres opened his mouth to speak, then settled for a nod and a hurried departure. Once out in the street, both men were silent until they reached the crossroads by Smithfield.

'Was he . . .?' Frizer began.

'As a serpent, coiled or otherwise,' Skeres agreed. 'Still –' he hefted the purse before stashing it in his belt – 'easy money, Ing, the easiest we'll earn in a long day's march.'

'Are we going to, you know, do it?'

'What?' Skeres was planning what he could spend his ill-gotten gains on and his mind was very much elsewhere.

'Be nasty about Master Marlowe?'

'Nah. What would be the point? But we'll treat ourselves to a penny show, shall we? Just to say hello. It would be as well to know what he looks like, at least.'

'Dinner, then a show,' Frizer said, linking arms with Skeres. 'That sounds like a plan.'

Ingram Frizer dashed away an errant tear, as Ned Alleyn, after much gasping and clutching at his breast, finally died.

'My body feels,' the actor groaned, 'my soul doth weep to see your sweet desires deprived my company. For Tamburlaine, the scourge of God, must die.'

Frizer sniffed, glancing at Skeres. 'Not such a bad old stick, was he?'

Nicholas Skeres, always more pragmatic, was simply glad that most people died more easily than that, with far less noise and fuss.

John Meres, as Amyras, stepped forward to close the play and, apart from Skeres', there was scarcely a dry eye in the house. 'Meet heaven and earth, and here let all things end, for earth hath spent the pride of all her fruit, and heaven consumed his choicest living fire! Let earth and heaven his timeless death deplore, for both their worths may equal him no more!'

The applause was thunderous, and even the seated gallery patrons were on their feet. Backstage, Philip Henslowe leaned on the back of a piece of the walls of Babylon and muttered his thanks to whoever up there was looking after him. The play had gone off without undue incident, just the odd heckler being ejected. Another full house! His mouth was almost watering at the thought of smashing all the penny pots. His backers were happy. His actors were happy. If this was what a murder could do, he might arrange one for every new play.

Marlowe, passing, poked him in the ribs. 'I know what you are thinking, Master Henslowe, but I must take some credit, surely?'

Henslowe came to with a start. 'Of course, Kit, of course. This wouldn't have happened with a bad play, not even with the shooting. No, no, this is your skill that has . . .'

Marlowe laughed. 'Spare me, Philip, please. Excuse me, I must just go through and meet the patrons. I had to calm down Lord Aumerle yesterday; he didn't at all enjoy being sprayed with blood in the execution scene.'

'Did you speak to Tom about that? We can't afford to be replacing clothes left, right and centre.'

'All done,' Sledd said, scurrying past with an armful of wood for running repairs.

'Good lad,' Henslowe said absently, and wandered off to the box office.

Marlowe bowed and complimented his way across the stage and was about to disappear behind some flats when two men approached him.

'Master Marlowe?'

He pinned on his most polite smile and turned round. 'Gentlemen?' he said. 'How may I help you?'

'We are here with compliments from Ma . . . Professor Harvey,' Skeres said.

'Really?' Marlowe's eyebrow rose. 'That is very . . . unexpected. Thank you.'

Ingram moved round to Marlowe's other shoulder, so that he was trapped between them. He looked closely at Frizer. 'But, I know you. We met in St Paul's.'

'That's right,' Skeres said. He had had his suspicions, but had not been sure. The lighting in the theatre was so different. He wished Harvey's task had been murder; it would have been a pleasure to take this popinjay down a proper peg or two.

Frizer recognized the signs and while he would not have minded doling out a few kidney punches then and there, on stage at the Rose was probably not the place. 'All's fair in love and war,' he said. 'No harm done.'

'No, indeed,' Marlowe said, extricating himself from them. He struck Frizer a friendly buffet on the shoulder. 'It's a shame we don't have time for a game of Find the Lady, eh?'

'Ha. Ha,' Skeres replied, mirthlessly, returning the blow, but nothing like as hard as his heart would have him do. 'Well, it was good to see you again, Master Marlowe. We will tell Professor Harvey we saw you.'

'And Robyn Greene? Is he a friend of yours, too?' Marlowe asked.

'Greene? Oh, no. Just Professor Harvey. Besides, Master Greene is not . . . about much at the moment.' Frizer suppressed a smile.

'Pardon?' If there was anyone who could understand a hidden meaning, it was Christopher Marlowe.

'Well, when we saw him this morning, he was just being arrested by Constable Harrison and his men. He would have been taken to –' he looked at Skeres for confirmation – 'Ludgate, from St Paul's.'

'What for, do you know?' A horrible suspicion was creeping over Marlowe. He was not a man much troubled by conscience, but if what he suspected was right, he would need to put things right. When he had the time.

Skeres shrugged. 'Who knows? Harrison and his men rarely get things right. He could be there for any reason, or none.' He clapped Marlowe on the back once more. 'We must be away. We'll give your regards to Professor Harvey, shall we?'

NINE

He crouched in the reeds while the early-morning mists still wreathed the water. He turned the key in the gun's mechanism slowly, watching the pool's edge where the dark waters lay matted with dead bulrushes. Here and there, a new green shoot rose like a promise from the brown. He nestled the pearl-inlaid butt against his shoulder and lined his eye up along the barrel. This gun was a bitch; he knew that of old, but he also knew it was worth a queen's ransom and he treated it with the respect it deserved.

Then he saw them, a pair of mallards in the morning, the drake, very like himself, in gorgeous colours, preening its feathers and diving to impress his lady love, the brown speckled drab who swam dutifully behind, looking coy and simple. It was spring in the marshes of Islington and the mallards, like Ned Alleyn who spied on them, had mating in mind.

'Alleyn!' The barking voice couldn't have been worse timed. It coincided with his finger squeezing the trigger and the shot went wide, the gun's butt thudding into his shoulder with such force that he dropped the thing and only just managed to rescue it from an expensive slide into the murky waters of the pond. The mallards, alarmed and reprieved at the same time, flapped noisily skyward to continue their courtship elsewhere.

The actor fumed, clutching his aching shoulder and clambering to his feet. A knot of black-clad officials was striding over the tussocks of grass, Hugh Thynne at their head. A clutch of constables. A cobbling of catchpoles. Alleyn was turning into Kit Marlowe. But he was also turning into Shepherd Lane. That was before Hugh Thynne stopped him with his cane. He prodded Alleyn in the chest with it and stood in front of him.

'You're a hard man to find, play-actor,' he said.

'Not really,' Alleyn smiled. 'It's Saturday. Everybody knows that Edward Alleyn hunts ducks at Islington Ponds on a Saturday. Gets me in the right mood for whatever part I'm playing.'

'Shot a lot of ducks, did he, Tamburlaine?' Thynne sneered.

Alleyn ignored the jibe. 'I assume you wanted me for something.'

'I might want you for murder,' Thynne told him. 'Or at the very least aiding and abetting a killer.'

'You have no writ, High Constable. This is Islington, in the county of Hertfordshire.' He tapped the man on the chest. 'You are out of your jurisdiction and out of your depth.'

'When it comes to murder,' Thynne said levelly, looking into the man's dark eyes, 'you'll find my writ runs everywhere. Show me the gun.'

Alleyn hauled it upright against his chest and threw it to him. Thynne caught it and looked at the thing. Heavy, ornate, richly lapped in silver and mother of pearl. 'Yours?' he asked the actor.

'On loan,' Alleyn said, 'from a patron. You may have heard of him. The Lord Admiral.'

Thynne smiled. 'We had a similar conversation the last time we met, Master Alleyn. Howard of Effingham didn't frighten me then; and he doesn't frighten me now. Where's Shakespeare?'

'Who?'

Thynne threw the wheel-lock back and Alleyn winced as it jarred against his already-bruised shoulder. 'The man accused in the murder of Eleanor Merchant. The man Robert Greene sprang from the Clink. Do you know where he is?'

Alleyn spread his arms wide. 'Perhaps your clods would like to search me,' he said, 'to see if I have any bit-players in my codpiece.'

'We've searched your house already,' Thynne told him.

'What?' Alleyn's jaw dropped along with his arms. 'You have no right . . .'

'We had every right,' Thynne corrected him. 'Williams – you made the list. What did we find in Master Alleyn's inner chamber?'

The Constable produced a paper from his purse and read aloud: 'Three fullams, sir.'

Thynne closed to Alleyn and whispered in his ear, 'That's dice loaded with quicksilver.'

'Eight gourds.'

'Dice hollowed on one side,' Thynne translated.

'Six bristles.'

'Dice doctored with horsehair so that they won't land straight.' He leaned back and the whisper turned to a bellow. 'And in the bedchamber?'

'Two morts,' the Constable told him, not needing to check his paper for this. 'One a blackamoor who gave the name of Ebony Sal. The other a country wench called Nell Bishop.'

'And what were these young ladies doing when we arrived, Constable Williams?'

'Painting their nipples, sir.'

'For what purpose?'

'To draw their clients, sir.'

'Where?'

'Anywhere they could, sir.'

'Specifically?'

'Up the smock alleys, sir. Petticoat Lane and the Spittle they said.'

'And for whom do these night-walkers work, Constable Williams?'

The man smiled and delivered his last line with a certain relish. 'One Edward Alleyn, sir.'

'You know,' Alleyn smiled back at him, 'you're rather good. Ever thought of acting?'

'You're in trouble, Alleyn.' Thynne wiped the smile off his face. Ned Alleyn was no stranger to the hospitality of London's prisons and he didn't care to repeat the experience.

'Oh, come now, High Constable.' He decided to brazen it out. 'These girls are just friends of mine. Doing . . . favours for other friends. You know how it is? As for the dice, well, let's not beat about the bush, shall we? Your lads planted them. You see, I've got rather a thing about gambling. Especially illegal gambling. Would you believe, some ill-educated souls in the audience actually play at Mumchance and Primero rather than watch the great Ned Alleyn in action?'

'Yes,' said Thynne, 'I would.' He tapped Alleyn on his bad shoulder with his cane. 'You keep a sharp look out for Shakespeare,' he said. 'If you see him, and if that sighting leads to an arrest, well, I think I can persuade Constable Williams here not to be *too* zealous in passing your name to the Recorder. Of course –'

he tapped the Lord Admiral's wheel-lock – 'you could save us all a lot of bother and just shoot Shakespeare yourself.'

Master Sackerson was confused. He was used to the smell of humans, leaning over his Pit, shouting, cursing, laughing. He was used to the smell of blood: his own; those of the mastiffs they unleashed against him; the butchered carcases they gave him in lieu of pay. But today, things were different. He could smell human. He could smell blood. But it was another kind of blood. It was human blood. He stood on his hind legs in his garden, nostrils quivering against the wind, his evil little eyes darting here and there, his head cocked to one side so that his one good ear could catch the sounds. Nothing unusual: the cries and shouts from the river, the church bells calling the faithful to prayer, the wind from the east.

That was the wind that scattered the dead man's papers into Sackerson's Garden, that sent them twirling and flying like leaves of the fall along Rose Alley and into Maiden Lane. Moll Devereux caught one as she stepped out from the Upright Man that Sunday morning. Her head thumped from the carousing of the night before and she'd spent so long on her back in an upstairs room that her legs weren't working any too well either. But Moll had been a good girl once and she knew how to read. She looked at the paper scrap in her hand. 'Abominations of the Devil,' she read aloud. 'Leave this place of Sodom and Gomorrah. Have done with the atheist Tamburlaine and turn to the Lord.'

Instead, Moll Devereux turned the corner. She saw the wall of the Bear Garden and that vicious old bastard Sackerson safely below in his Pit. But that was odd. The bear was on his hind legs, his hands raised as though in prayer, the matted fur swinging as he trod rhythmically from foot to foot. His mouth was open and he was growling, low in his throat. And he didn't take his eyes off something he had spotted, ahead of him, on his wall.

Instinctively, she followed his gaze. Lying on his back on the wall, his arms and head lolling into the Bear Pit, was a man. He was dead. Moll knew that because the man's face was ghastly white, like the make-up she wore on high days and holidays. She knew that because he wasn't moving. She knew that because there was a dagger thrust up to the ornate hilt in his heart.

'To the point, at least,' Hugh Thynne said as he peered over the corpse an hour or so later. The dead man was still sprawled awkwardly across the wall, his feet dangling over the roadway, his head arched backwards, his hands trailing just a little too high for Master Sackerson to make a meal of him.

The High Constable jerked his head and one of his headboroughs hauled the body off the wall so that it flopped unceremoniously on to Maiden Lane; another money-making opportunity for Philip Henslowe. 'First Finder?' Thynne straightened, looking at the little crowd that had gathered.

Another constable nudged the girl forward. Thynne looked at her. He knew her profession straight away. 'Name?' he asked her.

'Moll Devereux,' she told him sulkily, hands on hips. She knew this man and knew his reputation. How she wished that dagger had been tickling *his* ribs instead.

'You found this man?'

'Yes,' she told him.

Thynne leaned closer and whispered in her ear, 'It is customary to address the High Constable of London as "Sir".'

She fumed, but Moll Devereux had not been born yesterday. There were people you could afford to annoy, and those you couldn't. And the High Constable was certainly not one of those she went out of her way to irritate, though it went against the grain. 'Sir,' she said, curtseying as though the Queen herself had asked to meet her.

'Better,' Thynne said, standing back. 'So, you found him like that, over the wall?'

'I did . . . sir.'

'When was this?'

'Not an hour since. I heard the clock of St Benet strike the time. It was seven of the clock.'

'What's all this fuss here?' A voice called from the back of the rapidly growing crowd. 'If any of you are baiting my bear . . .'

Thynne half turned to face the new commotion. 'Well, well,'

he smiled. 'Master Henslowe. You seem to turn up whenever a body is found.'

Henslowe pushed his way to the front of the mob and saw the body on the ground. Instinctively, he stepped over it to make sure his bear was unharmed. Then he turned to the girl. 'Everything all right, Moll?' he asked.

'All right as it can be when you trip over a corpse first thing in the morning.'

'You know this woman, Master Henslowe?' Thynne asked.

'Of course I do,' the impresario snapped. He knew far more than the High Constable and wasn't at all happy at the way the morning was going. 'She works for me.' He could have bitten his tongue for letting that slip out, but it was too late now.

Thynne looked along the twisting lane to the sign of the Upright Man swaying gently in the breeze. 'Of course she does. I'd forgotten what a Johannes Factotum you were. Finger in every pie, eh?' He winked at Henslowe and nodded in Moll's direction at the same time. The High Constable turned to the crowd who eked a living of sorts on the Bishop of Winchester's ground. 'Anybody know this man?' he asked, pointing to the corpse at his feet.

There was a long pause, then Henslowe cleared his throat. 'I do,' he said.

Thynne turned to him again. 'This is better than any play,' he said. 'Who was he?'

'I don't know his name,' Henslowe assured him. 'But I know his calling. He was a Puritan, Presician, call them what you will. One of God's Elect.'

'Well, he's been well and truly elected now,' Thynne said. '*How* do you know him?'

A look of anguish passed briefly over Henslowe's face. Who'd run a theatre when the Godly walked the earth? 'I'd had him thrown out of the Rose,' he said. 'Twice.'

'Twice?' Thynne raised an eyebrow. 'I assume he didn't keep coming back to enjoy the show?'

'No,' Henslowe grumbled. 'He came to rant. Screaming nonsense about blasphemy, fornication, Godless ways. I ask you . . .' He absent-mindedly reached out and wrapped Moll Devereux's cloak around her, concealing the swell of her breasts.

'This kind of rant?' Thynne held up one of the scraps of paper that still lay strewn near the body. Henslowe looked at it. 'Sounds about right,' he nodded. 'Nice font, though. I wonder who his printer is.'

'Right,' Thynne said to his men, 'let's get this off the street. I happen to know that Master Henslowe here has ample space for the laying out of a body. Get him into the Rose.'

'Now, just a minute,' Henslowe protested. 'I've got a show to put on tomorrow afternoon.'

'Have you?' Thynne said through gritted teeth. 'Have you really? It would be ironic, wouldn't it, if I had to close your theatre down because of the death of a Puritan? Sort of . . . playing into his hands, if you will excuse the pun.' He lifted his cane and deftly parted Moll Devereux's cloak so that her cleavage graced the Southwark crowd again. 'Then there's the other little matter,' he said, 'of living off immoral earnings, that sort of thing. What a perfect pair you'd make,' he said, 'whipped at the cart's tail. What would Mistress Henslowe say? I understand she is beginning to make her mark on society, these days? My own wife mentioned that . . .'

Henslowe went white. He nodded to the constables and they hoisted the dead man on to their shoulders and made their way towards the theatre. 'By the way.' Thynne stepped forward and stopped them. 'Have you seen this dagger before, Master Henslowe?'

The impresario looked at it, the quicksilver curls of the hilt, the initials Ch. Ma. just below the ricasso. 'Never,' he said cheerily. 'Never.'

'Look, I'm really sorry about this, Ned,' Henslowe was nodding and smiling to the gallery commoners shuffling into their places as the orchestra warmed up, 'but the Tiring Room's a little crowded today.'

'Really?' Alleyn's mind was clearly elsewhere. He snapped his fingers and a lackey hurried to him, clutching a breast and back. He started buckling them around Alleyn who was already doing his breathing exercises.

'Yes. It's . . . well, there's no easy way to say this. It's another body, I'm afraid.'

Alleyn stopped breathing, at least in the theatrical sense, and held off the plumed helmet for a moment. 'What are you talking about, Philip?'

'It's that bloody Puritan – you know, the one I've had to throw out a couple of times. Moll found him, on the Bear Garden wall.'

'When was this?' Alleyn held on to the lackey's shoulder and proceeded to flex his knees and hold a foot up behind him, first the right, then the left.

'Yesterday morning. First thing.'

'Well,' Alleyn let the lackey buckle on his sword, 'if he was found in the street, what's he doing in here? And why is he *still* here?'

'Thynne insisted.'

'Thynne!' Alleyn bellowed and the theorbo player behind the curtain jumped and missed his note. 'That's twice in three days that interfering bastard . . . No, no.' He calmed himself. 'Nothing's going to ruffle me today, of all days. How did he die?'

'Well, that's the Devil of it.' Henslowe became conspiratorial, glancing around to make sure no one was too close. He shooed the lackey away. 'He was stabbed,' he hissed, 'with a knife.'

'That must reduce Thynne's suspects to a few thousand or so.'

'Actually, it reduces the suspects to one,' Henslowe murmured.

'One?' Alleyn was carefully combing his beard over his ruff. 'How so?'

'I saw the blade, Ned,' Henslowe said. 'It was Kit's dagger. Kit Marlowe's.'

This time Alleyn's eyes widened and his jaw dropped so that his careful combing had been rather a waste of time. 'Never!' he said. 'I don't believe it.'

The first trumpet sounded and the beginners were assembling behind the curtain. It wouldn't be long now. 'You'd better show me this body,' Alleyn said and Henslowe led the way. The pair ducked under the low lintel and down the steps into the Tiring Room. The noise of the audience here was louder than above, the thud and scrape of the groundlings shaking the Rose's timbers.

Alleyn collided with a serving wench with a large nose and an ill-disguised, straw-coloured beard. 'Who are you?' he asked.

The serving wench drew herself up to her full height. 'I am Richard Burbage.'

'Good for you.' Alleyn patted the man on the shoulder and carried on his way. 'Scraping the barrel a little, aren't we, Philip?' 'Oh, he's been hanging around for days, asking for a part. I relented in the end. You know me – all heart.' 'Oh, yes,' Alleyn agreed, rolling his eyes. 'I . . . Mother of God.' Alleyn crossed himself. It was an odd gesture from a Scythian shepherd. It was even odd for an innkeeper's son from Bishopsgate but shock took men in different ways. 'I *know* this man,' he said.

'You do?' Henslowe muttered, looking the body up and down, wondering if there was some identifying mark he'd missed.

'It's John Garrett. He's . . . was . . . a neighbour of mine, of sorts. A Puritan. There's a whole nest of them in Old Jewry. God's Word, that's what the Brethren call him.'

'Have you had any trouble from him?' Henslowe asked. 'At home, I mean? Presumably he knows you're an actor.'

Alleyn turned to him and clapped the plumed, gilded helmet on his head, careful to keep the ruff free. 'I am not *an* actor, Philip. I am *the* actor. I trust you'll remember that. Besides.' He glanced briefly at the dead man. 'Nothing, not even this, can dim my light today.' He strode up the step as the second trumpet shrilled. Henslowe followed him, bemused. Alleyn had got over the shock of knowing the corpse extremely quickly. But then, Henslowe knew actors. They could screw themselves up to raging giants and shrink to timid mice on the turn of a groat and Alleyn was the best of them.

'Not today.' He paused to silence a lackey who was about to say something. 'Later, son, later. Today, I stride among the tree tops.'

'Well, yes, the play's going well,' Henslowe enthused. 'Another packed house out there.'

'The play be hanged.' Alleyn adopted his magnificent entrance stance, hands on hips and head thrown back. 'Today, Mistress Constance and I are betrothed.'

There was a loud snort from a passing figure in the half-shadows. It was Thomas Sledd. Alleyn sneered at him. 'None of your cynicism, stage manager,' he said. 'I have found my way into Constance's heart. I am her lord . . . her King Edward.' He liked the sound of that.

'And that's not all, I'll wager,' Sledd muttered.

'What, sirrah?' Alleyn may have been unrufflable today but the little boy-actor-grown-too-big-for-his-breeches was just *beginning* to irritate.

'King Edward, eh?' Sledd turned to him, smiling. 'Well, my history doesn't run to much, but even I know William the Conqueror came before King Edward.'

The next thing Sledd knew, Ned Alleyn's hand had closed around his throat and he was pinning him up against the gates of Babylon, which shook and trembled with the impact. 'You've got three tickings of the clock to explain that, sirrah.'

'Well . . .' Sledd did his best to oblige, in a strangulated way. He didn't like the look on Ned Alleyn's face and he didn't like the size of his sword, either. 'Just a joke, Ned,' he managed. 'A one-liner. Kit's not here, so I thought I'd . . .'

'What did you mean, William the Conqueror?' Alleyn twisted the man's collar even tighter.

'It's . . . it's common knowledge, Ned. Constance Tyler is with child. And it's Will Shakespeare's.'

'How do you know that?'

'He told me,' he said. 'He was in his cups one night at rehearsals. I don't think you were there. He told me they were lovers. He wasn't sure quite how his wife would take it . . . Everybody knows, Ned. I thought you did too.'

Alleyn looked at the nearest cast members, ready for the third blast of the trumpet. 'It's true, Ned,' the Prologue said. 'I heard it too,' squeaked Zenocrate and there were nods from Tamburlaine's children and murmured agreements from everyone in the room. Then the trumpet. Alleyn let go of Sledd and the lad half collapsed to the floor. Tamburlaine looked around the assembled company.

'If anybody, *anybody* crosses me out there –' he pointed to the wooden O beyond the curtained doorway – 'God have mercy on their soul.'

And that was how it went. Calyphas was a little warier than usual of his father that afternoon. 'Villain,' Alleyn roared at him in Act Three, Scene Two. 'Art thou the son of Tamburlaine?' He punctuated each word with a slap that rang through the auditorium and brought gasps from the audience for their realism. He was even more alarmed when Alleyn overdid one bit and slashed his own arm with his knife. This was no fake blood – that packet lay unopened under his sleeve.

'One wound is nothing,' Alleyn bellowed, 'be it ne'er so deep.'

Celebinus suddenly dreaded his next line, to the extent that the Prompt had to say it for him. ''Tis nothing. Give me a wound, Father.'

'And me another,' Amyras whispered, hoping his dad wouldn't hear him.

'Come, sirrah,' Alleyn grunted, 'give me your arm.'

'Christ!' Celebinus hissed, his eyes wide in horror.

The Prompt tried to find that and put him right. 'Here, Father . . .'

Nothing. Celebinus stood there, his stare fluctuating between Alleyn's face and Alleyn's dagger.

'Here, Father,' the Prompt hissed, 'cut it bravely as you did your own.'

'You must be joking!' Celebinus exited left before Alleyn remembered how the rest of the scene went.

'My boy,' he called after the vanished actor, 'thou shalt not lose a drop of blood.' But Celebinus wasn't coming back to check.

By the time they had got to Act Four, Scene One, Harry Brickwell, playing Calyphas, the cowardly son, got so far into his part that when Alleyn advanced on him, sword in hand, to make him pay for his cowardice, the man just collapsed in a heap on the stage. It didn't matter. In fact, Henslowe decided he'd have a word with Marlowe about keeping it in. *So* terrible was Tamburlaine that men died of fright just looking at him. That had to be good, eh? What was not so good was the line-up at the end. The applause was thunderous as ever, the stage patrons on their feet with the groundlings and the gallery-commoners. But there was no Alleyn. When Zenocrate curtseyed and made room for him, the greatest tragedian of his day wasn't there. He had a meeting to go to.

Ned Alleyn wasn't signing autographs today. He wasn't making small talk with the watermen either. He'd torn off his Tamburlaine armour and swapped his third-rate stage-prop sword for a good one, another little present from the Lord Admiral. He'd wrapped his cloak around him against the cross-winds above the Bridge and once across, ran, pushed and jostled his way through the crowds, taking every back alley and ruined churchyard he knew to get where he was going. He dashed along the Cornhill, past the Merchant Taylor's Hall and into Bishopsgate Street. He ignored the trulls at the Hounds Ditch, even when one of them recognized him. ''Ere, didn't you used to be Edward Alleyn?' she called as he vanished round a corner. Then he was running across the level of Moor Fields where the ragged squatters sat under their canvas and leather, their smoky fires rising into the gathering evening sky.

Then, heart pounding, lungs bursting and with legs like lead weights, he was in Hog Lane and hammering on the oak door of the gabled house to his left. He didn't wait for Windlass to open it but burst in, leaving the man standing there with a dish-cloth in his hand as he made for the stairs.

'Shakespeare!' he roared with a volume that made Tamburlaine sound like a choirboy. 'You dung hill! Defend yourself!'

Will Shaxsper heard the commotion at once, and he knew the voice. Marlowe had impressed on him several times and Windlass had underlined it. He was to stay put. Make no move. And with luck . . . But luck wasn't with the Warwickshire man that day. He heard a thunder on the stairs and the next thing he knew, there was a scraping below his trap door and a sharp, rapid series of knocks.

'Do I have to burn you out, whoreson?' Alleyn bellowed.

It might be the last thing he ever did, but Shakespeare slid the bolt and raised the flap. After all, it was only Ned Alleyn. Good old Ned, fellow actor, man of letters. How often had they caroused the night away at the Punk Alice and the Upright Man? Rolled home, drunk as newts, down Damnation Alley? In truth, never, but just the same, it was only good old Ned. No cause for alarm.

Good old Ned was standing on the floor below, his face straight, his eyes cold. 'And bring your sword,' he said quietly.

Shaxsper did as he was told, lowering the wooden steps. He wasn't quite at the bottom when Alleyn grabbed him by the doublet sleeve and threw him the length of the room so he crashed through the door and on to the landing.

'Now, gentles!' Windlass was on the floor below, trying to talk some sense into them. He knew he was on to a losing bet from the start; there was no convincing an actor that he was in the wrong.

'Stow you, sirrah!' Alleyn snapped. 'Master Shakespeare and I have a little score to settle.'

'Ned.' Shakespeare picked himself up. 'Ned, what's the matter? And how did you know where to find me?'

'Kit Marlowe's got a heart as big as Smithfield,' Alleyn said. 'If anybody was going to get you out of the Clink, it would be him. And where would he take you, for safety? Here, of course. Oh, I'm sure it's only a matter of time before the High Constable adds all this up on his abacus too. But by then, you'll be the stuff the dogs fight over in the smock alleys. If you can use that thing –' he pointed to the sword lying by Shakespeare's leg – 'I suggest you do. What would you like? Italian school? Spanish? It's all one to me. All one to you?'

He lashed out with his boot so that Shakespeare felt a searing pain in his thigh and he struggled upright. For a moment he toyed with running. Alleyn was crouching in front of him, rapier in one hand, dagger in the other. Then he decided to try reason. 'Ned. Ned. Come on, what's all this about?'

'You know what it's all about, you filthy bung. My Constance.'

'*Your* Constance?' Had Shakespeare still had a hairline worth the mention, his eyebrows would have merged with it. 'I never took you for the jealous sort,' he said.

Alleyn took one step closer, two. Shakespeare retreated. He had no idea whether this was the Italian school or the Spanish. He only knew he had one weapon to Alleyn's two and days of sitting hunched in Marlowe's attic had given him cramps and seized up his joints. He winced with each move.

'No,' Alleyn hissed. 'You just took Constance. Had her while my back was turned. Make your peace with God, Shakespeare. You're going to die!' He lunged with the rapier. Shakespeare deflected the blade but his shoulder was exposed and Alleyn's blade shredded the velvet and the linen below, tracing a line of crimson on the material.

'Shit!' Shakespeare hissed and stumbled backwards, taking Alleyn's hammer blows on his blade.

'No, no, Master Shaxsper!' Windlass called. 'Parry of sixte. Sixte. Now quart. Sixte. Oh, mother of God.'

'How often did you rape her?' Alleyn shouted above the ringing steel.

'I didn't rape her,' Shakespeare lunged back, the unfair charge giving him renewed vigour. Alleyn batted his blade aside easily and their sword hilts clashed together.

'What are you saying?' Alleyn asked, banging his dagger on Shakespeare's quillons.

'I'm saying it was her idea.' Shakespeare gulped. Even without Alleyn's blade, he wasn't sure how long his legs and lungs could take this. He pushed Alleyn back and darted for the stairs, hurtling down them, tripping on the turn and measuring his length in the hall at Windlass' feet. He looked up at the man as he lay there fighting for breath. 'Are you just going to stand there?' he said, through clenched teeth.

Windlass shrugged. 'I am Master Marlowe's man, sir,' he said solemnly.

'Yes.' Shakespeare hailed himself upright, using Windlass as a crutch. 'But he's not here at the moment, is he? If he were, do you think I'd be doing this?' The flat of Alleyn's sword caught him high on the shoulder and he staggered sideways. A second later, the man who was Tamburlaine swirled his blade with such speed that Shakespeare's sword was knocked out of his grasp. The Warwickshire man stood there, eyes closed and a prayer on his lips. He couldn't, in the scheme of things, say he'd exactly lived by the sword. But now he was going to die by one, nevertheless.

The door crashed back and the High Constable of London stood there, flanked, as always, by his catchpoles. Alleyn half turned to face the intruders and the next thing he knew, everything went black.

'You're pretty handy with that,' Hugh Thynne said to Windlass, as the servant stood there, a lead-weighted cosh still in his hand. 'And you appear to be bleeding, Master Shakespeare.'

The actor opened his eyes, his chest heaving with exhaustion and shock. He was so grateful to Windlass, to the High Constable, that he was lost for words.

'Well, well.' Thynne smiled at the heap at his feet. 'Every picture tells a story, they say. Behold, lads,' he half turned to his minions, 'the great tragedian. A pity; I was hoping to find Master Marlowe.'

'Who, sir?' Windlass asked, straight-faced and concerned.

Thynne smiled bleakly. 'Don't push your luck,' he said. 'Or I might have to make something of your cowardly and wholly unwarranted attack on Master Alleyn here. Lads. Every room.'

'Just a minute . . .' Windlass began.

'I'm here, High Constable,' Shakespeare sighed. 'Ready to go with you.'

Thynne looked at him. 'Oh, that's not necessary,' he said, in a dismissive tone. 'In the criminal underworld which I am unwillingly forced to inhabit, the wheels turn fast. I am satisfied that you are not responsible for the murder of Eleanor Merchant. And I'm sorry I ever thought you were.'

'You are?'

'Yes,' Thynne said, watching his men get to work. 'Marlowe's my man.'

'Kit?' Shakespeare gulped. 'Impossible.'

'And then there's the little matter of extracting you from the Clink. Aiding and abetting a criminal.'

'But I'm not a criminal,' Shakespeare said, the rip in his arm starting to hurt like Hell. 'You just said so. And, besides, how do you know . . .?'

Thynne laughed coldly. 'I love these delicious arguments, don't you? The sort of thing they discuss until the cows come home in the Inns of Court. It'll take weeks to argue that one, perhaps months. And all the time, Master Marlowe will be rotting in Newgate. Of course, once he's found guilty of murder, he'll be on his way to the triple tree. Ever been there, Master Shakespeare? Tyburn, I mean?'

Shakespeare shook his head.

'You should go. It might lend some depth to your writing.' Shakespeare looked up, surprised. 'Oh, yes,' Thynne said. 'I know most things about most people. Tyburn has three tall posts, eighteen feet high in fact, with crossbeams nine feet long. Capable of hanging twenty felons at once, if needs be. I expect we can find some company for Master Marlowe.'

'Why would he kill Eleanor Merchant?' Shakespeare asked.

'Eleanor Merchant?' Thynne repeated. 'No, no. It's ironic, really. If I'd started my search here rather than at the Rose or Alleyn's place, I'd have found you all the sooner. And an innocent man would have gone to the gallows. No, you see, I've got Marlowe on two counts. Firstly, he used the name Robert Greene to spring you from the Clink. That's a felony in itself. Secondly, he killed a man named John Garrett. One of the Godly.'

'What?' Shakespeare was lost. 'What are you talking about? How do you know?'

'How do I know?' Thynne said. 'That's easy. Master Marlowe was careless enough to leave his dagger buried in the man's heart. That's as good as a signed confession.'

'No,' Shakespeare said. 'I mean, how do you know he got me out of the Clink?'

'Just as easy,' Thynne said. 'He left his mark on that little escapade as well. There are few men in London who would risk all that he risked for a friend, and take the opportunity to inconvenience – if I can call a spell in Ludgate Prison an inconvenience – another playwright at the same time. Marlowe is one of them.'

Shakespeare was doubtful that Marlowe would consider Greene another playwright, but other than that, he saw the logic. 'Kit is no murderer,' he said sullenly.

Thynne clapped him on his good shoulder. 'What a good friend you are, Master Shakespeare,' he said. 'A good friend, or the stupidest man I know. I would not like to have to choose which.'

TEN

Sir Francis Walsingham's house at Barn Elms stretched to the river, the lawns dotted with his apple trees with their dusting of new leaves and promise of pink white blossom. The two mastiffs by the river gate picked up their heavy heads and barked as the boat pulled nearer. The waterman was used to them. He had taken gentlemen of every political and religious persuasion to this house before and he was always well paid to keep his arm strong, his eyes averted and his mouth shut.

Kit Marlowe sat with him, huddled at one end of the boat with his cloak around him and his hood pulled up around his ears. It didn't matter when you travelled the river; the Thames had secret eddies and currents and cross-biting winds that chilled a man to the bone. He had seen the great house from far away, as soon as they'd rounded the river's bend by Putney church. It had chimneys twisted like barley sugar and its oak beams were cross-cut to form knot gardens of tracery over the front. It wasn't until he was nearer that Marlowe saw the man who had sent for him, the man who sauntered down the steps to the river level and silenced the dogs with a flick of his gloved hand.

'Nicholas Faunt,' Marlowe murmured as soon as he was on dry land and out of earshot of the waterman. 'It's been a while.'

'Any return goods, sir?' the waterman called, steadying his oars.

'Not today, sirrah.' Faunt waved him away and crossed to Marlowe, shaking the man's hand. 'Kit.' He half smiled in that enigmatic way that he had. The man was Francis Walsingham's secretary. And Walsingham was secretary to the Queen. And the stress on both those words was 'secret'.

'I'm sorry to drag you all the way out here. Man, you're frozen.' He looked at the playwright's pinched features, the light blue around the nostrils and the barely controlled shivering. A bittern flapped from the reeds on the far bank and Faunt caught the movement. 'You'll stay the night?' he asked.

Marlowe began to walk up the steps to the bowling green. 'Is Walsingham here?' he asked.

'No,' Faunt said. 'No, Sir Francis is attending the Queen tonight. She's at Nonsuch. She hasn't spoken to Burghley since that unfortunate business over the Queen of Scots, so poor old Sir Francis is having to bear the brunt. Her feathers have been ruffled by something or other. It'll take him a day or two to unruffle them.'

That kind of comment sounded uncomfortably like treason and it wasn't the first time that Marlowe had heard something similar from Nicholas Faunt. In the suspicious world in which both men moved, it could mean nothing. On the other hand, it could mean death.

'No.' Faunt ushered Marlowe in between the huge oak doors. 'No, I wanted to see you alone. Pick your brains, so to speak. Shall we?'

A manservant in the livery of the Queen took Marlowe's cloak and sword and disappeared into the oak panelling. 'You're travelling light,' Faunt said, tapping Marlowe lightly in the small of his back.

'My dagger?' Marlowe instinctively felt for it. 'Yes. Careless of me. I lost it.'

Faunt showed the man into an anteroom off the great hall. A huge canvas filled one wall, showing the family both men served, but two generations, as though they all shared the same room as adults. King Harry sat on his throne in the centre, his flat, expressionless face staring out at Marlowe. Beside him his son, Edward, the boy king, knelt in dutiful supplication to his father. Beyond him, the late Queen Mary, hard-faced and watchful, stood beside the swarthy chameleon who was Philip of Spain while Mars, the God of War, crashed into the scene with armed men at his back. But it was the figure on the right of the painting, to Harry's left, that held the attention of all who saw it. Gloriana, the Queen herself, as she had looked twenty years ago when Marlowe was in his hanging sleeves. The light shone from her forehead and her eyes and with her, olive branch in hand, walked the equally radiant Peace, a dove circling her golden head.

'Revolting, isn't it?' Faunt asked. He hadn't specifically seen Marlowe staring at the portraits. He just knew he was, just as everyone did who came into this room. That was why Walsingham had put it there. 'A present from the Queen.' Faunt handed Marlowe a goblet of Rhenish and raised his in a toast. 'God bless her!'

'The Queen.' Marlowe drank too. The rest of the room was in chaos. The grate was black and empty, the gilded Walsingham arms on the tiles green with neglect. The walls were lined with leather tomes, some of which Marlowe knew from his Cambridge days; others he didn't. On every conceivable surface there were bundles of papers, parchment, vellum. There were ribbons and wax and, in its red leather case, the Privy Seal.

Faunt saw Marlowe looking at this and threw it across the room at him. The playwright caught it and smiled at the royal insignia of the leopards and lilies. The lilies of France that the Queen didn't own any more. 'I often think what damage can be done using that,' Faunt said, sprawling in a chair by the hearth. 'What do you say, Kit? Shall we buy ourselves large houses in the country? Something near Canterbury for you, I shouldn't wonder. Me? I've always liked Oxford. And speaking of which, how about a Chancellorship of Cambridge University for you, eh? Or marriage to a foreign princess? Of course, if it's war you're after . . .' He stopped smiling. 'It can all be achieved by writing down your wishes and pressing *that* into a lump of wax at the bottom. That's power, eh? Riches beyond the dreams of avarice.'

Marlowe wasn't smiling. He threw the cipher back to Faunt and sat down in a carved wooden chair opposite him. 'What's all this about, Nicholas? My man Windlass gave me your summons, but I don't work for you any more – remember?'

Faunt chuckled. It was cold and bitter. 'You've never worked for me, Kit,' he said and nodded towards the portrait behind the playwright's head. 'You work for her. We all do.'

'Not any more,' Marlowe said.

Faunt paused. 'Oh, yes, of course.' He nodded, sipping his wine. 'The theatre. I hear *Tamburlaine*'s doing well. Men say you are the toast of London, the Muse's Darling. Pure spirit. All very gratifying.'

'It's my life now.' Marlowe shrugged.

Faunt was suddenly serious, leaning forward and staring into

Marlowe's dark eyes. 'Then what were you doing in Blackfriars?' he asked. 'The house in Water Lane.'

It was Marlowe's turn to pause. 'How did you know I was there?' he asked.

Faunt burst out laughing and even Marlowe found himself smiling. 'All right,' the playwright said, 'you had me followed. I must be slipping. I didn't notice.'

'Ah, you're just a bit rusty, that's all. But seriously, Kit, I need to know what you were doing there.'

'Why?'

'Secrets of State.' Faunt looked at him with a level gaze. If any phrase was guaranteed to bring a conversation to an end, that was it.

'All right.' Marlowe nodded. 'One confession for another. You tell me what you were doing at the Rose the other day and I'll tell you why I was at Blackfriars.'

'To see the play.' Faunt smiled. 'Your *Tamburlaine*. I was impressed.'

'Liar,' Marlowe said, folding his arms and waiting for more.

'You don't think I'd be impressed?'

'I don't think *Tamburlaine* is your sort of entertainment, Nicholas,' Marlowe said. 'And besides, there was no play on when you went with a gathering of backers into Philip Henslowe's box office.'

'Ah.' Faunt set his mouth in a rueful line. 'I take it all back. You're not rusty at all. What if I told you that I was at the theatre in connection with the house in Blackfriars?'

'Not a riddle, Nicholas, please.' Marlowe raised his free hand in supplication. 'It was a long journey in that boat and I was so cold I all but lost the will to live. Your note said it was urgent that you see me. So, what is it that it couldn't wait another minute?'

'The house in Blackfriars.'

Marlowe downed his goblet and stood up. 'I doubt I'll get a boat at this hour. Any chance of borrowing one of Walsingham's horses? I hear he's got sixty-nine of them in the stables.'

'All right,' Faunt relented. It wasn't something he did often and he didn't do it well. He refilled Marlowe's goblet and sat him down. He looked into the man's eyes. 'Can you keep a secret?' he asked.

Marlowe raised an eyebrow, but said nothing. He already knew the whereabouts of enough bodies to bury Nicholas Faunt and, quite possibly, Francis Walsingham too.

'The house in Blackfriars is a safe house. It belongs to us – the government, I mean. Oh, if you look up the lease in the Stationers' Office you'll find the owner is one Ralph Crabtree.'

'And?'

'Lord Burghley, to you.'

'I see.'

'The rent is paid to Roger Whetstone.'

'Francis Walsingham?'

'Christopher Hatton,' Faunt corrected him.

'So, various members of the Queen's Privy Council are hiring out property under assumed names to unknown actors and girls with a head full of air,' Marlowe reasoned. 'Bizarre, but hardly a crime.'

'No, you miss the point.' Faunt leaned forward. 'It's a *safe* house. It's a place we put people for interrogation purposes . . . Oh, not the unpleasant stuff – all that's a matter for Waad and Topcliffe at the Tower. No, it's a house where Walsingham has his little fireside chats. You've heard of Father Walter Gervaise?'

'The Jesuit.' Marlowe nodded. 'Tried to kill the Queen two years ago. He died while trying to escape.'

'You see, there you have it.' Faunt leaned back, sampling the Rhenish again. 'Wrong on all three counts. And you're supposed to be one of us.'

'I told you . . .'

'Yes, yes, I know.' Faunt cut the man short. 'You've left the service. Put it all behind you. Yes, I know.'

'So . . . Gervaise?' Despite himself Marlowe couldn't contain his curiosity.

'*Was* a Jesuit until Walsingham had a word in the house at Blackfriars. I don't know why we keep Topcliffe and his infernal machines. Just a word from Walsingham is all that's required. No, he didn't try to kill the Queen – that was just a story we put about, to smoke out a few others, as it were. As for the stories of his demise, well, they too are much exaggerated. He is currently – and I shouldn't really be telling you this – reporting on our behalf from Padua. When he's not there, he's living with Mistress

Gervaise and all the little Gervaises somewhere out on the Essex marshes. Well, you can't have everything.'

'I see.' Marlowe felt enlightened.

'I wonder if you do.' Faunt frowned. 'You didn't know about the house? Its purpose, I mean?'

'No,' Marlowe admitted. 'This is the first I've heard of it. I'd gone there over the Eleanor Merchant business.'

'Yes.' Faunt nodded solemnly. 'Eleanor. A great loss.'

'You knew her?'

'Of course,' Faunt said, reaching for one of Walsingham's pipes from the rack and looking around for a tobacco jar. 'She ran the house for us.'

'Did she?' Marlowe was sitting up now, frowning. 'Is that why someone killed her?'

'I thought Shakespeare killed her.'

'So does the High Constable,' Marlowe nodded, 'and half of London.'

'Do you drink smoke, Kit?' Faunt asked, ramming the tobacco into the bowl.

'All they that don't love tobacco are fools,' Marlowe said.

'Then light yourself a pipe. You and I have some secrets to swap, I believe.'

'You first.' Marlowe smiled, reaching for another of Walsingham's pipes.

Faunt smiled too. He could fence all night with Marlowe, with just a short break for supper. He recognized much of himself in the deadly young man sitting with him; as he had been ten or a dozen years ago, keen to make his mark in a dangerous world. He never underestimated men like Marlowe, perhaps because there weren't any men like Marlowe. Not at all. 'All right,' he said. 'So Eleanor Merchant was on our payroll; that made her a target. Especially given the nature of her house.'

'I took it to be a bawdy house,' Marlowe said. 'Night visitors. Whispers after dark.'

'That's what we hoped the world would think.' Faunt nodded. 'The problem was that, to put off the long noses of the Hugh Thynnes of this fair city of ours, we had to make it seem as if it was an outwardly respectable place – that's where friend

Shakespeare comes in. The only other lodger is a printer, a man named Calshott.'

'Not one of ours?'

Faunt showed the mild surprise in his face, wreathed in smoke as it was. *Ours.* Was the wayward sheep returning to the fold in spite of himself? 'No.' He shook his head. 'The man's an innocent. Works at the sign of the Moor's Head in Paternoster Row. If word got out that others used the house, everyone would assume what you did – that Mistress Merchant presided over a place of ill-repute. Eleanor's mistake, if that's what it was, is that she didn't take her simpler sister into her confidence. When I spoke to the girl she clearly didn't have a clue as to what was going on under what is now her own roof. We'll have to move on, of course. I've told Walsingham as much.'

'You said Eleanor was a target.' Marlowe blew rings to the ceiling. 'For whom?'

'Well, that's the Devil of it,' Faunt said. 'I don't know. Some pretty slippery customers have used that house over the years – and the outcome isn't always as happy for us as Father Gervaise. Some men have refused to be turned. Some have got away. Even so, even if they had some grievance, why pick on the woman who provided bed and board? Walsingham, certainly, and me, but Eleanor? No, this is not about revenge.'

'So what is it about?'

'You've been to the house. What did you make of it? The furniture and fittings, I mean?'

Marlowe thought back. 'Good,' he said. 'Expensive. I don't know what Shaxsper was paying in rent, but I doubt he could afford it. Of course, she had her salary from you.'

Faunt chuckled. 'Eleanor wasn't a field agent, Marlowe. What we paid her wouldn't feed one of Walsingham's horses for very long. It might not even feed one of his hawks.'

'But the jug . . .'

Faunt looked up. 'The jug? What jug?'

Marlowe knocked out the pipe on the hearth. He enjoyed drinking smoke but it didn't clear the head, as many men claimed. And he needed a clear head now. 'A silver jug,' he said, watching Faunt intently. 'Just less than a cubit high. Solid silver. Wrought with writhing figures and the Devil's face. Dee thought . . .'

'Dee?' Faunt sat upright. 'What has he to do with all this?'

Marlowe looked at him with a wry expression. 'John Dee has to do with everyone, Nicholas. Rather like your good self, in that respect.'

'He's at Whitehall, isn't he?'

'On his way abroad, yes. I showed him the jug.'

'Eleanor's jug?'

'Yes.'

'Why?'

'Because . . . because there is something about it. Something that says it is the reason – or part of the reason – Eleanor Merchant died. Constance told me the thing comes and goes. It is not always there.'

'Any more than Constance is,' Faunt murmured. 'What did she mean? The thing has magical properties? It disappears at will? You shouldn't spend too much time with John Dee, Kit; he'll turn your mind. Where is this jug now?'

'I left it with Dr Dee,' Marlowe said. 'He locked it away in a cupboard in his rooms. He plans to put it somewhere safe, or so he says. Whether he means to keep it safe from men or to keep men safe from it, I was by no means clear.'

A silence fell between the two as a servant crept into the room and lit the candles. He drew the curtains and waited while another came in carrying a tray of gingerbread and candied fruit. Faunt helped himself once the pair had gone. He waved to Marlowe to join him.

'The problem is,' he said, sinking his teeth into a sugar plum, 'this is not just about Eleanor Merchant, perplexing though her case is.'

'Not?' Marlowe paused and pointed to something on the tray. 'Is that Pine Apple?'

'Yes,' Faunt told him. 'Grown in the Queen's glass houses at Placentia. I can take it or leave it alone, to be honest, but Sir Francis loves it. Helps his ague, or so he says.'

Marlowe stayed his hand. The last thing he wanted to do was to eat Sir Francis Walsingham's last slice of Pine Apple.

'Do take it,' Faunt said. 'We have more than we can possibly eat in the kitchens. You were saying?'

'Not just about Eleanor Merchant? Why not?'

'At the moment, I'm more interested in John Garrett.'

'Who?'

'The Puritan found by Henslowe's Bear Garden yesterday morning.'

'Oh, yes. I heard about that. How do you know who he was? Windlass tells me he is unidentified.'

'Windlass needs to keep his gossip more up to date,' Faunt said. 'But, surely, Kit, I don't need to dignify that with an answer. We *are* the Queen's men.'

Marlowe smiled. Indeed they were.

'The man was mad, of course. I mean, we're all Protestants here, but he belongs to the Godly, that lunatic fringe. You must have come across them at Cambridge.'

'A few,' Marlowe said.

'Well, it wasn't just the Rose that Garrett was thrown out of, although that was where he was found the most. He was ejected from the Curtain too and made a thorough nuisance of himself in the stews of Southwark. London is apparently all the cities of the plain rolled into one and theatres . . . well. He'd have got round to you personally eventually – "the atheist Tamburlaine, the scourge of God".' Faunt crossed the room and picked up a pamphlet. 'Seen this? They found dozens of them near his body. Fell out of his satchel when he was attacked.'

'How did he die? I heard a knife.'

'That's right,' Faunt said. 'Through the heart. As clean as a whistle.'

'Another soul who was a target,' Marlowe said. 'He must have made more enemies on both sides of the river than the King of Spain has ships.'

'Oh, I'm sure he did,' Faunt said. 'But it's the method, you see. Quick. Clean. Almost . . . scientific.'

'I don't follow.' Marlowe took a sip of Rhenish and grimaced. It didn't follow candied Pine Apple any too well.

'If God's Word Garrett had upset a theatre owner – Henslowe, say. If he'd annoyed a brothel keeper – well, that's Henslowe again, isn't it? If he'd started spouting his religious claptrap at St Paul's Cross – in any of these situations, I'd expect some roughs to work him over. Hell, you can hire half a dozen Apprentices for the cost of that fruit you're eating. And they'd use clubs. It would be messy, loud and not fatal. They like to leave them alive to encourage the others. No, this was neat. Orderly. And the message here is not "we'll hurt you". No it was "you will die". Just like Eleanor died. Neat and quick.'

'And I know how that was done,' Marlowe said. 'She was killed with a most singular weapon – well, almost singular. It is one of only two in the world. A snaphaunce.'

'Marlowe!' Faunt was leaning forward, his supper forgotten. 'Are you telling me there's a new kind of gun out there and we don't know about it?'

'Apparently so,' Marlowe said, 'judging by your reaction. It was smuggled somehow into the Rose on the afternoon in question and fired from the orchestra's corner. The problem is that one of the two snaphaunces is safe in the Tower under the care of Sir William Waad.'

'I think we can rule him out, somehow,' Faunt said.

'I agree.' Marlowe nodded. 'But what about the other one?'

'Is anything known?' Faunt asked.

'Well, Sir William didn't know any details, but one thing had stuck in his mind because it was so unexpected. He couldn't work out how the man could have afforded it. It was bought by a tobacconist . . .'

Faunt was instantly on his feet, crossing the room in a couple of strides. He began rummaging in the pile of papers on a side table, destroying Walsingham's careful but idiosyncratic filing system in seconds. He found a piece of parchment and slapped it with his open hand. 'I *knew* it!' he shouted. 'They found a body in the Thames over a week ago. Beyond the Bridge, but it had gone in somewhere upstream. He was unidentified for a while, but now we know he was Simon Bancroft. He was a tobacconist.'

'Was he now?'

Faunt ran his finger along the line. 'Inquest verdict . . . Oh, now, that's a surprise. Suicide.'

'Not through money worries, it would seem. Or would it?' Marlowe tapped his finger on his cheek.

Faunt returned to his chair, topping up Marlowe's wine. 'Kit,' he said, 'I wouldn't normally ask it of you . . .'

'But could I look into the late Master Bancroft?' Marlowe

smiled. 'And while I'm at it, get the measure of God's Word Garrett? All in a day's work, I suppose.'

'You'd be doing your friend Shaxsper a favour,' Faunt said.

Marlowe laughed. 'Nobody has friends in the theatre, Nicholas, just rivals. You're only as good as your last caesura.'

'I'd offer to help,' Faunt said, 'but Spain . . . Well, I can't say more at the moment. You'll have the full backing of the Department, of course.'

'Of course.' Marlowe smiled. 'I wouldn't have it any other way.'

ELEVEN

'If you could just tell me what you are looking for, sir.' The old man was wringing his hands in John Garrett's parlour. It had been the worst week of his life. He thought he had seen it all. They'd whitewashed the walls of his parish church when he was a boy and taught him to read from an English prayer book. Then they'd brought them back, the brass eagles, the wooden saints, the stained glass and priests spoke to him in Latin again – '*Hocus Pocus*'. Now . . . now he lived with the Godly and the world had turned again. The words of Master Calvin rang in his ears: 'It is your duty to proclaim the word of God.' And that is what the old man had done for the last twenty years. 'I don't know what you want.'

'Stow you, ancient.' Enoch Harrison was in no mood for old idiots this morning. 'I have the High Constable's writ. Your master is dead. We need to know why.'

'It is God's will, sir,' the old man said. 'He cares for the fall of every sparrow. We shouldn't look more closely than that.'

'Shouldn't we?' Harrison had never stood in the house of one of the Elect before. He'd moved on several of them at street corners and listened to the rubbish they spouted at Paul's Cross. It was much as he expected though; drab, comfortless, grey and cold. 'Has this place got a cellar?' he asked.

The old man nodded.

'Right. I'll start down there. Rogers – take the attic.'

Under Constable Rogers didn't like his job. Unlike Harrison, who relished it, and the High Constable, who did it for a living, Ben Rogers had taken it on for a year as his civic duty. He was a cordwainer really and already he missed his leather and his workbench. If anyone had told him what a full-time job being Under Constable would be, he would never have taken it on. He found the stairs and climbed to the dusty little room under the eaves. The windows were at floor level and the light flooded the floorboards but little else. Under Constable Rogers was a keen observer and he could make out a rectangular shape in the dust of the far corner.

The old man had followed Rogers up the rickety stairs. The dust testified to the fact that he hadn't been to the top of the house in a long time. His old limbs, twisted by age, couldn't manage it any more. But this was different. Now the old man's master was dead – butchered, men said, in a Bear Garden – and there were headboroughs tramping all over his master's house and him not yet in his grave.

'What was here?' Rogers asked him.

The old man had to squint to see what the Under Constable was talking about. 'Er . . . a chest, sir,' he said.

'What was in it?'

'I believe Master Garrett kept his Bibles in there, sir, his Scriptures and Notices.'

'Notices?'

'Sermons, sir, I suppose you'd call them.'

'Where's the chest now?'

'I don't know, sir. This was the Master's study. I didn't meddle.'

If truth be told – and when *was* it told in London in that year of the Queen's grace? – Under Constable Rogers was wasted as a cordwainer. He was a perfectly competent craftsman, but he had an eye for detail, for what was amiss, especially in little rooms. If this was Garrett's study, where were his books, his inkwells and quills? Where were his papers? The room was altogether too empty.

Rogers tapped on the linen fold cupboard. 'Is there a key for this?' he asked the old man.

'The Master had it, sir. Kept it round his neck, I seem to remember.'

Rogers nodded. He'd seen the man's corpse laid out at the Rose; stripped of his shirt and cap, a deep, dark gash marking the entrance to his heart. And the key had still been there, tied to a leather thong. He hauled out his tipstaff and smashed the wood around the lock. Much to the old man's alarm, splinters flew everywhere and Rogers let the door swing wide. Inside the recess was a gown, coal black in keeping with the dead man's religious persuasion and, tucked almost out of sight, a chest. It had a domed top and was covered in brass studs. Rogers dragged the chest out of the cupboard and stepped to one side to allow what light there was to fall on it. On closer inspection, Rogers could make out the words the studs spelled out. 'God helps those who help themselves,' he read, half aloud. This was locked too, but a quick tap with the tipstaff was all that was needed to smash off the brass lock.

Rogers squeezed his fingertips into the gap between lid and box and eased the lid up. Looking down into the box, he expected to find books, Gospels, other tokens of the Godly. Instead, he could hardly believe his eyes. There was money. So much money. He ran his fingers through it, letting the gold and silver trickle through them. There was a queen's ransom here, more than he could make in a lifetime stitching somebody else's leather.

'Did you know about this?' Rogers asked the old man.

'No, sir,' he told him, wide-eyed and shaking. He put out a hand to the softly glowing gold, but then withdrew it, as if he feared the coins would bite. He could hardly believe that the floorboards had borne the weight of it all.

'What's your name?' Rogers asked the old man.

'Partridge, sir. Thomas Partridge.'

'How long have you been Master Garrett's man, Partridge?' Rogers said.

'All my life, sir. I worked on his father's estates in the country before he saw the light.'

'Saw the light?'

'Of God's bounty, sir. The Master – that's Master Garrett's father, I mean – gave away all he had to serve the Lord.'

'Gave it all away?' Rogers repeated. 'So what's all this, then?'

'As God is my judge, sir, I have no idea.'

'What did your master actually *do*, Partridge? When he wasn't screaming at people in theatres, that is?'

'He was a guildsman, sir, of the Haberdasher's Company.'

'Lot of money in that, is there?' Rogers asked, still stroking and fondling the coins. 'In haberdashery?'

Partridge came closer to look at the contents of the chest. 'I didn't know there was this much money in the world, sir, and that's a fact.'

Rogers rocked back on his heels. None of this made sense. Garrett's house may have been new to him, but it was no more than he expected of the Godly. The furnishings were scant and worn, the plaster peeling in the corners, where the damp had penetrated. Draughts whistled past every door jamb and rattled loose window panes as the sneaky spring wind came in from the south-west. Old Partridge didn't look as if he had had a square meal in years and his clothes were older even than he was.

'What was he going to do with this, do you know?'

'As I told you, sir, I didn't know it existed until now. The Master did say he would leave money in his will for sermons to be read in his name.'

'How many sermons?'

'Four or five,' the old man told him, with a shrug.

Rogers knew that was a pittance in the scheme of things.

'Of course . . .' Partridge had suddenly remembered something.

'Yes?' Rogers looked at him.

'Well, the Master had a dream, sir. He wanted to quit London. Pandemonium, he called it, the gateway to Hell. He'd read that Captain Frobisher has found a new land – Terra Incognita, it's called. It is a land of purity, sir, all ice and snow, the colour of innocence. He and the Brethren often talked of it. A brave new world, he called it. A chance to begin again in a new-found land, where there are no theatres, no drink, no cut-purses or bawdy houses. A place a man can walk and talk with God.'

Rogers nodded. 'But in the real world,' he said, 'such paradises would, I think, cost a fortune to set up.' He looked at the heap of coins. '*This* fortune.'

'Rogers!' he heard Harrison call from the floor below. 'Anything?'

'Up here, sir,' the Under Constable said. He moved closer to Partridge. 'What becomes of you now, old man?' he asked.

Partridge shrugged. 'I am a Masterless man, sir. The Brethren will take over the house and give it to another of their number to live in. Once we have interred the Master, my duty is done.'

Rogers came to a split-second decision. He grabbed two handfuls of coins and stuffed them into the pocket at the front of the old man's apron. 'Find yourself that new land,' he whispered quietly. 'That Terra Incognita. The Master would have wanted it.'

Enoch Harrison's head popped up through the floor space. There had been a movement he hadn't quite caught. Had Rogers just slipped something to the serving man? He couldn't be sure. But a second later his eyes were elsewhere. They focussed on God's Word Garrett's chest and they lit up.

It took the High Constable's clerk nearly three hours to count all the money from John Garrett's chest. That was because Sam Renton was meticulous and he did it three times, as was the High Constable's order whenever it came to money.

'Tell me again.' Hugh Thynne was puffing on his pipe in the low-ceilinged room over the stables.

Enoch Harrison sat facing him. He'd been on his feet since just after dawn and wasn't feeling at one with the world. He knew the High Constable of old and knew that Thynne would want every one of Garrett's pennies accounted for. That was why he had helped himself to a third of it. As soon as Rogers and the old man had gone, Harrison had been on his knees scooping handfuls of coins out of the Puritan's chest and into his purse and wallets. He waited until the pair had left the building before he moved, for fear of clinking too loudly with his booty. It was safe now, stashed under the eaves of his house in the lee of the Crutched Friars, hard by Goodman's Fields.

'Nothing to tell.' He shrugged. 'The old serving man told Rogers that the Presician had this dream, of setting up some sort of kingdom of the Godly. The only problem is he wanted to do it in some Godless land, far away.'

'Did the old man say where the money came from?'

Harrison shook his head. 'Claimed never to have seen it before.'

'And you believed him?'

''Course I didn't. If I'd had my way I'd have kicked the old bastard down the stairs and trod on his fingers until he came clean. But Rogers was there.'

'Oh. Yes.' Thynne remembered. 'Under Constable, isn't he? Pretty bright fellow, I understand.'

'Bright, my arse,' Harrison grumbled. 'The man's an idiot. Doesn't understand how the world turns. Now you and I are men of the world, sir. We know a hawk from a handsaw.'

'Indeed we do, Constable.' Thynne was elsewhere, watching

the smoke curling away to the plastered ceiling. 'Indeed we do. Whatever that means – I've always wondered.'

'Any news, sir,' Harrison said after a while, 'on the Bancroft case? Eleanor Merchant?'

Thynne sat up straight and he looked at the man. 'Now, what makes you ask about them?' he wondered.

'Oh, just idly curious,' the Constable said. 'Just doing my job.'

'I was a bit surprised, to be honest,' Thynne commented.

'What, about me asking about those murders?'

'No. About how little, for a man going to start a New World, God's Word Garrett had in his attic.'

Marlowe often spent the night other than in his own bed and in the last few years of his life had slept under wagons, in hayricks, standing up and in the saddle. But he had never spent a worse night than the one he had just spent at Walsingham's house at Barn Elms. With the master of the house so often away, the staff had grown not just lax but downright disrespectful and once Faunt had left to make his way back to his own home upriver, Marlowe was left to the mercy of a footman and a maidservant who were so dismissive of their guest that he almost expected them to give him their boots to clean, rather than the other way about. Breakfast had been the same as supper, with the bitten bits cut away, and this was served by leaving a tray outside his room, in itself little more than a garret up in the eaves of the West Wing. In short, he was glad to find himself aboard a boat, heading for the Bancroft house at Queenshythe. No sailor, he was nevertheless happy to be going somewhere where there may be something worth eating and someone who would at least wish him the time of day without a sneer.

The boat bumped gently against the jetty at the bottom of the grounds of the Bancroft house and, while the waterman tied up, Marlowe took in the view. The lawns were not spacious and no deer cropped the grass, but the whole had been designed to give an impression of space and grandeur and Marlowe was impressed. It was almost unbelievable that this house was less than half a mile from St Paul's, as the crow flew, and that wharves and jetties jostled its garden walls up and down stream. It could have been a country estate anywhere in the kingdom, in miniature. The house was so new that there was still a workman precariously balanced on a ladder and being berated by a foreman standing below on the ground. The man had one foot on a pediment below a window and he was putting a final touch to some elaborate strapwork on a gable end. Marlowe would have wished him good morning, but had a definite dislike of seeing men plummet from ladders, so crept quietly past and round to the front of the house.

At the front, the house was less countrified, but still quite distinct from its neighbours. The tobacco trade was clearly doing well. He knocked on the door with his knuckles; there was something about the huge Italianate lion's head knocker that was quite off-putting and its pristine gloss suggested that most other callers felt the same. The sound of a lute, issuing from an open window above his head, stopped, but not until it had wound up the figure to a harmonious conclusion. The choirboy still inside the playwright gave thanks; without that courtesy, he would have had the threads of the tune in his head all day.

The door was pulled open on its stiff new hinges by an over-dressed maidservant. She had a white cap on her head and a stuff gown, with a boned bodice which must surely have made any kind of housework all but impossible. She looked with wide eyes at Marlowe, but didn't speak. He put her out of her misery. 'Christopher Marlowe,' he said. 'Here to see Mistress Bancroft.'

The girl still stood as though turned to stone, but was relieved of her duty by a man's voice from halfway up the curving stair. 'Thank you, Lettice. I will see to the gentleman. You may get back to your work.' Bobbing a curtsey, the girl disappeared through a door at the rear of the hall.

'You must excuse Lettice,' the man said, coming down the last few steps. 'She's new. We find it difficult to keep staff here, being out of town, as they see it. How can I help you? I am Thaddeus Bancroft . . . but, wait. You are Christopher Marlowe!' He shook his visitor's hand.

'I am indeed,' Marlowe said. 'And I know your face from somewhere . . .'

'I am an investor in the Rose!' Bancroft told him. 'How extraordinary you should be here. And, did I hear correctly, you want to speak to my cousin, Mistress Bancroft?'

'I want to speak to Mistress Bancroft. I didn't know she was your cousin.'

'Well, to be more precise, the relict of my cousin Simon. Simon Bancroft. He has recently . . .' He dropped his voice. 'He has recently died. More than that, I fear. I believe he –' and here he dispensed with sound altogether and mouthed – 'took his own life.'

Marlowe feigned astonishment. 'My condolences. I am very sorry for your loss and in such circumstances.'

'Thank you, Master Marlowe,' the tobacconist said. 'His widow is still prostrate and also, naturally, protesting that he would have done no such thing. But of course, a death is in itself hard to bear, without that added stigma. No funeral or what have you to assuage the pain.'

'I understand. She is lucky to have you to comfort her.'

Bancroft lowered his head and coloured slightly. 'I do what I can,' he said. 'Mary and I have always been . . . close, and I hope to make her closer still. When she is out of mourning, I intend to make her my wife.'

Marlowe, the man of the world, was stuck for what to say. With her husband hardly cold and by his own hand, any kind of congratulations seemed a little out of place. He settled for a smile.

'Yes, indeed. My wife. I look forward to it. I have never married, Master Marlowe. The Bancrofts are not emotional by nature. We have all, my brothers, my cousins and I, been brought up to live in the world of money. We have not all been fortunate. My brother Thomas, for example . . . But I digress. It was not until I saw how Simon's coldness distressed Mary that I realized how little money means, in the end. Then, there he lay, dead and cold on that slab in that horrible little room, consigned to the worms in some unconsecrated corner of a churchyard who knows where. And there was Mary, crying for him anyway . . . I realized then . . .' He seemed to come to his senses and coughed to cover his confusion. 'Well, anyway, Master Marlowe, as a playwright you are obviously a man of some emotion. You know how I felt. How I feel.'

Marlowe was still mulling over what kind of man would be lying in wait for his cousin's widow, but he managed to nod.

'And now, you are here to see Mary. May I ask why?'

'I can tell you something of why I need to speak to her, but if you have lived here for some time, you may be able to tell me yourself. If she is still upset, that is.'

'I have always lived with Simon and Mary. It is cheaper to live together if one can.'

'Yes, indeed. Then you can help me. I believe your cousin may have purchased a snaphaunce . . .'

'A what?' Bancroft looked puzzled.

'A snaphaunce. A kind of gun. A pair was given to the Queen. One is in the Tower. Your cousin may have purchased the other. We know it was purchased by a tobacconist, and, as your cousin has recently been found dead . . . well, it is a chance I thought it was worth following up.'

'I am also a tobacconist.' Bancroft made the statement with no inflection.

Marlowe opened his eyes wide and stared at the man. 'You are *also* a tobacconist?' Was there no limit to what these cousins shared?

'Yes. But I didn't purchase the sn . . . what did you say?'

'Snaphaunce.'

'I did not purchase it. I have no interest in firearms and I am not as free with my money as Simon was. He may have bought it. If so, it will be in his ledger.'

'Simon Bancroft kept a ledger? Of his personal purchases?'

Bancroft looked at him as though he were mad. 'Of course. Doesn't everyone?'

Marlowe shrugged. The Bancroft house was not just out of town. It was in a different world. 'May I see it?'

'Of course,' Bancroft said. 'Follow me.' He took Marlowe upstairs and showed him in to a beautiful room with a wide window overlooking the river. A book lay on a desk in front of the glass. Marlowe suspected that should he ever have such a room, with such a desk in it, he would not write quite so fast; most of his time would be spent on the view.

'I will leave you to look through it,' Bancroft said. 'Just come downstairs when you have finished. I would love to discuss *Tamburlaine* with you.'

Marlowe opened the book and started looking through,

backwards, to save time. He had not gone many pages, wading through details of loaves of bread, maids' wages and pounds of raisins – Bancroft had annotated the raisins in a crabbed hand '3d a lb; ruinous' – before he found the entry he was looking for. 'Snaphaunce. Bought from the Queen's Wardrobe.' It was there, clearly enough, but someone had scored through it neatly with a quill, taking extra care to erase the cost. Now, what could that mean? Marlowe raised his head and looked out down to the river. The boats flickered up and down stream like dragonflies and the shouts of the foreman in the garden came up as a distant hum. The door opened behind him and he turned, to be enveloped in the naked embrace of a woman, who clamped her lips to his as her breasts pressed against his chest. Without looking into his face, she put her cheek to his and whispered in his ear, 'Oh, Thaddy. Come back to bed. Who was that at the . . . Oh!' She pulled away and gave a little scream. 'You're not Thaddy!'

'Mistress Bancroft, I presume,' Marlowe said, dropping his gaze politely, then, realizing it could be misconstrued, up at a bookcase in a distant corner. He didn't look round until he heard the door slam and running feet go down the landing. He turned his gaze to the window to meet the startled eyes of the plasterer and watched in horror as he lost his grip on the window moulding. It had obviously been in his fate today to see a man fall off a ladder, but at least he knew who had bought the snaphaunce. And also, he suspected, he now knew why Simon Bancroft had thrown himself in the river.

Marlowe could do with a lie down in his own bed and something half decent to eat. Delicious though it was, he wasn't sure that Pine Apple on a stomach full of Rhenish was a good idea. But he had to get on and there was also the issue of Shaxsper. He was beginning to dread going home; what with Windlass on one side complaining about Shaxsper and Shaxsper on the other complaining about Windlass he felt like a parent saddled with two squabbling toddlers, but without the cuteness to offset the irritation. So he decided to go to the Rose instead. He had been meaning to speak to the orchestra but simply hadn't had the time. Today would be as good a day as any and if he knew his musicians they would have various eatables disposed about their persons, for snacking on between scenes.

Arriving at the theatre, he had to battle his way through the line of people who had arrived early to be sure of a seat. Sellers of various sweet meats and drinks were patrolling, selling from trays around their necks. Most of them worked for Philip Henslowe and had been pulled in to do extra shifts to cater to the queue. They usually sold food at the bear and dog fights, so this was much more pleasant, as well as being in daylight, a nice change for once. He paused to buy a pie from a seller who looked marginally cleaner than the others. He hoped the pie was younger than the stories he had heard backstage at the Rose had implied. It tasted all right, so he trusted to luck.

He was licking his fingers to clean up the gravy when he arrived at the orchestra gallery. The musicians were there, tuning up their instruments and arguing about what to practise. The tambour player, never as exercised over the music as the rest, was sitting at the back staring into space, hitting himself on the head now and again with his instrument. He was chewing on an empty pipe and looked as though he hadn't a brain in his head. The theorbo player was trying to restring his instrument single-handedly and was failing miserably. Without a second person to keep the tension on the incredibly thick strings, he couldn't get them wound around the peg properly and although he kept tutting and looking around hopefully, no one was taking any notice of him. Marlowe thought that this may be a way to start the conversation.

'Can I help you, er . . . Barnaby, isn't it?'

The man stopped his tutting and smiled with pleasure. 'It is, Master Marlowe. Fancy you remembering.' He pulled a triumphant face at the crumhorn player, which said, *Look at me. The playwright knows my name.*

'What do I have to do?'

'If you could just hold this end, Master Marlowe, sir, while I wrap the string round the peg. If *no one helps me –*' he looked pointedly at the tambour player who remained oblivious – 'I won't be done when the play starts.'

Marlowe held the end of the string in place and watched while the theorbo player deftly threaded and tensioned his string.

'Thank you,' Barnaby said. 'I just have to tune it now.'

There was a snort from the shawm player. 'Tune! Hark at him. He wouldn't know a tune if it bit him in the leg.'

Barnaby, who by carting his enormous instrument around had developed rather startling muscles, feinted a step forward, causing the crumhorn player to hide behind Marlowe. 'At least I always turn up, for rehearsals *and* performances,' he said, peering round Marlowe to catch the woodwind player's eye.

'*I* always turn up,' the man retorted. 'I'm here, aren't I?'

'You are *now*,' sneered Barnaby. 'But where were you on the first performance? The one where the woman got shot. The one where Miles here swallowed that fly.'

A snort from the drummer let them know that he was not dead, but merely on another plane. 'That was funny, Miles,' he said. 'I dropped my clapper, I was laughing that hard.'

Miles grinned. There was no point denying it. Once he had coughed up the fly, he had seen the funny side. But he could have died.

Marlowe stopped them. He was a musician, although only a despised vocalist. He knew these arguments could run for weeks. 'Can we just get everything straight for a moment?' he said. 'Before you get all creative on me, no one is in trouble. I just need to get a few things sorted out. It's for Master Shakespeare.'

'I hear that Constable's looking for him,' Barnaby chanced.

'I heard he'd caught him and strung him up.' The crumhorn player was a misery by nature.

'No, no, now will you listen for a moment?' Marlowe said. 'Then you can get back to your rehearsal. I need to talk to you about that first performance. The one where the woman was shot.'

'The one where old Miles swallowed a fly.'

'The one where you weren't here,' Marlowe said, turning to the crumhorn player. 'What's your name, by the way? Gerard, is it?'

The musician nodded sullenly.

'So, if you weren't here, how did the rest of the orchestra manage? Had you rewritten your parts?' he asked the band in general.

'We didn't have to,' Barnaby the theorbo player chimed in. 'There was another bloke playing the crumhorn. Not bad, actually. Played a bum note in the introduction to Act Four, but then, we're used to that.' He pulled a face at Gerard again.

'So . . .' Marlowe turned back to Gerard. His scalp was prickling. He was so near Eleanor Merchant's murderer, he could almost smell his sweat. Then, his eyes focussed beyond the man's shoulder and saw something else to make his hair stand on end. Thynne, with Harrison at his back and two burly men behind him, were advancing on the stage. This could only mean that they had found Shakespeare and had come for him now. He would have to be quick. 'So,' he began again, 'you had a friend stand in for you. Who was it?'

Gerard licked his lips. 'Um . . . not a friend.' He looked in desperation around the rest of the musicians, but they avoided his eyes. 'A man . . . a man met me as I was leaving the theatre the night before. We had had a late rehearsal. Well, that bit you wrote, Master Marlowe, that bit with the bloke and his wife . . .'

'Tamburlaine and Zenocrate,' Marlowe corrected him automatically.

'Them, yes. Well, the music is really tricky in that bit and we needed to run through it, so we were here late. Weren't we, boys?'

There were reluctant grunts of agreement.

'So?' Marlowe said, with a look over his shoulder. Thynne had turned and was talking to Harrison. Now was his chance and he took it. He ducked down behind the theorbo, much to its player's astonishment. 'Just someone I don't want to see,' he explained. 'Keep talking, everyone, but don't look at me. Where was I? Yes, so, Gerard. Who was this man?'

'I don't know. He said he always wanted to play in a theatre orchestra, but he was a gentleman and couldn't lower himself to do it for a living.'

This time the grunt from the rest of the musicians was in harmony.

'But he really wanted to play at the opening of the great Kit Marlowe's second *Tamburlaine*. He offered me an angel.' He shrugged. 'I took it. It takes me nearly two weeks to earn that as a rule.'

Miles had taken umbrage. 'You didn't stop to ask him if he could play, I suppose?' he said.

Gerard looked surprised. 'I took that for granted. Why would he want to play with the orchestra if he couldn't play? It makes no sense.'

'And he could play,' Marlowe said. 'Couldn't he? Apart from one bum note in the introduction to Act Four, that is to say.'

'Yes. He was all right. Sat at the back . . . that was my idea,' Barnaby said. 'When I realized that we had a new boy on board, I wanted to keep him out of the way. In case we had to kick him out halfway through.'

Marlowe smiled grimly. At the back was where the murderer would want to be and they gave it to him without demur. He must have thought God was on his side when that happened.

'What did he look like?'

Everyone looked at everyone else, sketching in a bland face, small eyes, perhaps. Big nose? No, average nose. Beard, though. Definitely a beard. Not trimmed, like Marlowe's. Big. Odd kind of beard for town. They muttered on and came at last to the conclusion that he was just ordinary.

'Did he speak?'

Again, looks, mutters and the majority decision that no, not really. Gerard had heard him speak, but the street was noisy and he had whispered, so he didn't really know how he sounded.

'Old? Young?'

Just average.

Now Marlowe came to the difficult bit. Had the man, the average, ordinary man, made any odd noises, any strange movements throughout the play? He knew the answer before they gave it. No. Nothing, not really.

'Except . . .' The tambour player held up a finger and looked down at Marlowe, then quickly looked up in response to his frantic gesture.

'Well,' he said slowly, after the fashion of tambour players who always sounded as though they were listening to the beat of a different drummer, 'who made the gun noise?'

'Pardon?' Marlowe felt the trickle of ice across his scalp again.

'I make the gun noise, with my clapper. But I dropped it when old Miles breathed in his fly and I couldn't reach it. It went down between the boards and I had to crawl to get it out. But there *was* a gun noise. It nearly deafened me.'

Keeping his voice level, Marlowe asked, 'Could it have been Master Shakespeare's gun?'

'Do you mind?' said the tambour player. 'I am a musician! I have perfect hearing. If I say it came from behind me, that's where it came from.'

'He's not wrong,' Barnaby agreed. 'Not about being a musician, of course. But he's great on direction, is Tobias. Can't fault him on his directions.' The other two nodded.

Marlowe could hardly keep his voice level. 'So, a complete stranger took the place of Gerard and there was the sound of a gun going off when there should be no gun. Meanwhile, someone in the audience was shot. And you didn't think this was worth mentioning?'

'Well, Shakespeare done it, didn't he?' Tobias asked, tapping himself gently on the head with his tambour again.

Marlowe sighed and rubbed his face with his hands. Giving them something to do stopped him from using them to strangle the band. Eventually, he sighed and got up on to his knees. 'Gather round, lads,' he said. 'I want to go backstage.' And he crawled between their legs, not standing up until he was beyond the curtain.

Christopher Marlowe had vanished like a will o' the wisp sparkling over the Islington Ponds. One minute, Thynne had him in his sights, chatting to the orchestra; the next, he had gone. He glanced at his men – Dimwit and Didn't Notice; no help there, then. He continued towards the stage but before he reached it, a man he'd met before came bounding across it and jumped down into the groundlings' pit, landing neatly in front of him.

'Where is he?' Thynne asked him. 'Where did he go?'

'Who, sir?' Jack Windlass could be as obtuse as any of Thynne's Constables when he had a mind. And, unlike them, he had a mind.

'Don't waste my time, lackey. I want Marlowe.'

'Ah,' Windlass was smiling but his hand was firmly on the chest of the High Constable. 'Autographs. Of course. Perhaps if you came back this afternoon, for the show. I'm sure Master Marlowe will be only too happy . . .'

Thynne pressed closer. He was half a head taller than Windlass. 'You *do* know who I am, sirrah?' he grated.

'Oh, yes,' Windlass nodded. 'But I don't think you know who I am.'

Thynne let out an explosive laugh. 'You're Marlowe's dogsbody,' he said. 'I scrape things like you off my pattens every day of the week.'

'Oh, I doubt that,' Windlass said and held up a badge. It was gold and worked with the Queen's arms.

'Where did you get that?' Thynne wanted to know. 'Mine –' he hauled a similar device out of his robe – 'was given to me. You stole yours.'

'Given to you?' Windlass said. 'By whom?'

This was getting irritating, but Thynne decided to humour the idiot a while longer. 'The Lord Mayor of London,' he said.

'Ah.' Windlass nodded solemnly. 'That's good. But a knave doesn't beat an ace, does it?' He spun the badge to reveal a different crest altogether, the quartered arms of Lord Burghley.

He stepped closer to the High Constable and whispered in his ear. 'You see, *sirrah*, I am Master Marlowe's man for today, but I will be the Principal Secretary's man for ever. And it is his wish – no, let me rephrase that; it is his order – that Master Marlowe is to be left alone.'

'But he's guilty of murder,' Thynne protested.

'So's the Pope,' Windlass shrugged. 'Why don't you go and arrest him?'

For a split second, Thynne's temper threatened to get the better of him. But he checked himself. Windlass presented no problem, but Burghley? The High Constable might as well fill his Venetians with stones and walk into the Thames. He jabbed a finger towards Windlass' face. 'This isn't over,' he said. And he turned on his heel, his confused constabulary at his back.

'Kit.' Philip Henslowe hovered at the playwright's elbow. 'A word?'

Marlowe had made his way up to the Heavens, the star-studded awning stretching above him. He had just witnessed a bizarre scene. Down below, on the ground, High Constable Thynne had just left. High Constable Thynne, who had been making a beeline for him only moments ago. And he'd been talking, of all people, to Windlass, whom Marlowe hadn't realized was in the theatre at all. What was going on?

'Kit?'

'Sorry, Philip.' Marlowe turned to him. 'I was miles away. What's the problem?'

Henslowe's eyes widened at the same time as his arms spread wide. 'You mean apart from the fact that my leading man is currently lying in your bed with a lump on his head the size of a capon's egg and muttering nonsense?'

'What? I was away last night. What happened?'

'The detail doesn't matter,' Henslowe said. 'Even though I fear the Devil was in it. Your man Windlass put me in the picture, so to speak. Did I see Thynne here a few minutes ago?'

Marlowe looked down again. 'You did.'

'He's looking for you.'

'Yes, I know. He's not a stupid man. He could have realized it was I who sprung Shakespeare, not Robert Greene.'

'No, Kit. You've got it all wrong. He doesn't want you for that. He wants you for murder.'

'What?' Marlowe spun to face the man. While he'd been chewing the fat with Nicholas Faunt at Barn Elms, all Hell seemed to have been let loose.

'Your dagger, Kit,' Henslowe whispered, making doubly sure they were alone on that balcony. 'Where is it?'

'I lost it.' The playwright frowned. That was the second time he'd been asked that question.

'Yes.' Henslowe nodded. 'You lost it in the chest of God's Word Garrett.'

'What?' Marlowe slapped his forehead. 'Skeres,' he said. 'Or Frizer. Or both. They're good – I'll give them that.'

'What are you talking about?'

'The last time I still had my dagger was here, in the theatre. Two gentlemen of the road came to congratulate me. I'd met them before – in Paul's Walk – and I didn't fall for them then.'

'The Ratsey Lay?' Henslowe had been there himself.

'I sensed we'd have gone on to that,' Marlowe smiled. 'No, it was Find the Lady. I pulled out before I lost any money.'

'And now?'

'Now, I've lost my dagger.'

Henslowe's mind was whirring. 'So . . . what are you saying, that these two coney-catchers killed Garrett?'

'I don't know, Philip.' Marlowe said. 'But I'm going to find out.'

'What will you do?' Henslowe called as Marlowe made for the stairs.

'Do you mean apart from finding those two and squeezing them until their pips squeak? And, obviously, I shall give them over to the authorities and trust that my God will help me.'

Philip Henslowe rested his elbows on the balcony rail and looked at all his people bustling about below. He watched the playwright stride across the stage and drop into the groundlings' yard, calling for Windlass as he did so. 'Your God, Kit Marlowe?' he murmured to himself. 'And who might that be? And since when did you do anything that involved trusting the authorities?'

Philip Henslowe didn't like his players to know that he talked to himself. To be fair, he didn't do it often and to be fairer still, he hadn't realized that Richard Burbage was there, hovering like the plaque in the shadows of the Heavens.

'I couldn't help overhearing . . .' the third maid said.

'What?' Henslowe grabbed the man's lapels. 'What did you overhear?'

Burbage was a little flustered. He hadn't really seen Henslowe on the edge before and the sight was a little unnerving, the impresario's eyes bulging and swivelling in all directions. 'Er . . . about Alleyn, being incommoded.'

Henslowe relented, not realizing that if Burbage had overheard that bit, he had overheard the rest too. 'What of it?' he snapped.

'Well,' Burbage's eyes shone like a man who had just glimpsed Paradise. 'I know the part.'

'What part?' Henslowe wasn't following this conversation.

'Tamburlaine,' Burbage explained and broke straight into it. '"Now, bright Zenocrate, the world's fair eye, Whose beams illuminate the lamps of heaven, Whose cheerful . . ."'

But Henslowe had gone, clattering down the stairs to the stage.

'I know it,' Burbage shouted, running after him. 'Word for word.'

'Yes,' Henslowe said. 'Probably better than Alleyn does, if

truth be told. But, well, I mean, third handmaiden to leading man – it's a bit . . . meteoric, isn't it?'

'Some,' said Burbage solemnly, as though he'd just offered to be shot in Henslowe's place, 'have greatness thrust upon them.'

Henslowe dithered. And Burbage knew already that when Henslowe dithered, you'd got him. 'Oh, very well,' the impresario said, 'but only until Alleyn's better. And only because I'm desperate.'

The groundlings were making their way past the Bear Garden later that day and Henslowe had a near mutiny on his hands. Almost everybody was higher in the stand-in pecking order than Burbage and by half past one of the clock only Thomas Sledd was still talking to Henslowe.

'There could be trouble,' the stage manager said from his grave old vantage point of twenty years, 'when the riff-raff realize Ned's not on today. Could be serious trouble.'

'Yes, thank you, Master Sledd!' Henslowe hissed. He knew, of course, that the man was right, but he didn't need Sledd's flashes of the obvious this afternoon. He looked through the slats at the crowd coming in and he glanced to his right. Richard Burbage was warming up, already in Tamburlaine's magnificent armour, flexing his knees and making strange humming noises at the back of his throat.

The last fanfare sounded and the crowd roared as the Prologue burst on to centre stage. There was no Marlowe today to be applauded, but Zenocrate took her curtsey as usual and some anonymous fellow came on as Tamburlaine. The cheering died when Burbage swept off his helmet and the fruit began to fly.

'Get 'em on, Tom,' Henslowe hissed. 'Beginners. Quickly, man!' And the show began.

Henslowe was in danger of chewing his fingernails down to his knuckles by the third scene. In a moment or two, Tamburlaine would be on as part of the action and there would be a riot. He would have to give them their money back; they'd throw him in the river; burn the Rose down . . . There was a commotion behind the flats and Henslowe heard the most magical, the happiest sound in the world.

'Get that armour off, you snivelling pizzle! What do you think this is, some Mystery Play?'

He heard a slap and a corresponding 'Ow!' and moments later, Ned Alleyn hurtled past him, buckling himself into the armour Richard Burbage had just kindly vacated. He caught Henslowe's eye. 'My head feels as if it's locked in a vice, Philip,' he said, 'but the show must go on. We'll have a little chat about whoever that was in my costume later.' The trumpets sounded and Alleyn grabbed George Beaumont's hand and the royal pair paraded round the stage, nodding to the gentry gathered there, the greatest actor careful to keep his helmet in the crook of his arm so that the audience could see that Ned Alleyn was back.

'Mr Henslowe, Mr Henslowe!' a voice hissed at the back of the stage and a scruffy sweet-meat seller was tugging at the impresario's Venetians. 'Now that Master Burbage is unconscious, any chance I can play third handmaiden, please?'

TWELVE

I t was a very different Kit Marlowe who crossed the Bridge the next morning. He had left his rapier at home in the care of Windlass, who would not be drawn on the nature of his conversation with the High Constable at the theatre, and he had swapped his silk and velvet for a plain black fustian. He tucked his hair under a simple square cap and left off his pattens so that his shoes squelched in the mud.

Under his arm he carried a pocket edition of the Geneva Bible which he'd bought in Paternoster Row that morning and he hailed his brothers and sisters along the Bridge in the way the Godly did, happy to be here, happy to be alive. He was doubly happy as he reached the gate at the southern end because above him rotted the traitors' heads on their spikes, leather-brown in the weather with dark holes where their eyes had been, long ago trophies of the kites and rooks, some of which still spiralled overhead, still hopeful of a new titbit. Marlowe was happy because his head was not among them.

His journey took him east, away from the Rose, Master Sackerson's Garden and the stews of the Winchester ground, to the altogether more wholesome air of St Olave's church. Black- and brown-robed mourners were drawn to the squat, grey building like iron filings to a magnet. They greeted each other with cries of rapture. One or two of them hugged each other with tears streaming down their faces. Pale children were dragged along too, under the clanging of the passing bell.

Inside, the church was a spiritual wasteland. There were no pews and no rood screen, although Marlowe had long since stopped looking for those in any church in the land. No saint of gilt or plaster looked down from his niche. No brass eagle held the Bible in its outstretched wings. The smell of incense had last drifted out of St Olave's plain-glass windows before Kit Marlowe was born and the tombs of the long departed had been smashed and removed. Ahead of him on the cold, polished stone an indented couple lay side by side, a knight and his lady, once flesh and blood, their effigies once chiselled in brass with their children kneeling below them. Now they were slight depressions in the ground, because the Godly did not approve of them.

'Good afternoon, Brother!' A cheery man with a snub nose hailed Marlowe. 'Sad times, eh?'

'Yes,' said Marlowe solemnly. 'Sad indeed.'

'How did you know God's Word?' the man asked.

Somebody left my knife in his heart, Marlowe wanted to say, but he thought it might spoil the mood of the moment. 'Oh, you know,' he said. 'Ships that pass in the night.'

'Hmm.' The snub-nosed man nodded, extending a hand. 'Killsin Jenkins,' he introduced himself.

'Delighted,' said Marlowe. He knew what was coming next.

'And you are . . .?'

'Distraught, of course. I had to pay my respects.'

'No,' Jenkins chuckled. 'I mean, your name. God . . .' He suddenly caught sight of the Bible in Marlowe's grasp, and became conspiratorial. 'You're not an Anabaptist, are you?'

'Perish the thought!' Marlowe shuddered.

'Well.' Jenkins looked around him to make sure the coast was clear. 'You can't be too careful, can you? There was a whole nest of them in Aldgate a couple of years ago. Let the side down, don't they? Oh, they were hanged, of course, but that's not the point.'

'Quite.'

'No, what the unGodly don't realize is that we are not an identical mass – and I hate using the "m" word, even in this context. What is it they call us? Puritans? Well, it takes all sorts, Brother, it takes all sorts. We are actually fifty shades of grey when all is said and done.'

'You and God's Word were close?' Marlowe asked.

'Lord, no.' Jenkins leaned in closer, talking out of the corner of his mouth. 'Couldn't stand the man.' He rubbed his thumb and forefinger together.

'Er . . .?' Marlowe wanted to be sure he understood the sign.

'Exactly,' Jenkins said. 'Mammon. Oh, we all have to live, Brother. I, for instance, am a girdler, from a long line of girdlers. I live comfortably, but I have a wife and six children to feed.

God's Word had no one but himself and old Partridge over there. And I happen to know he paid the man a pittance. No,' he shook his head, looking at Partridge, 'not worth all those tears, old man.'

Marlowe frowned, warming to his part. 'Isn't that a little unkind, Brother?' he asked. 'Fifty shades we may be, but we are all brothers here, cast in the image of the Father.'

'Hallelujah,' a voice echoed his sentiments. 'Praise ye the Lord. Good God!'

Marlowe thrust out his hand to the newcomer. 'Martin Marprelate,' the playwright said.

The newcomer blinked. His mouth was open and he seemed a little on the simple side. 'Um . . . Philip Henslowe,' he said.

'Killsin Jenkins,' the other man added his hand too. 'Praise ye the Lord, indeed. Are you a friend?'

'Er . . .'

'Killsin.' Marlowe smiled. 'Will you excuse us? Don't you think Master Henslowe looks a little pale? He's overcome, as we all are. A little fresh air. That would be best. We'll be back anon.'

Jenkins bowed his head and clutched Marlowe's arm. 'You are a true Christian, Master Marprelate,' he said. 'Walking in the steps of the Lord. Hallelujah.'

'Hallelujah!' Marlowe agreed, and left, towing Henslowe behind him into the churchyard where the dead kept their secrets. 'Kit!' the man hissed when they were clear of the Godly. 'What the Hell's going on? Martin Marprelate? What's all that about?'

'I was about to ask you the same thing,' Marlowe whispered, watching the last of the Elect disappear inside the church. 'You might at least have dressed the part.' He flicked Henslowe's ostentatious lace, the stuff he'd just bought on the strength of *Tamburlaine.*

'I'm not pretending to *be* one of these misfits,' Henslowe blurted out, then regained his composure. 'I just came to find out if there was any chance of anybody here suing me. After all, it was *my* Bear Garden wall they found him on.'

'Yes, and it was *my* dagger that kept him there,' Marlowe said. 'For your information, I am trying to find out why. Or I would have been if you hadn't put your great pattens into it all.'

'Sorry,' Henslowe muttered. 'I had no idea.'

'Tell me about it.' Marlowe untucked the heavy Bible from under his arm. 'Here. I'm going back in there and I'm tired of carrying this about.' He tapped the leather and passed it to Henslowe. 'Let me know your views on this.' He winked. 'I think it could catch on.'

So Martin Marprelate returned to the flock that Wednesday afternoon. He joined in with a vengeance, testifying with all the others but drawing the line at rolling on the ground as some of them did. For all they were there to see him off, nobody had a good word to say for God's Word Garrett. Nobody except a little old man who had known him since he was a boy. And even he had to concede that latterly, God's Word had come into a great deal of money, which the constables had appropriated. He hadn't a clue where that had come from. Neither did he tell Marlowe where some of it had gone. Into every rain a little life must fall.

'You haven't heard the last of this!' A furious Robert Greene was thrown out of Ludgate Gaol with as little ceremony as he had been thrown in. Passers-by looked at him oddly because to see anyone emerging from those grim, grey walls was a rarity. He tried to compose himself as he strode towards the Fleet Ditch, tying his doublet points and adjusting his codpiece. His hat and Collyweston cloak had disappeared in the prison yard, bartered in exchange for food. Every minute of the time he had served, he regretted having given his last groat to those charlatans Frizer and Skeres. Had he hung on to that, he might have lived quite royally in Ludgate.

So now Robert Greene had another score to settle. And yet again, it was with Kit Marlowe. He straightened his shoulders as he trudged along Fleet Street, moving west. He was Dominus Greene, for God's sake, a Cambridge graduate. All right, he had no sword at the moment and no dagger, but he still had the . . . Oh, bugger! He felt his left earlobe for the gold-mounted pearl that hung there. Except it didn't. He ran through his mind the various people who might have taken it. There was the Tom O'Bedlam who dribbled all over him and peed on his pattens. There was the harlot with the big teeth who was willing to let him have a little on account, against the day when Master Greene, poet and playwright, would be out again, earning some money. There was the Presician who tried to convert him and prayed for his soul. Any one of them could have taken the pearl. It couldn't have been Big Robbie from the border town of Berwick – he'd have taken Greene's ear as well.

All right, so Robert Greene had no sword, no dagger and no ear-ring, but what he did have kept him going as he argued with the guards at Temple Bar was his burning hatred for Kit Marlowe. Praise for the man still rang in his ears. At every corner, he heard the name. It was Marlowe this and Marlowe that. *Tamburlaine. Tamburlaine. Tamburlaine.* Had everyone in London been to see that bloody play? By the time he got to Gabriel Harvey at the sign of the Coiled Serpent, Greene was incandescent.

'That bastard Marlowe had me arrested!' he screamed, waving his arms in imitation of a windmill. 'He sprang Shakespeare from the Clink and gave *my* name. Mine!'

Harvey looked up from his brain pie, dusted the pastry crumbs from his fingers and smiled. 'Good morning, Robyn,' he said.

Robyn? Greene stood there open-mouthed. The smell of Ludgate still clung to him and he didn't even know if his lodgings in the Vintry were still available, should he wish to wash any of it off. *Robyn?* Gabriel Harvey was using his pet name again. What was going on? Had the world gone quietly mad while Greene was inside?

'I can't see anything good about it,' he fumed, dragging up a stool, uninvited, and sitting down.

'Ah.' Harvey was still smiling. 'Have a brain pie? No? They're a speciality of the house.' He looked down at the half-eaten food on his plate with affection. 'It takes the brains of six capons just to make one bite, you know.' He licked his thumb and used it to pick up crumbs of pastry, which he transferred to his mouth. 'Lovely.' He looked up at Greene. 'Sorry, I digress. You can see nothing good, because you've been away. I heard.'

'Well, then . . .'

'Well, it's not all doom and gloom, dear boy, not by a goose feather. You see, there's a warrant out for Marlowe's arrest.'

'There is?' Greene's scowl turned to a smile. 'For impersonating me? Marvellous.'

'No, not for that, Robert. Kit Marlowe is wanted for murder.'

'Good God!'

'It's all thanks to those two rascals you found, Robyn. Skeres and Frizer. I'll stake my huge reputation on it.'

'What . . . you mean . . . Marlowe didn't do it?'

'Whether he did or not is utterly immaterial, dear boy. I wanted his name smeared the length and breadth of London and that, these two have achieved. How they did it is of course no concern to me.'

'So he'll hang, then?' Greene enthused, his eyes gleaming.

'Well, when they catch him, yes,' Harvey said. 'And I've been thinking about that, wrestling with my conscience, so to speak.'

'Who won?' Greene grinned.

Harvey ignored him. 'I didn't want Marlowe hurt. I mean, I'm a scholar, an academic, I don't do all that physical stuff. But then, I thought, wait a minute. This isn't actually my problem, is it? Marlowe's got himself into deep water and if he was nudged a little by friends Frizer and Skeres . . . Well, that, as Richard Hakluyt would say, is Africa.'

'So . . . it *was* all too pat, after all?'

'Sir?' Jack Windlass wasn't often startled, but the sudden strike of the flint surprised him. He hadn't seen Marlowe sitting in the fireside nook in complete darkness.

The playwright chuckled. 'Don't give me that wide-eyed look, Windlass.'

'I don't follow,' Windlass said as Marlowe lit one candle, then a second.

'You do a mean shin of beef, Jack,' he said.

'Thank you, sir.' Windlass half-bobbed.

'And from what I hear from Will Shaxsper, you're very handy with a lead cosh.'

'Lucky strike.' Windlass shrugged.

'Perhaps.' Marlowe sank back into his chair. 'But there's nothing lucky about deflecting the High Constable, is there?'

'No.' Windlass was shaking his head. 'No, you've lost me.'

'He was at the Rose,' Marlowe reminded him, 'on his way, I suspect, to arrest me. Until you had a word. Then he left. I know he'd seen me, so what could you have said that made him leave?

"No, High Constable, that fellow over there just *looks* like Kit Marlowe." Or "Don't bother him now, sir, he's a little busy." Perhaps it was "But my master is such a nice man, sir, *and* a genius. Let him off just this once. Ah, go on!" None of this sounds quite right, does it, Jack? And as I said, it was all too pat – you being a masterless man at the very time I was looking for a servant and you bumping into me in Paternoster Row that day. So.' He folded his arms. 'Time for the truth, I think.'

Windlass knew when the game was up. He pulled the badge from his doublet and flicked it to reveal the coat of arms on the back. Marlowe nodded. 'Burghley,' he said, grimly. 'What is it that you do, exactly? Apart from shin of beef, that is?'

'Whatever's needed, Master Marlowe,' Windlass said, sitting opposite him. 'I am paid to watch your back.'

'Gratifying,' said Marlowe, 'if unnecessary.'

'Ah.' Windlass wagged a finger at him. 'That's what they all say. John Winthrop said something similar before the Dons got him. And of course, Hector Moncrieff dispensed with my services the day before they found what was left of him in Damnation Alley. And I don't want to think about Peter Hopton . . .'

'If this is a list of your previous "gentlemen", Windlass, it's not exactly impressing me. If I remember you had a character from a Henry Goring.'

'Also known as Nicholas Faunt.' Windlass smiled. 'And please note that disasters only befell my gentlemen when I was variously unavailable. As long as I'm around . . .'

'As long as you're around,' Marlowe interrupted, 'you may as well help me dispense with this bottle of claret and talk me through a murder or two.'

Windlass smiled and wrestled with the bung before pouring the burgundy liquid into goblets. 'I don't usually do murders, sir,' he said.

'Glad to hear it. Indulge me, however. Eleanor Merchant. Where did she die?'

'At the Rose, sir.'

Marlowe nodded. 'Shot – and not by accident – by a temporary replacement among the orchestra. We can rule out Shaxsper. Our killer had to be someone who knew *Tamburlaine* well enough to know there was an execution scene involving guns.'

'Someone with a theatrical bent?' Windlass hazarded.

'Don't get me started,' Marlowe muttered. 'Yes, it could have been any member of the cast, although most of them were on stage at the time and highly visible. Backstage crew? Possibly. The truth is that all plays are read in advance – censored, if you will – by the Master of Revels.'

'Sir Edmund Tilney,' Windlass enthused. 'I always had him down as a wrong 'un.'

'Then there are the compositors and printers.'

'Sneaky lot. Those apprentices aren't called Devils for nothing.' Windlass nodded. Marlowe was starting to list half of London.

'And of course, a lot of them go upstairs.'

'Upstairs, sir?'

'To Walsingham, even Burghley himself, looking for anything Papist, blasphemous, unpatriotic. Everybody has servants – saving your presence, Jack – who have friends, wives, sweethearts. It's quite conceivable rather a lot of people knew there were guns in *Tamburlaine*. Will was just a convenient idiot.' He looked at Windlass. 'But since it turns out we're in the same business you and I, safety-of-the-realm-wise, what do we know about Eleanor?'

'She ran a safe house,' Windlass said. 'In Blackfriars.'

'A safe house where the disaffected paid visits, men of dubious reputation, men on the run, double agents . . . Men perhaps with murder in their hearts.'

'So we are looking for a Catholic spy,' Windlass reasoned. 'One of the Mission, perhaps, a Jesuit?'

'Perhaps,' Marlowe nodded. 'But then there's God's Word Garrett. What links has he with the safe house?'

'But he *was* a Puritan,' Windlass said, rubbing his finger absentmindedly around the rim of his goblet. 'A Jesuit might well have him in his sights too.'

Marlowe shook his head. 'No, if that were the case, why not get a few more of them? Send one of William Waad's bristle bombs to St Olave's and bring the roof down? No, John Garrett died for another reason.'

'This was the Bear Garden, wasn't it?' Windlass was thinking aloud. 'Down from the Rose.'

Marlowe nodded, knowing the way this was going. 'So we're back to the theatre.'

'Stands to reason.' Windlass shrugged.

'Nicholas Faunt points to the neatness of the killings,' Marlowe said. 'A single shot for Eleanor. A clean stab for God's Word.'

'What's his point?' Windlass asked.

'He was ruling out street crime,' Marlowe told him. 'The daily casual violence in this great city of ours.'

'Oh, that,' Windlass snorted. It was something both men lived with.

'But then,' Marlowe poured himself another drink, 'he wasn't including Simon Bancroft in that.'

'Who?'

'A tobacconist found in the river with his head caved in.'

'Yes.' Windlass nodded. 'That's more casual.'

'His cousin is a backer at the Rose,' Marlowe said.

'So it *is* about the theatre!' Windlass looked triumphant.

'No, Jack.' Marlowe shook his head. 'No, I don't think so. What do a tobacconist, the runner of a safe house and a Puritan have in common?'

Windlass had heard jokes like this before, except that he knew there was nothing funny about this one. He shrugged.

'Money,' Marlowe said. 'Think about it. The tobacco trade is doing well, but not well enough to enable a man to buy an extremely costly gun, almost one of a kind. Your master, Burghley, pays a tolerable salary to the keeper of a safe house, but not enough for her to buy a unique jug of solid silver that even the Queen's Magus is afraid of. And as for the Puritan who should care nothing for the riches of the world, why does he have a chest of gold that could buy an entire Terra Incognita. No, Jack, *that's* what this is all about. Too much money.'

The Bancrofts' tobacco warehouse at Three Crane's Wharf was easy to find. The family name was proudly emblazoned across the front, which was certainly one clue. But the other was a row of men standing outside by the loading bay doors, smoking pipes of tobacco, in the concentrated way of those who wanted – no, *needed* – to drink some smoke and only had five minutes in which to do it. As Marlowe approached, he saw them all knock out the embers on the soles of their shoes and solemnly troop back inside, leaving just some crawling sparks in the ash and the whiff of the weed in the air.

Marlowe followed them inside to find that they had all gone back to their tasks of weighing out damp wedges of the packed leaves on to squares of sacking, which they then folded into a tight package with practised hands and closed with a few stitches of coarse linen thread, which also attached a label. They then turned over a piece of thin paper from a pile and impaled it on a wicked-looking spike, set into a block of wood on each desk. There was no talking, just the thick silence of men helping someone else make a lot of money. Marlowe hovered in the doorway for a moment, not certain which of the men, if any, was in charge, but he was saved from disturbing one of them by a familiar voice calling his name.

'Master Marlowe!' He turned to see Thaddeus Bancroft clattering down some stairs precariously attached to the far wall. On a gallery above the stacked bales of tobacco, there was a walled-in area, positioned so as to command a view across the open space of the warehouse. 'Come on up.' He gestured to the stairs. 'I assume you want to speak to me, rather than simply buy some tobacco in bulk?' He smiled and Marlowe remembered that, unless the man's inamorata had told him, he knew nothing of the little contretemps back at his house, although he could scarcely have missed the drama of the plummeting workman. Marlowe crossed the floor of the tobacco store and followed him up the stairs.

On the gallery was a snug room which had clearly grown as the business had grown. The basic structure was of rough wood, cut to length and closed in with what, on closer examination, were sections of the packaging in which the huge tobacco blocks arrived, simply stretched and nailed over the carcase. But inside this box was a chair, carved and embellished with stylized tobacco leaves and softened with two enormous pillows, indented though they were by the shape of the man who spent most of the day sitting there, engrossed in the ledger open on the desk in front of it. Bancroft had the slightly cross-eyed air of a bookkeeper who had been too long at his books and he flopped back into the cushions, moulded to another body altogether, waving Marlowe into another, less well-used chair, with relief.

'I have been trying to run my business and Simon's from our different warehouses since he . . . since he died,' he said. 'I decided yesterday to move everything into this one, as he has a rather better working space than my own.' He glanced around. 'I am going through his books,' he added.

'I rather thought that you shared a warehouse,' Marlowe said. After all, he thought, they seemed to share everything else.

'No, dear me, no,' Bancroft said. 'Our businesses are side by side, as you see, but Simon had gone down a rather different path. *I* simply import the tobacco and then sell it on almost as it arrives in my warehouse, to certain people throughout the country. My profits are lower –' he tapped the ledger – 'and as it turns out, considerably lower, than Simon's, but I only need two men to help me, so my overheads are lower also. The rest is down to factors and packhorses – not my problem. Simon sells – sold – his tobacco in smaller amounts, mainly to men who sell it in their ale houses or even just by the roadside, to anyone who wants a fill of a pipe. With every transaction a little is added, of course. Simon was able to charge more, but he had more men to pay, I suppose, so it all evens out in the end. But, even with his extra income, I am finding it hard to work out how he was so *rich*. The stock here is not so much greater than mine, he had no more ships than I do and yet . . .' He looked up, hopefully. 'Do you understand finance, Master Marlowe? Along with your many other talents?'

'Master Bancroft,' Marlowe said, regretfully, 'I understand what money does to a man, to what crimes it can drive him. But sadly, although I can sum a line of numbers, I don't understand how one man can make more than another, doing the same thing. Unless . . .'

Bancroft looked at him, one eyebrow raised. 'Unless that man is involved in something underhand,' he completed the sentence. 'Something criminal, even.'

Marlowe shrugged. 'You knew your cousin, Master Bancroft, where I did not. Do *you* think he was involved in something underhand?'

'My cousin was a meticulous bookkeeper,' Bancroft said, with the air of someone embarking on a lecture. 'As you saw, he wrote down even the smallest transaction and Mary – his widow, as I am sure you remember –' Marlowe was not likely to forget, but Thaddeus Bancroft didn't know that – 'Mary often said that he would stay up all night worrying over a ledger if there was so much as a ha'penny unaccounted for. So, I have gone over every page of this ledger to find where his extra income – and I believe it to be quite substantial, Master Marlowe – came from.' He twiddled the goose feather between his finger and thumb. 'I need to know, because Mary has become rather used to that kind of life. I don't want her to have to go back to how she lived before.'

'Which was?' Marlowe had seen the light of the professional whore in the woman's face before she had fled.

'I believe . . . I believe Simon met her when he was employing her services. I see no reason to hide that fact, Master Marlowe. She is a dear, good woman who had fallen into a life of sin. It could happen to anyone.'

Perhaps not anyone, exactly, Marlowe thought, but he got the general gist. Without wishing to be rude, he felt he had to add a comment. 'This would be a while ago, though, surely. Mary is not . . .'

'Not in the first flush of youth, perhaps not, no. She and Simon had been married for ten years or more when he . . . when he died. But it is only in the last few years that his fortunes have been on the rise. However, I digress. My main worry is that I simply can't find where his money has been coming from.' He dropped the quill and massaged his temples, leaving inky thumb prints on his jaw.

'Might there not be another ledger, a private one?' Marlowe asked him.

'That occurred to me,' Bancroft said. 'I have searched the house from top to bottom. All I could find was his household ledger and that balances to the last farthing. I even went so far as to check the food in the pantry – the cook was livid and threatened to give notice. But everything that was there was in the ledger.'

'And you've searched here, of course,' Marlowe prompted. The room would not offer much of a challenge. It was so small that the desk and chair almost filled it and the ledgers on the single shelf had not been touched for years, if the dust and cobwebs were anything to go by.

'Not yet,' Bancroft said. 'I thought I would go through the ledger first.'

'And therein lies the main difference between us,' Marlowe said with a smile. 'You are a man for adding columns. I am a man for turning out drawers. Let's put our talents together. I will search and you can go through anything I find. Does that seem to be a good plan?'

Bancroft nodded and smiled his diffident smile. 'That seems like a very good plan,' he said. 'Where do you want to start?'

Marlowe had not been wasting his time whilst Bancroft had been sharing his innermost thoughts, which he seemed to do without too much persuasion. Master Topcliffe's talents would be wasted on this man; he would have told all before the pincers were even warm. He had already decided that the old ledgers on the shelf were not likely to yield much information. The desk was very simple, with just one drawer. It didn't seem to fit very well, which was rather at odds with the carving on the legs, which suggested expense. 'Let's start in the desk drawer,' he suggested and Bancroft pushed the chair back and pulled the drawer open. For such a relatively large space, there was very little in it, just some goose feathers and a penknife, against the day when a new quill needed to be fashioned.

'Well,' Bancroft said, disappointed, 'I didn't think it could possibly be that easy.'

'May I?' Marlowe got up and went over to the desk and looked more closely at the drawer. 'Does it look rather shallow to you?' he asked the tobacco importer.

'A false bottom!' Bancroft said. 'Simon's father, my Uncle Reynold, had a desk with a false drawer. I'll wager this one is the same. There is a knob at the back.' He reached in, running his fingers along the wood. 'There is a knob at the back,' he repeated, then sat back, defeated. 'There doesn't seem to be a knob at the back, Master Marlowe. It's clearly just a very badly made drawer.'

Marlowe set him gently aside. 'I think we are just being a little too clever, Master Bancroft,' he said and took the sharp little knife from the drawer. Then, leaning down, he felt under the bottom and there was a soft twang as he cut a string. A small book fell to the ground, face down. It was bound in soft leather and was smaller than the palm of a man's hand.

'How did you know it was there?' Bancroft asked, amazed.

Marlowe shrugged. He could hardly tell the man of the things he had done, the things he had seen since he turned twenty. The priest holes where the Jesuits crouched in their silent terror, not daring to breathe; the secret places where men hid their darkest thoughts. 'The drawer didn't close properly. It seemed to catch halfway. It was the string, stretched between the sides, which was snagging on the runner. You'd have found it eventually.' He smiled encouragingly and, picking up the little book, handed it to him. 'Come on, you're the money man. We've already agreed that.'

Bancroft picked up the flint from the desk top and lit another candle. Drawing it closer, he opened the book, flicking through it to find the last page with writing on. 'Look,' he said, pointing at the date. 'The tenth of March; the last day we saw him alive.'

Marlowe looked over the man's shoulder and examined the page. It was ruled downwards to create columns. In the left-hand column was the date. The page was almost full and it had seven dates on it, each one with several entries. The second column was wider and had the same three letters in it – KTJ. Bancroft pointed. 'What does this mean? Someone's initials?'

'Let's just try and get the general flavour first, Master Bancroft,' Marlowe said, 'before we go into details. All of the figures in the third column are the same look. Twenty, followed by the letter "l".'

'Twenty pounds,' Bancroft said, automatically. 'Simon always wrote sums like that when it was monies of account.'

'Meaning?'

Bancroft blew out his cheeks in a huge sigh. 'Money isn't always money, Master Marlowe. Sometimes, it is money as you have it in your purse, angels, groats, perhaps the odd ryal still knocking around. Monies of account is . . .' He glanced up into Marlowe's face, which had assumed the bland politeness of someone who was drifting away from the conversation in hand, no matter how important it might be. Bancroft decided to shorten his lecture. 'Monies of account are amounts that you don't actually own, or at least not for long enough for it to matter. In other words, if someone paid you an angel they owed you and you immediately paid it to me, in payment of another debt, that would be monies of account. Do you see?'

'I do believe I do,' Marlowe said happily. 'So that third column stands for money that passes through Simon's hands, no matter how briefly.'

'Correct!' Bancroft said cheerfully. 'Or near enough. Now,' he drew his finger along the line, 'there are no more entries on that line. But look above, to the date preceding it, and you will see that there are more entries. And so it goes,' he flicked back the pages, 'right to the beginning of the book. So, looking at the entry above, in the fourth column, but one line down, is the same entry, twenty pounds, in Simon's manner, with a little tiny . . . what is that? Is it a letter "h", do you think? Then, in the fifth and final column, a number two. Note, there is no "l". I think this is money that Simon received.' He looked back a page. 'Look, at the bottom, the totals only represent the twos, not the twenties.' He tapped his teeth with a forefinger. 'This looks like . . . It's on the tip of my tongue.'

'May I?' Marlowe said, holding his hand out. Bancroft handed over the book, with some reluctance. The page before the last was the same in every particular, except that it was full and at the bottom, two boxes were ruled. In the right-hand one was the figure 20, which didn't take long to work out was the total of all of the twos. In the other box, was the number 502. He flicked back further. The larger figure was clearly a cumulative one, he could see. 'What kind of profit do you make a year?' he asked Bancroft.

'In general, or from tobacco?' Bancroft asked. 'The success of your plays has had a very gratifying effect on my income.'

'From tobacco, just for the moment.'

'Umm . . .' Bancroft cast up his eyes and seemed to be working something out in his head. 'Approximately six hundred pounds. Give or take.'

'So, here,' Marlowe pointed, 'is that profit again. Give or take.'

Bancroft craned round to see. 'Yes. So it seems.'

Marlowe looked at the first date in the book. 'This goes back longer than a year,' he said, 'but even so. A nice little extra, I think you'd agree.'

'May I?' Bancroft held out his hand for the book. 'I *know* what these figures mean, I'm sure of it. My father made sure I knew all about how to keep accounts, before he died. His old bookkeeper knew all there was to know and he . . . Oh, my head is like a sieve sometimes.' He bent his head, shaking it slowly and making little tutting noises. For his part, Marlowe was in a similar quandary about the initials. They must mean something – or someone. Suddenly, his heart was in his mouth. Bancroft had leapt up from his seat and was hugging Marlowe round the chest and bouncing them both up and down. He felt the flimsy floor shake with his gambolling and down below a parcel of tobacco for Lyme Regis ended up with a good layer of wood dust in the mixture.

'I am an idiot, indeed I am, Master Marlowe.'

Marlowe knew that, and not just because he couldn't remember what rows of figures reminded him of.

'Double stoccado, that's what it is.'

'Double . . .?'

'Stoccado, yes. It's a moneylender's scam, so that there is interest paid many, many times any legal limit. It's very simple, really.' His face clouded and he stopped hugging Marlowe, to the playwright's relief. He had now been hugged by both of the* surviving Bancrofts and it was two too many. 'I am distressed that Simon should stoop to it, even so,' he said, sadly.

'You'll have to excuse my ignorance, Master Bancroft. Explain as to a child.' Marlowe could only sympathize when he knew what the man was talking about.

'It doesn't need simplification, Master Marlowe. It is simplicity itself. I will tell it as though it involves the two of us, then it will be easier to follow. If I may?'

Marlowe nodded assent.

'Well, let's say you need to borrow . . . let's say fifty pounds, quickly. You are well-to-do but with few liquid assets. You come to me and ask to borrow the sum. I say that I can't lend you such an amount as a pure loan, the laws of Usury being what they are, but I can sell you something in my possession, which is worth the sum in question. You give me your promissory note for fifty pounds, signed and witnessed, often by a servant of the house. I know a friend who will buy the item from you for fifty pounds, forty five at the very least. You are happy to do that – all you want is the money. So, we go to my friend's house with the item . . .'

Marlowe clicked his fingers. 'Let's call it a Knights' Templar jug, shall we?' he said, quietly.

Bancroft smiled in spite of himself. 'Master Marlowe, you must make everything a tale, I see. Very well, we go to my friend's house with this jug and he looks at it carefully, then says he can buy it, will buy it with pleasure, but the price is only forty pounds, perhaps, or thirty or even less if I am greedy. He gives you the money, usually after an argument because it is much less than you need, after all. At a later date, or even that same day, I go to see my friend and give him back his forty, or thirty or whatever the sum was, plus a commission. Looking back through this book, it looks like ten per cent. I also retrieve my jug, or whatever the item in question may be. Do you see?'

'But . . .' Marlowe was working it out, and failing. 'You are down twenty-two pounds . . . aren't you?'

'In the short term. But I have your promissory note for far more. And if you don't pay me I can do one of two things. I can sell the note for a little less than its face value to someone less scrupulous than myself, who will use strong-arm tactics to get the money. Or I take you to court and take, if necessary, all you have.'

A light went on behind Marlowe's eyes. 'I *see*! So you have charged me interest of—'

Bancroft broke in. 'Anything up to fifty per cent for as little as a week or a month. Taken over the year, that is thousands of per cent. Totally illegal, of course, but effective and in use every day, somewhere in London and doubtless everywhere men need to borrow money.'

Marlowe was so busy tying up loose ends, he could hardly form the words to take his leave of Bancroft, but, taking the book, he half ran, half fell down the stairs. He needed to talk this through with someone who would understand it, before he forgot how it worked. He would have to find Nicholas Faunt.

THIRTEEN

I f Nicholas Faunt had an address, Marlowe didn't know it. He was one of those men who was just suddenly there, sitting in a Cambridge inn or dancing, masked, at a country house. He could be the man praying beside you in church, riding through a tangled wood with his hawk as you hunted. And he could be the man on the other end of a knife that was sticking in your ribs.

But one thing was certain; Nicholas Faunt was never far from Francis Walsingham. Marlowe had found him last at Barn Elms because Faunt had sent for him. What was it Faunt had said? 'You'll have the full backing of the Department, of course.' Well, Marlowe would put that to the test. Walsingham *was* the Department. He could be at Placentia or Nonsuch or Whitehall or Hampton Court, wherever the Queen commanded 'her moor' to attend her. On the other hand, he could be at his house at Seething Lane, hard by the Tower.

The end of March was not kind to Francis Walsingham. His old trouble came back with the crisis over the Queen of Scots and now the Spanish business, and his stomach felt as though he was permanently locked into Skeffington's Gyves, his nose touching his knees.

He looked straight enough to Nicholas Faunt that day, but Faunt had always believed that Walsingham would live forever and minor ailments he could overlook.

'Any news of twenty-two?' He took Walsingham's proffered glass, checking the Burgundy for its clarity and any traces of sediment. He trusted Walsingham with his life, except when it came to accepting a drink from the man. The Spymaster looked up at him from his crabbed position behind the huge desk, the eyes heavy, the black beard flecked with grey.

'You don't have to use code here, Nicholas,' the man said quietly. 'I have personally had removed the ears these walls once owned. We are alone.'

After the tranquillity of Barn Elms, where the river lapped and the curlews called, Seething Lane was chaotic. In the hall and passageways below, clerks of every hue bustled backwards and forwards, whatever the hour, laden with maps, documents, ciphers, letters, assiduously oiling the cogs that kept the machinery of government turning. Even so, Walsingham was right. Up here, under the heavy eaves, there was a reassuring stillness. Out of the window, through which the last light of evening crept, the Tower stood square and imposing. Whoever wanted to get to the Queen's Spymaster would have to get past the Queen's arsenal first.

'Very well.' Faunt sipped his wine. 'What news of Francis Drake?'

'When Drake has accomplished something,' Walsingham sighed, leaning back against his chair, 'I am sure I will be the last to know. He's promised to, as he puts it, singe the King of Spain's beard.'

'Has he, by God?' Faunt laughed.

'If he does,' the old Puritan said with a solemn face, 'it will be by God, yes.'

Faunt shifted a little. He was less than happy when Walsingham came over all religious. Such men were dangerous. 'I actually came to talk to you,' he said, 'about Blackfriars.'

'The safe house in Water Lane?' Walsingham dipped his quill back into the inkwell.

'Safe no longer, I fear,' Faunt said. 'It's been compromised. We'll have to move on.'

Walsingham nodded. 'Any ideas?'

'I wondered about Marlowe's place,' Faunt suggested. 'Hog Lane. Norton Folgate. It's in the Liberties, rather less busy, shall we say, than Blackfriars.'

The Spymaster knew that Faunt had a point. 'What will Marlowe think of it?' he asked.

'Marlowe might not mind,' a voice said behind them. 'But you should know that the house in Hog Lane is simply lousy with mice.' The two men turned to look at their visitor. Walsingham was out of his seat. Faunt had a dagger in his hand. 'Sir Francis, Master Faunt,' Marlowe said, sketching a bow. 'I am pleased to have found you so quickly. I thought I might have had to scour London and beyond.'

'How did you get in?' Walsingham wanted to know. 'It's not possible.'

'Isn't that why you employ me?' Marlowe asked. 'To do the impossible?'

'It's not like you to be looking for us, Master Marlowe,' Walsingham said with a small smile, acknowledging a point well made. 'The boot is usually very much on the other foot.'

'I need to speak to Master Faunt,' Marlowe said, watching the man slip his dagger away with the same ease with which he had drawn it. 'If you will excuse me, Sir Francis. It is in connection with something we have spoken of before.'

'Yes, yes,' Walsingham said, with an impatient wave of his hand. 'The death of Eleanor Merchant. We were discussing that when you arrived.'

Faunt shot him a look, but needn't have worried. Walsingham was too wily a fox to let anything out of the bag before its time.

'Her death, yes, of course,' Marlowe said, perching on a hard chair between the two men, but leaning forward as though anxious to be away. 'But also of two others – two others we know of, that is – and the link between them.'

'Explain.' Walsingham never used three words where one would do as well.

Marlowe explained all he and Faunt knew to the Spymaster, saving the best until the last. 'But now,' he said, ferreting in his purse for the tiny ledger, 'we also have this.' He flourished it and handed it to Faunt, as the one with the better eyesight. Even he had to take it over to a candle on the table and turn it to the light.

'It's a ledger,' he said. He turned it in his hand. 'A very small ledger. So what is your point, Kit?'

Marlowe was about to reply when Walsingham held out his hand. 'Don't spoil the game, Master Marlowe,' he said. 'Let me see if I can work it out.' He took the book from Faunt and weighed it thoughtfully in his hand. He stroked the soft leather covers and flicked the pages, then smelled the open book. He too turned to the candlelight and ran his finger down a line of figures. 'Is this the best you can do to test the old man?' he asked. 'I haven't seen one of these for a long time. In fact, not many people choose to keep a ledger of such dealings. Whoever

wrote these figures is dabbling –' he looked at the totals – 'I
should say more than dabbling, perhaps, in double stoccado.'

Marlowe visibly wilted.

'Well,' the older man said, throwing the book back to the
playwright, 'am I right?' He looked closely into Marlowe's eyes.
He slapped his knee. 'I *am* right. I haven't lost the touch, eh,
Nicholas? So, who is this blackguard? Mind you.' He flicked
through the pages. 'He only seems to be keeping around ten per
cent and on very small amounts. Not much harm done there, I
don't think. The sums loaned are paid back quickly –' again, the
flick through the pages – 'very quickly, looking at these dates.'
He frowned at Marlowe. 'Explain.'

'I have only just had this double stoccado explained to me,'
Marlowe said, 'and as I walked here, I thought it through.
Thaddeus Bancroft seemed quite sure that his cousin was not an
out and out rogue and I agree that as far as a moneylender goes,
he seems to get his money back very quickly. The same day, as
Sir Francis has noticed, very often.' Faunt seemed about to speak,
but Marlowe forestalled him. 'You can tell by the dates on the
bottom of one page and the top of another, Nicholas. The summing
works too well for there to have been a gap – there would have
been sums carried over, that kind of thing. I think, anyway.' He
raised an eyebrow at Walsingham, who nodded. 'So I think that
Simon Bancroft was the second person, the "friend", to whom
the borrower is taken. He may not have known how much money
was being made by the principal.'

Faunt had picked up the book again and was looking through
it, page by page, holding each one up to the light. Finally, on
the last but one, he breathed a triumphant, 'Ah ha.'

'What have you found there, Nicholas?' the old Spymaster
asked.

'Here, on this page, pricked with a pin. Hold a minute, it is
not well done . . .'

Walsingham turned to Marlowe with an indulgent smile.
'Nicholas is master of the pricked message. Anything less than
perfection irks him.'

'This is not . . . no, I have it. "H. Crutched Friars". That's all.'

'That could be the moneylender, do you think?'

'The Crutched Friars,' said Walsingham. 'Just around the

corner. It is the kind of address where a moneylender might live, I suppose . . . but why are we worrying ourselves over this? Why would a moneylender be killing – I think this is what you are saying, Kit – killing the people who help him? Did they steal from him, perhaps? Did they try to keep the valuable goods that they were "buying" each time? Surely not. They would know that they couldn't get away with that. And, besides, if these initials denote the item . . .?' Marlowe nodded. 'Then it is clearly used over and over again.'

'Is someone else killing them?' Marlowe suggested. 'Because they want to be part of the scheme and are not chosen, because . . . No, that won't work. If that was all, then why kill three?'

'Blackmail!' Faunt said, clicking his fingers.

'My boy,' Walsingham said indulgently, 'you are working too hard. Blackmailers don't kill their victims.'

'No,' Marlowe said to Walsingham, 'but victims kill their blackmailers. If the moneylender was being blackmailed, he would assume it would be someone who knew all about his business. And who better but one of his partners, if we can call them that?'

'Precisely so,' Faunt said. 'But he didn't know which one it was, so he is killing them one by one, until the blackmail stops.'

'In that case,' Walsingham said, rather cold-heartedly, 'why are we using precious breath by discussing it? A moneylender, his cronies and a blackmailer. Let them bludgeon and shoot each other until they are all extinct. The air of London will be the sweeter for it, surely?'

'That is certainly one way of looking at it,' Marlowe said. 'But so far a woman is widowed, three children are orphaned and . . .' He was a little stuck for a sob-story on the Puritan, so let the sentence hang. 'While this man is killing his partners, he is killing people guilty of nothing more than trying to make some money on the side and who can argue with that? Simon Bancroft wanted his wife to have a comfortable life. Eleanor Merchant was trying to get back the money squandered by her husband. Even God's Word Garrett was trying to do good, to set up a new life for the Godly away from England. Why should they die?'

Faunt and Marlowe were looking at each other with glittering eyes. The game was afoot and they were eager for the chase. Walsingham looked at them as they sat there, hardly able to keep still. 'You remind me of greyhounds in the slips,' he said at last, rising painfully from his chair. 'I am for my bed. I have boxes of papers to read before I sleep, so I'll say good night.' He smiled at the two and made for the door. 'I think that if I know nothing of your plans I will sleep the better for it. Wait until I am down the stairs; my hearing is excellent.'

The two men waited, listening for the old man's footsteps to die away. Faunt relaxed back in his chair and extended a hand. 'You first, Kit,' he said.

Seething Lane was as quiet as it ever got, with just a flickering candle in Walsingham's bedroom on the first floor. The old house was shifting as it cooled, clerks bedding down under their desks, the kitchen range clicking as the embers died one by one. Two men, cloaked in black, oozed out of a door tucked round the side of the building and pressed themselves into the shadow of the wall.

'Ready, Kit?' breathed Faunt. He was excited – as only a man of action lately tied to paperwork and plotting could be – at last, to be doing something active. There would be blood; and if he wasn't exactly hoping for it, if the prophecy came true, he wouldn't be sorry.

'Ready.' Like Faunt, Marlowe could feel his heart beating just that bit faster and his brain was fizzing. A play with your name on it was all very fine and well, but there was nothing quite like the thrill of the chase. 'Crutched Friars; I don't know it well. Are there many houses in it? How will we find the one we want?'

Faunt raised a shoulder. Who knew? That was what working in the field was all about, after all. They trod on silent shoes until they reached the corner and creeping round it found they were suddenly not alone. A bellman stood there, raising his dark lantern to shine into their faces. He knew a couple of felons when he saw them, although quite what he could do against two strong young men, and one armed to the teeth at that, he wasn't so sure. But still, the City paid him to keep watch, and so keep watch he would.

'May I help you gentlemen?' he said, in as brave a voice as

he could manage. He estimated that their cumulative ages came nowhere near his own.

'Hush.' Faunt's admonishment came out as almost a breath.

The bellman had many admirable qualities, but sharp hearing was not among them; ringing a bell next to his ear for ten years straight had not helped the situation. 'Eh?' he said loudly, inclining his head.

Marlowe leaned in and whispered as loudly as he could. 'Pray, be quiet. We are trying to take someone by surprise.'

'Party, is it?' the bellman said. Now he looked more closely, they were more roisterer than felon.

Faunt sighed and reached into his doublet and showed the man the Queen's badge. He took him by the sleeve and pulled him back round the corner. Tilting the man's lantern so it shone on his own lips, Faunt enunciated clearly, but quietly. 'We need to be quiet. We need to find a house in the Crutched Friars. Do you understand? Just nod.'

The man nodded. This was better; if only people always spoke this clearly.

'Your lantern will be helpful. May we borrow it?'

No nodding this time. 'Oh, no,' the bellman said. 'We have to buy our lanterns with our own money. You're not taking that.'

Marlowe moved the lantern over and continued the conversation. He sensed that Faunt had a very low threshold when it came to dealing with the stupid elderly deaf. 'If you come with us, you must be quiet. Whatever you see us do, you mustn't try to intervene. Can you do that? If not, then I'm afraid that my friend here will have to take your lantern by force.' Without prompting, Faunt had unsheathed his dagger and held it under the light. 'So, may we have your lantern?' Against his better judgement, the old man shook his head. 'So, you'll come with us, but be quiet.' There was a pause, then a reluctant nod. 'Well then, off we go.'

'It will be time soon for me to ring my bell and tell everyone all is well.' The man was stupid, perhaps, but very conscientious; a dangerous combination in these circumstances. 'All *is* well, isn't it?'

Faunt pulled his face close to his own and spoke in a normal tone. 'Yes and no,' he said, 'but if you do, that bell is going down your throat. Do you understand?' As well as he could with

Faunt's hand on his collar, the bellman nodded. 'Well, then, let's try again.'

In single file, with Marlowe at their head and Faunt bringing up the rear, they crept round into Crutched Friars, the rabbit warren of hovels where the monastery used to stand in the days of King Harry. Marlowe's heart fell. The houses had been built over the years, piecemeal and at random. Some were almost derelict with neglect, others spick and span, but there was nothing to denote where 'H' might live. He looked round and caught sight of Faunt's expression. He was obviously thinking the same.

Holding the bellman's sleeve to show that they were going to be stationary for a moment, Marlowe went close to Faunt and whispered in his ear. 'Which house?'

'I have no idea. There must be a mark of some kind. Let's see if there is anything that might guide us.'

Marlowe prised the lantern from the bellman's grip and, holding it aloft, they slowly started on their examination of the doors along the riverwards side of the street. Faunt, an expert in discovering the undiscoverable, ran his fingers along the mullions of the windows, feeling the stone or wood for incised signs. They found nothing, but crossed to start again in the other direction. Neither wanted to believe they could fail this early in the enterprise. But all along the northern side, there wasn't a sign of an 'H' on any door or window.

Pulling the bellman with them, they huddled together round the corner. 'Now what?' Faunt asked. 'Look again?'

'Perhaps the bellman knows someone whose name begins with H,' Marlowe suggested. 'Perhaps . . .' He glanced at the man, who was staring vacantly into the distance. As distant church bells began to ring, his hand kept straying vaguely to his belt where his muffled bell hung, waiting. 'Or, perhaps not,' he conceded.

'Let's go the other way round,' Faunt suggested. 'Widdershins.'

'How would that help?' Marlowe asked. He was cold and disappointed that they had got nowhere.

'Perhaps if we come at the houses from another direction, we will see something we missed before.' Faunt shrugged. 'It's worth a try, surely?'

Marlowe nodded and the three men trudged slowly along the

northern edge of the street, going widdershins with the lantern bobbing at eye level. Marlowe was finding it hard to keep his concentration on the job in hand. His imagination had already finished the night with the murderer in the Compter and he and Faunt celebrating their success with Walsingham's Burgundy. Feeling people's windows had not been in the story in his head at all. He looked up at the sky; the clouds were gathering. All they needed to make the night perfect was rain. Then he saw it and he stopped dead. The bellman stepped on the back of his heel and jabbed him sharply between the shoulder blades with his chin. Marlowe pointed to the corner of a door frame, above his head. 'Look, there.'

He raised the lantern high, risking opening its shutters a little to give more light. And there, as clear as day, was what Faunt had taken for an H. It was an heraldic ermine symbol, as near to an H as made no difference, the upstrokes fused together at the top.

Faunt clapped him on the back. 'That's it,' he whispered. 'That's what it was in the book. I just thought it was an H, badly done. Good work.'

Marlowe turned to the bellman and mouthed, 'Thank you. You have done the Queen a great service tonight.'

The man snatched back his lantern and made off round the corner. They half expected him to ring the hour and assure the populace that all was well, but he was clearly confused on the matter and was silent. The moment had gone. His shadow lengthened and then disappeared.

Faunt turned to Marlowe and whispered, 'Next stage. Ready?'

Marlowe nodded. He disappeared into the shadow of the doorway and heard Faunt tap gently on the door with the ermine mark.

The door creaked open and a voice said, guardedly, 'Yes?'

Faunt answered in a voice Marlowe had not heard him use before. He sounded rather stupid, but well bred and sophisticated. There was something about the sibilants in his speech that hinted at a dilettante lisp. 'My man, I am in need of . . . funds. Gaming losses, I'm afraid. A friend told me you could help.'

'A friend?' the voice said from behind the door. 'Does your friend have a name?'

''Fraid not. Well, he does, of course. But I don't know whether
he would like me giving it to voices behind doors.'

Marlowe clenched his teeth. Faunt was a loss to the stage, he
could see, but he was antagonizing the man. A slammed door
now might mean the end of everything.

'Fair enough. You have a name, though?'

'I certainly do. My name is Sir Oliver Blennerhaysett. From
Warwickshire, you know. Down in London for the Horse Fair
and I seem to have lost all my money at dice.'

The voice behind the door sounded amused. 'You country
gentlemen! You will do it, won't you? I don't do any moneylending here, but if you go down this street to the end, then turn
north . . .' The voice reconsidered the man's rural status. 'That's
to the left. Then not the first street, nor the second, but the third
on your right, that's where you need to go. See this sign above
my door? You'll see another such, halfway along, on the left.
Knock there.' And with no further ado, the door scraped closed
and Faunt was left on the doorstep.

'Kit?' he whispered. 'Did you get that?'

Marlowe leaned out from the doorway and waved a reply.
They had planned to leave a minute or so between them, so that
if anyone decided to follow Faunt, Marlowe would be behind
them, the old coney-catching trick. He waited in his doorway
while Faunt made his way along the street to the end. No one
came out of the door with the mark of the ermine, so he fell in
behind.

Following Faunt was like following the wind. He was silent
as he ran through the streets, his cloak snapping behind him like
a sail. At the end of the third street on the right, he stopped and
straightened his doublet, ran a hand through his hair and pulled
up his hood. Then he walked swiftly and, looking up to check
he was at the right house, tapped on the door. He stepped back
two paces, looking up at the windows on the floor above. He
risked a glance to his left to check that Marlowe was there and
he saw a shadow move slightly two doorways down. Being
followed by Marlowe was like being followed by the wind; you
didn't know he was there until he suddenly blew you over.

Marlowe saw Faunt's head turn sharply and heard a voice ask
who was there.

'Sir Oliver Blennerhaysett,' Faunt said, in his foolish voice. 'To borrow some money, if you would be so kind.'

An arm shot out and dragged him inside. Marlowe edged closer and crouched under the nearest window. There was the faintest glimmer of light showing through the shutters and he could hear voices, but not what was being said. Then the voices stopped and the light went out. The playwright scurried back to his doorway and pressed himself back against the cold stone. With luck, the men wouldn't pass him, but if they did they would hopefully be so deep in conversation that they wouldn't even notice him standing there, still and as silent as a statue.

There was no conversation as they left the house and Marlowe could hear just one set of footsteps, going away from him. Whoever Faunt was with didn't mind making a noise, the nails in the soles of his boots ringing on the flags. Faunt, as usual, flannel-footed as a cat, was padding alongside in silence. Marlowe risked looking out from his doorway and saw the men outlined against the faint grey of the starlit sky as they reached the top of the sloping street. Faunt was wiry and strong, walking on the inside, against the walls of the houses. The man he walked beside was taller, wider at the shoulder but didn't walk so smoothly. Marlowe guessed he was a little older, just that touch stiffer in his walk. Both had hoods to their cloaks, but Faunt's was thrown back, showing his close-cropped dark head. The other had his hood pulled down. Marlowe could see the edge of it well forward of his face when they turned to the left at the top of the hill. As soon as they turned the corner, he ran forward to make up some time. Pausing at the turn in the street, he heard a soft tap at a door. Peeping round carefully, he saw the two waiting outside an imposing doorway, decorated in the new Italian style with lions' masks and roundels. As he watched, the two men stepped inside.

Inside, Faunt could see little beyond a tapestry hanging on the wall beyond the curving stair. A manservant stood there, with a nightstick in his hand and a nightshirt trailing almost to the floor. He looked Faunt up and down with faint derision in his eyes. Sir Oliver Blennerhaysett put his thumb firmly on Nicholas Faunt and stopped him from punching the man right between the eyes.

Faunt was used to playing a long game but his blood was up and
the chase was over. He had his moneylender and now his partner
in crime. The day was his. Nevertheless, he waited quietly, trying
to look like a gentleman of the shires, down on his luck in
London.

'The master will be down shortly,' the manservant said, placing
the candle from the nightstick in a sconce on the wall. The
moneylender turned his face away, so it was still shielded by the
hood. There was a soft footfall on the stairs and a white stock-
inged toe came round the corner, with a long white nightshirt
above it. A hand slid along the polished banister rail and the
master came slowly and carefully down the stair and into view.

Faunt caught his breath.

The master of the house stopped and peered into the hall, then
straightened up. 'Nicholas Faunt?' he said, in disbelieving tones.
'Nicholas Faunt? I always thought you did quite well for a living.
Never out of business, in your line, I should have thought. Thynne,
what were you thinking, bringing Master Faunt here?'

'Sir William.' Faunt sketched a bow and put his hand on the
dagger at his back. 'I'm afraid you can't blame Master Thynne.
I told him I was Sir Oliver Blennerhaysett of Warwickshire.'

Sir William Danby, Coroner to the Queen, carried on down
the stairs and allowed himself a dry chuckle. 'Sir Oliver would
be flattered,' he told Faunt. 'He must be eighty if he is a day
and hasn't left his estates in at least twenty years, to my knowledge. But I repeat, Thynne, what were you thinking? A man in
your position should know all the important people in London.'
He nodded at Faunt, who nodded back. Two men who knew just
what was what and who was who.

Thynne had thrown back his hood and stood with his back to
the door, like a stag at bay. Walsingham's greyhound had chased
him into this covert and there was no way out, except by his
tongue.

'Let me explain—' he began, but Faunt stopped him.

'There is someone outside who needs to hear your explan-
ation,' he said. 'If you will just excuse me, Master Thynne.' He
pushed past him and opened the door. 'Kit?' He raised his voice
so the men inside could hear him.

Marlowe sighed. This was happening far too quickly to be

good. They must have been barking up the wrong tree. He moved out of his shadow and edged round the half-open door.

Thynne slammed the door behind him and leaned on it again. It seemed to give him some kind of comfort. 'You!' he spat. 'What are you doing here?'

'Chasing you, Master Thynne,' Marlowe said.

'I admit that usury is not an attractive way to make a living,' Thynne said, spreading his hands. 'But I hardly think it warrants you –' he pointed at Faunt – 'impersonating a gentleman of the shires, or you –' he pointed at Marlowe – 'following me. Not only that, Sir William,' he said to Danby, 'but this man is a wanted felon. He murdered a man outside the Rose Theatre and I have been hunting him ever since.'

Danby came down the last few steps and silenced Thynne with a raised hand. 'Hugh,' he said, condescension dripping from his tongue like honey, 'I think we'll have to consider you caught, fair and square. I myself,' he paused for a small smile, 'am above suspicion, of course, and if you try to involve me in this,' he looked from face to face, 'if any of you try to involve me in this, it will go the worse for you. I know you, Faunt, have friends in high places, but mine are even higher.' He paused and puffed out his chest. 'I was at the Inns of Court with Lord Burghley.' No one pulled rank like Sir William Danby. 'I can help you escape the full penalty of the law, Hugh, if you agree to admit everything to these gentlemen. Is that fair? After all, High Constables don't grow on trees.' He spoke directly to Faunt this time.

'It's not that simple, Sir . . . William?' Marlowe began.

'That's right, Master Marlowe,' Danby said. 'Coroner William Danby, at your service. I think your plays are masterly, if I may digress for a moment. Simply masterly. They read as well as they play. I am fortunate enough to be among those who are sent copies, before they appear. For reasons beyond my comprehension, the High Constable gets a copy too, don't you, Hugh? We check for libel. Obscenity. Things of that nature. And of course –' he smiled again, that mirthless smile that lawyers share, a smile that first appeared on the serpent in Eden – 'of course, I find both libel *and* obscenity, and usually much more besides. I'm sorry. Yet again, I digress. It's not that simple, you say.'

'No, Sir William,' Marlowe continued. 'I have reason to believe that Master Thynne here is a murderer, with at least three deaths on his conscience.'

'Assuming he has a conscience,' Danby put in.

'Assuming that, yes. So,' Marlowe turned to Thynne, 'what have you to say for yourself?'

'I lend money,' Thynne said flatly. 'I lend money at huge interest. That is a crime. I don't deny it. How can I deny it? You and your accomplice here have trapped me and it's all up with me. My family will starve. My honour is taken from me. But murder? Why should I murder anyone?'

Danby looked at Marlowe, then Faunt. 'He has you there,' he said. 'Hip and thigh. Have you any proof as such?'

'Not proof,' Marlowe said. 'But enough evidence, when stacked one piece on another, surely adds up to proof in the end. The three people dead were like you, Sir William, accomplices in his moneylending scheme. Perhaps you would have been next. Why should he stop at three?'

'I have never had another partner but Sir William,' Thynne protested. 'I have brought all my business to him.'

Danby compressed his lips and shook his head. 'Hugh, Hugh, Hugh,' he said, sadly. 'You must take me for a fool. Like Master Faunt's, my eyes are everywhere. I knew that you were doing business all over London, otherwise how could you live as you do? One of my men has followed you, off and on, for months and has seen what you are about. Oh,' he turned to Marlowe, 'this may be bad for your case, Master Marlowe. It may be that I, in doubting Master Thynne, have inadvertently given him alibis for the nights in question. If so, I am sorry.'

Thynne was silent, still pressing back against the door. He licked his lips and spoke, with an effort. 'I know who your murderer is,' he said. 'And I can take you to him.'

Faunt and Marlowe exchanged glances. 'I think we have him already,' Faunt said. He turned to Danby. 'If one of your servants can run to Sir Francis Walsingham's house, to bring some men, we can take Master Thynne to the Compter. He'll be among old friends there.'

Danby looked doubtful. 'Master Faunt,' he said. 'I would love to help, but with Her Majesty at Whitehall tonight, we are in the

Verge. Could you either go elsewhere to arrest him, or wait until tomorrow afternoon, when she moves out to Nonsuch and takes the problem with her?' He looked at them and explained. 'I would have to officiate, you see, and . . . well, surely you can see my predicament? Why not humour Master Thynne? Let him take you to his murderer. Who knows –' the coroner allowed himself a chuckle – 'he may be telling the truth.'

'I am,' Thynne agreed. 'I am telling the truth.'

Marlowe thought for a moment, then agreed. 'We must bind his arms,' he said. 'I don't fancy chasing him through the streets, not after having him so close.'

Danby called over his shoulder. 'Pursglove! Pursglove! Bring some rope, will you?'

'Don't tie my hands,' Thynne pleaded. 'I won't run, I promise. I want this foul murderer brought to book as well as you do. And I am still, for the moment, High Constable.'

The manservant arrived, with a short piece of light rope coiled elegantly on a silver tray. 'Rope, Sir William,' he said, with as much dignity as he could muster, given that he was still in his nightshirt.

Marlowe came to a decision. 'We'll take the rope, in case we need it,' he said. 'We're trusting you, Thynne.'

'I won't run,' the High Constable said. 'You have my word. But, for the look of the thing, may I bring my cane of office? So that the world will see the High Constable out walking with two gentlemen?'

Faunt unsheathed his dagger. 'I can throw this as well as I can use it in my hand, Master Thynne. Running would not be wise.'

Danby was running out of patience. This evening had not gone well. Not only was he now at risk of Faunt and Marlowe speaking out of turn, but he would have to find another way of making some extra money. It was experience, one way and another, being the Coroner Royal. The sooner these men were gone, the sooner he could fix the damage. 'I think we have discussed all we can discuss, gentlemen,' he said. 'Pursglove, show these gentlemen out.'

And as if a pleasant evening had wound itself happily to a close and old friends were parting to go their various ways, Pursglove opened the door to allow the three men to leave. Danby called goodnight and they were out on the street. Faunt took up position behind Thynne, his dagger tickling him in the small of his back.

'Take us to the murderer, Master Thynne, if you please,' Marlowe said, with just a hint of irony. 'We can't wait to find out who it might be.'

'You know who it is, Master Marlowe,' Thynne said. 'It just needs a moment's thought. I'm astonished that a man with your reputation for brilliance has entirely missed the point. In this life, or so I have found,' he continued, leading the way back down the street in the direction in which they had come, 'there are always people who are envious about what one has. When I was a child, I had a little wooden horse which my father carved for me. My brother wanted one the same, but before our father could make one, he had taken mine and broken it. Then, my father refused to finish the horse he was making and so neither of us had one. Jealousy is a terrible thing, Master Marlowe, Master Faunt. Just ask Alleyn and Shakespeare. Given another five minutes at your house, Marlowe, and they would have finished my job for me. They were beating each other to death, over a woman. In my line of work, I see all kinds of crime, sometimes for the slightest of reasons.'

'And what is your point?' Faunt asked, giving him a none-too-gentle prod.

'That despite the fact that my money came from a complex and totally illegal method of moneylending which gave me little peace, what with the worry and keeping it from my wife and the men I mix with in society, I know that some were jealous of me. And one such has decided to murder my accomplices, so that in time the trail will lead back to me.'

'As it has,' conceded Marlowe.

'As it has. And then, with me swinging at Tyburn, the murderer can step in and take over my business and get to my position in the world.'

'That's not much of a position, though, is it, Master Thynne?' Faunt ventured. 'The High Constable is only high compared with other constables. I have never noticed you at any of the tables where even I, a humble servant of Her Majesty, eat. So, your position in society isn't anything to be envious of really, is it?'

'Turn right here,' Thynne said. 'And you will see envy writ large. Enoch Harrison. My senior constable. This is his house.' He stopped and faced the door. 'Do you want me to knock? We have a code.' Faunt and Marlowe knew all about codes.

The playwright frowned up at the door. 'But this is where we came to ask for you,' he said. 'The address in Bancroft's book. The ermine sign.'

'Or,' Faunt felt it fair to point out, 'a very badly drawn H, for Harrison.'

Thynne asked again. 'Do you want me to knock?'

Marlowe nodded and Thynne beat out a rapid and complex tattoo on the door. Marlowe and Faunt stepped aside; there was no point in presenting a target to whoever was inside.

Harrison's giant factotum Peach stood there, almost filling the tiny hallway, his fists bunched in readiness.

'Peach,' Thynne said, the tone of insolent command back in his voice. 'Where's Harrison?'

A door to his left opened and Harrison stood just inside the room, firelight behind him and a candle burning in a sconce on the wall. 'Master Thynne? What is all this?' Marlowe and Faunt burst through the still open door and slammed it shut.

Thynne pointed with a hysterical, trembling finger. 'There he is!' he told them. 'There's your murderer!'

Harrison's face turned to a thundercloud. 'What!' he roared. 'You dare say that about me, you conniving, lying dog? Peach! Kill him.'

Peach did not have lightning reflexes. He was good at taking orders, but making decisions was not one of his talents. He moved from one foot to the other, but that was all.

'Peach!' Thynne joined the confusion. 'Don't listen to him. You know he killed those people. Grab him. Give him in charge to these gentlemen. They know what to do with murdering pigs like him.'

Harrison stepped away from the doorway and revealed his right hand for the first time. In it, he had a deadly knife, which he held in front of him as he walked slowly forward, towards Thynne. 'What have you been saying about me, you welching, greedy bastard?' he said through gritted teeth. Not taking his eyes off Thynne, he spoke to Marlowe and Faunt. 'While he was lording it over all of us, telling us to run here, run there, do this, do that, he was worse than any felon we took in charge. He was making interest on loans that would make your eyes water, taking money for protection – protection from his own men, I might tell you. He was dealing in stolen goods, he was—'

'Shut up!' Thynne screamed in his face. 'That was all you. It's over, can't you see that?'

Marlowe stepped forward. 'This isn't getting anyone anywhere,' he said. 'It doesn't take a genius to see that Master Faunt and I are outnumbered, assuming you thieves stick together. Sir William Danby, the Queen's Coroner, knows where we are and who with. And if I tell you that Master Faunt here is Sir Francis Walsingham's man, you know that if you so much as harm a hair on his head, *your* heads will be on the Bridge before cock-shut time tomorrow. So, less screaming from both of you. Let's settle this like gentlemen, shall we?'

Harrison took a reluctant step back, but kept his knife raised. Peach managed to reposition himself so as to be completely detached from the constables, High or otherwise, no mean feat in the tiny space.

'Now,' Marlowe said. 'Let's start with Master Simon Bancroft, shall we?'

'Who?' Harrison asked.

'Very clever,' hissed Thynne. 'You know perfectly well who he is, since you killed him.'

'The tobacconist,' Marlowe said, calmly. 'Found in the river.'

Harrison shrugged his shoulders. A voice which sounded as though it came from the inside of a mountain sounded behind Marlowe. 'That was Frizer and Skeres,' Peach said. 'I gave them the money and the name. It was writ on a piece of parchment, wrapped round the gold. It was sealed with his seal.' He pointed to Thynne.

'Well, that's not evidence, is it?' Thynne said. 'My seal is on my desk. Anyone could use it.' He pointed to Harrison. '*He* uses it all the time.'

Peach had more. 'And that Puritan bloke. They done for him and all. Same thing. Parchment, gold, seal.' He mimed the parcel with hands like trussed geese.

'Same thing indeed,' Thynne said. 'Peach, you have the brain of a slug.'

Harrison was not denying the accusations any longer. He stood with the knife held out, but with the other hand on his hip, as though listening to an interesting story – fiction, but interesting.

'What about Eleanor Merchant?' Marlowe asked Peach.

'Dunno. Somebody else might've give them the parcel. I ain't always here.'

'No,' Marlowe said. 'I don't think it was Frizer and Skeres who did that one. It was a little fancy for them.'

'Do you *know* these people?' Faunt asked.

'In a manner of speaking,' Marlowe said. 'I don't think they had the brains to carry out the murder of Eleanor Merchant. That was . . . well, one of these two gentlemen, I suppose we should say.'

'Him,' Thynne and Harrison said, as well as any Chorus.

'I know Constable Harrison was at the play when that woman died,' Peach said. 'He likes a play, Enoch does.'

'I don't deny it,' Harrison said. 'But I was in with the other groundlings because *certain people* don't give me enough money to pay for the gallery. How could I shoot her from there? I know the crowd can get a bit raucous at times, but not so they wouldn't notice me or anyone else turn a gun on someone.'

'Can you prove you were with the groundlings?' Marlowe said.

'Er . . .' Harrison gave it some thought. 'I was standing near that woman that shouted "That's the stuff" or something. They threw her out.'

'That's not much of an answer,' Marlowe said. 'Someone always shouts out something like that. Try again.'

'I'm thinking,' Harrison said and he really seemed to be working at pummelling his brain into action.

'He can't prove a thing,' Thynne shouted, triumphantly. 'Because he *did* it!'

'I remember!' Harrison said. 'Some woman shouted "Yes, indeed" during . . . the Prologue, was it? It was after that useless shawm player buggered up the fanfare.'

'He inhaled a fly,' Thynne said, then stopped abruptly, eyes swivelling from man to man. 'That's what I heard, anyway. When I questioned the orchestra after the murder.'

'He inhaled a fly?' Marlowe asked, quietly. 'Even I didn't know that until the other day. Tell me, Master Thynne, are you musical at all?'

'Ha!' Thynne said. 'I can't carry a tune in a bucket, everyone says so.'

Peach gave his preparatory rumble again. 'That ain't true, Master Thynne,' he said. 'You've got a nice singing voice and you played that whatsit, that thing what that woman brought in the other day, you played it to make sure it worked. Lovely, it was.' He nodded at Faunt and Marlowe. 'Just a snatch, like, but really nice.' He hummed a bar.

'So,' Marlowe mused, not taking his eyes off Thynne. 'We have a conundrum, Nicholas. Is our murderer Enoch Harrison, he whose name begins with an "H"?' He crossed slowly to the High Constable. 'Or is it a man who is still a member of the Worshipful Company of Skinners whose badge is an ermine?' He flicked aside Thynne's cloak to reveal the embroidered badge glinting in the half light.

Things seemed to happen as though everyone was embalmed in liquid amber. Harrison took a step forward at the speed of a glacier, lunging with elephantine slowness at Thynne. Suddenly the High Constable sped up to the normal tick of the universe, turned and was gone out of the door to the street, batting Marlowe aside.

'Get after him, Kit. You're faster than I am,' Faunt said and Marlowe hurtled into the night.

'Now, Master . . . Peach, is it? It was a little careless of Master Marlowe to let slip that I am Sir Francis Walsingham's man, but in essence he is right. That rope there –' he pointed to it coiled on the floor – 'would you like to see it around your neck or Constable Harrison's wrists?'

It was wonderful what a choice like that did for a man like Peach. Harrison was flat on his face in a heartbeat and a very large ex-employee was lashing his hands together.

FOURTEEN

Thynne was a will o' the wisp as they chased him through sleeping St Dunstan's. What moon there was hid behind clouds and ducked below the angled gables of the tall houses. Faunt had caught up with Marlowe and they had to be careful. It was the experience of both of them that the only sleeping people in London were the honest souls who had finished their day's work, said their prayers and gone to bed. Everybody else was still on the streets, the footpads lurking around every corner, loitering in every square.

'He's going south,' Faunt said, finding it difficult to keep pace with the younger man with his longer strides.

'The river,' agreed Marlowe. 'Then what?'

'One thing we can be sure of,' Faunt wheezed. 'The High Constable is not the sort to take his own life in a fit of remorse and shoot the Bridge.'

'He's not going for the Bridge.' Marlowe saw their quarry's cloak flying as his boots clattered into Petty Wales. 'He's going for the Wool Wharf. For a boat.'

'He'll be lucky,' Faunt grunted. 'At this time of night.'

'He's the High Constable of London, Nicholas. He'll just flash his badge and he'll have a whole fleet of ferrymen at his disposal.'

'Shit!' Faunt caught his foot on an uneven cobblestone and checked himself against a wall. 'We need some light.'

'Ho, bellman!' Marlowe saw a glimmer floating past the empty wool stalls yards away and prayed that its carrier wasn't as stupid as the man they'd left at the Crutched Friars. He left Faunt to hobble on as best he could and dashed across the open space where the Carthusians had once knelt in prayer. 'Your lantern if you please.' It hadn't worked last time and it didn't work now.

'I cannot, sir,' the man said, standing as tall as he could and holding his horn lantern aloft to see Marlowe's face. 'Not even for Christopher Marlowe.'

'You know me?' Marlowe was amazed.

'The author of *Tamburlaine*?' the bellman said. 'I most certainly do. Me and the missus have seen it three times now. The missus, well, she goes to watch that Ned Alleyn. Me, I go for the poetry of it all. Brilliant.'

'Thank you,' Marlowe said, momentarily thrown by this surreal conversation. 'Then you'll let me have the lantern?'

'Oh, I couldn't do that, sir.' The bellman shook his head solemnly. 'It's more than my job's worth.'

'You heard about the shooting at the theatre?'

'Heard about it?' the bellman said. 'I was there. Me and the missus. Shocking.'

'Well, what if I told you we're after the bastard who did it?'

'You are?' The bellman looked across to where Nicholas Faunt was sitting on the ground, nursing a twisted ankle.

'Yes.' Marlowe felt he had to underline it. 'So, can I have the lantern?'

'No, sir.' The bellman was still on his dignity. 'But you can have me *and* the lantern.'

Marlowe looked at the man. He was older than Faunt, older than Methuselah perhaps, but he looked solid enough and he carried a staff. He didn't seem to be deaf. Most importantly of all, he carried a lantern. 'Fair enough,' he said and slapped his arm before dashing back to Faunt.

'Leave me, Kit,' the man said. 'I'll only slow you up. Get after him, man. You'll lose him. Here, you might need this.' And he threw him his glittering badge of office.

Marlowe and the bellman clattered away.

Twice, before they reached the Wool Wharf, Marlowe thought that Faunt was right – he had lost him. But each time he caught sight of a running man. The bellman's lungs felt like bursting but he matched Marlowe stride for stride – as long as he didn't need to speak as well – the lantern, its shutters full open, throwing lurid shafts of light off the cranes and the bales of wool.

Far out across the river a solitary light bobbed on the ebb tide. Marlowe took a gamble. Where was Thynne going? If he'd gone downstream, he could have been making for Deptford, to take a ship bound for anywhere in the wide world. But for that he would need the wind and the tide and a captain accommodating enough to take on board a man breathing hard as if Hell followed him. If Thynne turned upstream he'd meet the Bridge and that was impassable for any wherry no matter how determined. No, the man was making for Southwark and the rolling Surrey countryside beyond it. There'd be time enough to lose himself in the forests of the Weald or find the coast anywhere he liked. After that, no power on earth could get him back.

Marlowe dashed out on to the jetty. 'Ho, waterman!' he shouted. Two or three men asleep in their boats under blankets and canvas lifted tired heads. 'Southwark!' Marlowe commanded.

'Look, sirrah,' the nearest waterman said, 'it's nearly two of the clock. You won't get in to the Punk Alice now and anything still wandering the streets, believe me, you don't want to know.'

'Do you know this, sirrah?' Marlowe dropped to one knee on the planks and all but pushed the *Semper Eadem* up the man's nose. 'The badge of the Queen?'

'Er . . . yessir.' The waterman was suddenly the most loyal subject in the realm. He threw off his blankets and lit his lantern, steadying the boat as Marlowe clambered aboard.

'Thanks, bellman,' he said. 'Next time you and the missus come to see *Tamburlaine*, be sure to let them know you're a friend of Kit Marlowe. I'll make sure you get two of the best seats, on the house.'

'That's gratifying, sir,' the bellman said. 'But I offered my services to help you catch that bastard. Besides, it's a dodgy place, south of the river. You don't want to be there after dark.'

Kit Marlowe had lost count of the times he'd been south of the river after dark, but he smiled and turned his face to the wind as the waterman took up his oars. 'Southward ho!' he called to the lonely night.

They saw Thynne's boat reach the Southwark mud and a dark, cloaked figure jump ashore. The man was going west, towards the bulk of St Olave's, its spire black against the purple of the night. Marlowe was out of his boat first, sinking up to his calves in the clawing ground and wading up to the road. The bellman was half a step behind him as they leapt the graves around the church. The dead of Southwark watched them go, past all caring who trampled over them now.

And now Marlowe knew exactly where Thynne was going. He couldn't have planned for this, to have all his complex plans unravelled like a sleeve in the still watches of the night. He would need money, wherever he planned to run to out of London; that would be vital. And Thynne knew just where to find it – the little room at the top of the Rose where Philip Henslowe slept most nights with his broken clay pots and his coffer full of silver. If Henslowe wasn't there, there would be nothing to stop Thynne. A man like him knew his way round locks; he would just smash his way in. If Henslowe was there, the High Constable would add another to his list of people who made the regrettable mistake of getting in his way. And Philip Henslowe was no match for Hugh Thynne.

The Rose loomed out of the darkness, the bare flagpole standing tall above the roof where Henslowe planned to build his tower with the proceeds of *Tamburlaine*. There was a shrill cackle in the shadows of Rose Alley. A Winchester goose was fumbling with a man, stuffing her breasts away at the arrival of the men from north of the river. Marlowe half turned, but he was too slow and he saw the lantern sprawl across the road, dropped from the bellman's grasp. The man sank to his knees, felled by a blow from Thynne's lead-headed cane, and he lay groaning in the mud.

Marlowe was suddenly alone. The fumbling couple had gone. The bellman was sleeping soundly. And for the first time, Marlowe realized he was unarmed. In a way, that made sense. A man running with a rapier through the London night was likely to hit every obstacle in sight as well as trip himself up at the first difficult turn. But now . . . Thynne emerged from the shadow of the Rose's entrance way, the cane held out in front of him. With dazzling speed, he swept off the Malacca and a long blade glinted wickedly in the half light. There was no need for Marlowe to feel for the sheathed dagger at his back. He had had no time to replace the one Frizer and Skeres had borrowed. Why hadn't Faunt thrown him something more useful than . . .? He gripped the badge and threw it at Thynne, who saw it coming and batted it aside with his blade. Marlowe rolled to his right and snatched up the bellman's staff as he scrabbled upright again.

He heard Thynne chuckle. 'What are you going to do with that stick, playwright?' he asked.

Marlowe decided to show him and, twirling the thing in both hands, smashed it again and again on Thynne's blade, driving him back to the Rose's wall. Thynne cursed and lunged, the steel slicing through Marlowe's left sleeve and Marlowe's left arm. Now Marlowe was against the wall and he paused for breath.

'One thing I need to know,' he said, feeling the blood trickle under his shirt.

'You don't need to know anything where you're going,' Thynne said, the point of his sword circling in the Southwark night.

'Indulge me,' Marlowe hissed and swung the staff again. Thynne caught it on his blade and batted it aside but Marlowe was faster and shoulder-barged the man, who staggered back, temporarily winded. In a split second, the blade-tip was there again, probing for Marlowe's chest.

'Eleanor Merchant,' Marlowe said. 'I know you hired those two coney-catchers to kill Bancroft and Garrett. Why the switch for Eleanor?'

'Would you believe,' Thynne smiled, 'honour among thieves? Yes. I'll never understand it either. All my years hunting evil. They still surprise me, the gallows-fodder. Skeres and Frizer drew the line, they said, at killing a woman. I could line up as many men for them to knock down as I liked, but a woman . . . no. I told them she was blackmailing me, but they still refused.'

'*Was* she blackmailing you?' It made no difference, but Marlowe wanted to know anyway.

'Somebody was. I thought it was her. First I thought it was Bancroft, of course. He was just too . . . pleasant to my face. He gave me a gun – priceless, it was. But you know that. It's in pieces now, at the bottom of the river. Now destroying it, *that* was a crime. But when he was dead, well, the blackmail went on. So I killed Eleanor Merchant, then had Garrett killed. And still the blackmail went on, but now, there was more to blackmail me about. And all the time, it was Harrison. I realized that tonight. God's teeth, I was stupid! Why couldn't I see what was in front of my face?'

There was a strange sound that, at first, neither man could place. Then Marlowe realized what it was. Far below them, to Thynne's right, Master Sackerson was awake and scenting the night air. His eyes glittered evil in the darkness and he smelt that curious smell again, the smell of human blood. Something fascinating. Something taboo. He snorted and snuffled in his throat, standing on his hind legs with his forepaws raised as if in prayer.

Thynne lunged at Marlowe's face, the blade grazing his cheek and shearing off a hank of hair. The playwright knew he might not survive another attack like that and he swung the staff horizontally, cracking against Thynne's right leg and bringing him to his knees. Then he swung again, smashing the wood into the man's temple. Thynne jabbed at him again, cutting points from his doublet and then jumped away from the staff blow he knew would follow.

But he had jumped too high and missed his footing entirely, falling through the blackness, his blade clattering on the roadway high above. He landed badly, the breath knocked out of him for a moment and he struggled to his knees, disoriented and dizzy. He was in an enclosure with a high wall all round and there was a horrible, indefinable smell. He half turned to see something large towering over him.

Master Sackerson growled and opened his jaws.

FIFTEEN

The *St John of Lubeck* ploughed the sea roads beyond Tilbury on a sunny spring afternoon. The rigging creaked in its housing and the canvas snapped as the hopeful gulls wheeled. Everywhere was the smell of wool and pitch and the new wood-shavings of the running repairs.

Ingram Frizer stood on the aft deck with Nicholas Skeres at his elbow watching Essex disappearing into a grey memory off to port.

'I'm going to miss the old place, Nick,' Frizer said. It was one of his more wistful moments.

'Ah, we'll be back, Ing.' Skeres clapped a friendly arm around the other man's shoulder. 'Don't you worry. When it's all blown over.'

'Did you pay that bill, by the way? That ordinary in Deptford Strand?'

'Nah,' Skeres scowled. 'You?'

'Nah.'

Skeres felt in the small of his back and adjusted the ornate dagger, the one that belonged to Kit Marlowe. It had been good of Constable Harrison to return it. His fingers ferreted beyond it and he found the little pack of cards nestling there. He turned to the length of the ship and his eyes alighted on the helmsman, correcting his trim, his mind clearly elsewhere. 'Find the Lady, Ing?' He cocked his head.

Frizer laughed quietly. 'I thought you'd never ask,' he said.

Three disconsolate actors sat on Philip Henslowe's stage at the Rose, their legs dangling down over the edge, their heads in their hands. One was Ned Alleyn, Tamburlaine, the greatest tragedian of his day, nursing the prize headache that Jack Windlass' cosh had given him. Another was William Shakespeare, reinstated as Theridias, King of Argier, complete with stiff and bandaged arm courtesy of Ned Alleyn. The third was

Richard Burbage, who had just lost his role as third handmaiden on account of the fact that the sweet-meat seller was more convincing.

'Lads, lads.' Kit Marlowe was striding across the groundlings' space towards them, stepping nimbly round dropped vegetables and other nameless detritus left behind by the audience. 'Such glum faces. We've a play towards. Just getting through the queue outside was a nightmare. Ned, they come for you.'

'I've lost her, Kit,' the tragedian moaned. 'Constance.' He turned with a scowl to Shakespeare. 'Thanks to someone sitting not a million yards from me as I speak.'

'I told you, Ned,' Shakespeare said. 'We've both lost her. She's taken up with young George Beaumont, of all people.'

'And please don't take it out on him on stage, Ned,' Marlowe begged. 'A threat unprofessional, don't you think?'

'I suppose so,' Alleyn muttered.

Marlowe looked at the three of them sitting there sunk in gloom. It couldn't go on; it was affecting everyone to do with the theatre. 'Barabbas,' he said, to Alleyn.

'I beg your pardon?' Alleyn said. It sounded like a complicated religious insult, if he was any judge.

'It's a character I'm thinking of for a new play. Barabbas, the Jew of Malta. It's got Ned Alleyn written all over it.'

Alleyn straightened, despite the pain in his head, despite the pain in his heart. A new play by Kit Marlowe, *another* chance to fret his hour upon the stage. 'Has it?' he smiled. 'Tell me more.'

'And you, Will Shaxsper,' Marlowe taunted him. 'When you and I first met you told me you wanted to be a playwright. Here it is, then. My challenge to you. I'm writing a play about a Jew. Why don't you do the same? See which one the groundlings flock to see.'

It was Shakespeare's turn to straighten. 'Do you know,' he said, flexing his wounded arm, the one that held a quill, 'I think I will.'

And the two of them were gone, arm in arm, gabbling away like two old gossips in the Cheap. Richard Burbage sat alone. The balm that was Christopher Marlowe hadn't touched him yet.

'Tom,' Marlowe shouted and beckoned the stage manager over. He sat down next to Burbage and Tom Sledd sat down next to him. 'Tell Master Burbage here what happened when you lost your virginity.'

'You what?' Sledd felt Marlowe's elbow sharply in his ribs.

'To your acting career. You know.' Nobody winked like Kit Marlowe when he had a point to make.

'Oh, that. Yes, well, it was a shame really.' Sledd was in full flow already. 'I could really have been somebody – Queen Boadicea, Lady Godiva, but no, I had to dip my wick, didn't I? And that was it.'

'What was?' Burbage wasn't following any of this.

'Well, didn't you know? As soon as you dip your wick, your balls drop and your voice goes with them. End of career.'

'So . . .' Burbage was trying to tie this piece of nonsense into some kind of logic.

'So.' Marlowe leaned into him. 'George Beaumont is sharing Constance Tyler's bed. Which I gather involves very regular wick dipping, if you catch my meaning. What do you reckon, Tom? Two days?'

'For his voice to go? Couldn't be more.'

'And then, Dick,' Marlowe said. 'I can call you Dick, can I? Then,' he whispered quietly, 'Master Henslowe will have a crying need for a new Zenocrate.'

Richard Burbage's eyes lit up and he dashed away, turning at the edge of the O for one last curtsey of gratitude to Christopher Marlowe.

Kit Marlowe wandered away from the Rose as a golden sun died in the west. He walked along Maiden Lane to the walls of the Bear Pit. Below him, Master Sackerson took his ease, rolling first to one side, then the other. Someone had said to Philip Henslowe that the beast would have to die now that it had tasted human blood. So Philip Henslowe had walked into the Pit and planted a kiss firmly on Master Sackerson's snout. Just because he could.

Marlowe wasn't sure of the direction at first. It was the tapping of a cane, he was sure of that, and he turned in the golden glow to see a cloaked figure coming out of the sun.

'We've been looking for you, Kit.' Nicholas Faunt leaned on Sackerson's wall, to take the weight off his twisted ankle.

'We have,' echoed Sir Francis Walsingham, sidling up on Marlowe's other side.

'If it's autographs you're after . . .' The playwright smiled.

'Look behind you, Kit,' Walsingham said. 'What do you see? Between the houses, I mean?'

Marlowe turned, to the darkling river and the skyline topped by the granite square of St Paul's. 'London,' he said.

Walsingham nodded. 'I see London burning, Kit,' he said softly. 'And I see them coming up the river from the sea roads of the west.'

'The galleons of Spain, Kit,' Faunt whispered. 'He sees the galleons of Spain.'

Marlowe looked from one to the other. 'What have I to do with these visions, gentlemen?' he asked.

'Nothing, Kit, nothing,' Faunt shrugged, folding his arms as he leaned against the wall.

'Or everything,' Walsingham said.

There was a silence until Master Sackerson ended it with a gentle snore.

'Everything or nothing,' Walsingham said, looking out over the river. Then he turned to the playwright. 'Well, Kit. Which is it to be?'